What Happens When You Break

What Happens When You Break

G. L. STRONG

To my Rose... For motivating me to be the best I can be.
—G.L. Strong

Prologue

Maya

"Aren't you nervous?" I look over at my best friend Abby, and take in her perfectly blown out brown hair and stylish outfit. She looks like she belongs here. Like this isn't our first day as freshmen in high school. The crop top and high waisted shorts she sports show off her curvy frame. She filled out this summer, unlike me.

I know what I look like. Like a ten year old boy. I'm wearing my usual outfit of black gym shorts and a white soccer t-shirt. My blonde hair is tied back tight in a long braid, showing off my chubby cheeks and pale, freckled forehead. I don't look like I'm fourteen, since the sports bra I'm always wearing isn't a necessity at this point.

"No way, M, this is what we've been waitin' for! Today's the day that determines the rest of our lives. It's so excitin'!" I can't help but roll my eyes at her melodrama. I highly doubt the first day of freshman year is the most important day of my life.

"That's a bit nerve-wrackin', don't you think?" Her arm loops around mine and she drags me forward through the massive halls filled with people at their lockers. I tried opening mine during orientation and I couldn't get it open, so I'm dreading having to try again this morning.

"We got this. As long as we stick together, we will be—"

"Abby!" The squeaky voice I've grown to hate engulfs my ears. I cringe at the sound and look towards the bouncing blonde running towards us. She's everything I'm not. She's tall, curvy, pretty, and popular. Her golden highlights shine in the fluorescent light as if the sun was beaming down on her and her tan skin is flawlessly done with makeup.

"Ahhh! Tay! I missed you so much, girl!" I watch as Abby lets go of me and runs to the girl in question before they start air kissing each other's cheeks. Taylor is two years older than us. She does dance with Abby in a program outside of the school and they have gotten close the last few months. It's a weird coincidence that Taylor only started talking to Abby the minute her boobs and hips came in. Now that I look at them, they look almost identical minus Abby's brown hair.

"I'm so happy you're finally a freshman, I've been waitin' for like ever!" I feel awkward standing here watching the interaction, but I'm also so nervous to be on my own that I can't will myself to walk away.

"I know! Now we can hangout like all the time!" They squeal at each other and I can't help but compare their sounds to pigs being slaughtered. I wish I was one of those pigs right now.

"You have to sit with me and my friends at lunch. You're gonna fit in perfectly, girl!" I watch as Taylor looks around like she wants to make sure no one is listening. She doesn't even see me even though I'm standing a few feet away from them. I'm invisible. "Wanna come smoke a cig with me in the girl's bathroom? One of the windows is broken and it opens just enough for us to blow the smoke out the crack. All of the cool kids are doin' it now."

I wait for my best friend since preschool to tell her no, that she would never smoke a cigarette, especially at school. "Totes! Let's go before the bell rings!" Her response makes my mouth fall open. I watch them bounce away, leaving me in their dust, before they both turn a corner and disappear from view.

I look around the huge hall around me and shrink into myself. There are people everywhere. Their laughter and loud chatter attack my ears and make it hard for me to breathe. I gulp down my nerves and throw myself forward through the crowd of people. I walk through the maze of hallways, praying silently that I manage to find my locker. I don't remember where it is with how big this school is. There are thousands of lockers and every hallway looks the same.

I round a corner and hit a wall. Except, the wall grabs my shoulders and prevents me from falling. I bring my eyes off the ground and let them trail up the person in front of me. Blue jeans hug his huge thighs and a letterman jacket hangs over the tight white t-shirt that does a terrible job at hiding the tan abs underneath. The same abs I've seen at my house mowing the fields and helping with the horses.

I finally look at his face, a good foot and a half above my own, and my heart does the same pathetic flutter it always does. His hazel eyes sparkle with sparks of golden light as they look at me. The brown hair on his head is short for easy maintenance. His sharp jaw and chiseled cheek bones make him appear both effortlessly perfect and rugged at the same time.

"Hey, where are you runnin' off to so quick?" His slight southern accent only adds to the beauty of Colton James Grant.

The man I write about in my diary every night. The man I have been obsessed with since he became my brother's best friend years ago.

"I'm tryin' to find my locker. These halls all look the same." I sigh while his hands hold my shoulders and when his thumb rubs up and down on my bare skin, I feel one hundred times more relaxed.

"What's the number? It will get a lot easier to find your way around, I promise." He lets go of my arms and I feel instantly colder. If he ever knew how obsessed with him I am, he'd probably never talk to me again. I'm just his best friend's little sister. Nothing more, nothing less.

"It's 1124." My voice cracks with the number and I want to curl into a ball and hide away.

"Alright, Mayo, let's get you to your locker." The nickname he came up with when I was eight makes me grit my teeth. It's a horrible nickname that he started calling me when he found out I hate mayonnaise and he hasn't stopped since.

"You don't have to… I'm sure you have better things to do."

"I can assure you there is nothin' more important than helpin' you feel a little less stressed on your first day. You only have me and Andrew for one year before we rid this place for good and go off to college, so you should probably take advantage of me as much as you can." His shoulder bumps into mine and I feel my cheeks heat from where my mind went with his words.

I clear my throat as we walk forward. "I have a feelin' Drew is gonna pretend I don't exist all year. I think I embarrass him."

"You? Embarrassin'? Not a chance, Mayonnaise." I groan at the name.

"Could you please not call me that here? You're right. I'm not embarrassin', you are." His laugh bubbles through the hall and it's the only thing I can hear through the loud talking around us. I notice a few people glancing our way, probably wondering why the gorgeous, popular, captain of the football team is talking to a little boy.

"Alright, I'll save that nickname for when we're alone." He winks at me and my mouth dries at the sight of it. "So, what should I call you?"

"Well, you might not know this, but my name is Maya."

"You sure? You sound more like a smart ass to me." It's my turn to laugh and for the first time all day, I feel calm and stress free.

"Takes one to know one." I stick my tongue out at him and he shakes his head with a smirk.

"Touché, little Turner, touché."

"I don't like little Turner either." I grimace at the use of my last name and how it makes me sound like a baby.

"You're a hard girl to please. Alright, Maya it is… for now. But one day I'm gonna come up with another nickname for you and it's gonna be the best nickname you've ever heard." He stops in front of a locker and I realize I have no idea which way we went to get here. Great, I'm just as lost as I was five minutes ago.

"Thank you for helpin' me, Colt." I grab for the slip of paper in my backpack that has my combination on it and before I can look at it, Colton rips it from my hands and uses it to effortlessly open my locker on the first try.

"I'll always be here for my favorite Turner. I've gotta get to class but I'll see you later, Maya. Good luck on your first day, you're gonna kill it!" He squeezes my shoulder reassuringly before striding down the hall and away from me.

I throw my head back with a huff. He's right. I'm going to kill something. But it's most likely going to be myself.

Chapter

ONE

Maya

Twelve years later…

"**M**s. Turner, you have a call on line two waiting for you." Carol's exhausted voice surprises me over my intercom. I didn't realize anyone else was in the office with me this late. I can't help but flip off her invisible voice, dreading this conversation. The exhaustion I feel can't be described. Between a double homicide case, planning my wedding which is two months away, and finding out my dad's pancreatic cancer has metastasized, the last few weeks have been a blur.

Groaning, I grab the phone and wait for Detective Bronson's obnoxious voice to fill my ear. Every time I get a call, it's him. He hasn't left me alone since the first call I got regarding this case.

John Wickins brutally murdered his wife and twelve year old son in the middle of their living room. Just one of the many murder cases I have to deal with living in New York City. I know he's guilty. I can see it on the sick man's face every time I see him. He's going to rot in jail for life if it's the last thing I do.

"Detective, it's nearly nine pm, can't this wait until the morning?"

"You've called me a lot of names, little sis, but detective has never been one of them." Andrew's deep voice comes through the phone and I hate that no relief comes from it. I'd almost rather hear from Detective Flirts-a-Lot.

"Drew, sorry. I thought you were someone else."

"I tried to call your cell, but it went straight to voicemail. Figured you were at the office still." He pauses before continuing. "Also, is it normal for detectives to be callin' you this late at night?" The protective tone of his voice almost makes me laugh.

"Unfortunately, crime doesn't stop when we go to bed. It's not a normal occurrence but this detective is a bit… thorough?" The word comes out as a question since I couldn't come up with the proper word to describe Detective Bronson. He knows I'm engaged and yet, his persistence never leaves.

"If you ever need anythin' you know I'm here to help you, Maya." I actually laugh this time. I can't hold it back.

"Drew, I haven't seen you in eight years. You live across the country. You couldn't help me even if I asked."

"And who's fault is that? You're the one who had to leave Texas and live in the big city. Texas has crime too, ya know. We need prosecutors just as much as the rest of the country." I sigh and put my fingers at the bridge of my nose.

"I'm fine, Andrew. If there was ever a problem, I know how to take care of myself."

"Shouldn't your fiancé be the one takin' care of you?" Crap. Why didn't I say Claude would take care of me?

"Right. Him too."

"I don't like that guy." His judgement flows through the receiver and I have to bite my tongue so I don't swear at him.

"You've never even met him."

"Exactly. You've been with him for two years and he's never met any of your family."

"That's my doing. I don't want you guys to meet him. You'll just scare him away." I put the phone between my ear and my shoulder and close one of the files I have open on my desk. I'm not getting anything else done tonight.

"Don't you think it's a problem that he'd get scared off so easily? We're just a charmin' southern family." His accent comes out thicker and I roll my eyes at the statement.

"Yeah, charming my ass."

"What kind of name is Claude, anyway? And what kind of man stays at home while his soon to be wife works a twelve hour day?"

"Did you really call me to discuss my fiancé's daily routine?" I hate that his words hit me deep. I feel the same way. Claude was the top chef at a French restaurant when we first met. He was motivated and sexy and his French accent definitely won him a few points.

But, after the restaurant changed owners, the entire kitchen staff was fired and Claude has been unemployed ever since. I know any kitchen would hire him in a heartbeat, but he's been lazy and unmotivated since it happened. His excuse is he doesn't want to take on anything new before the wedding. He wants to focus on making our day perfect instead. I guess that includes sleeping in until eleven, working out for hours, and playing sports video games.

"No. I called because of Dad." I freeze where I sit, the folder on my desk forgotten. "He asked for you, Maya."

"What do you mean asked for me?" I can feel emotions welling up in my throat. I haven't seen my family in years, but I used to be close to them. My dad's the one that taught me how to play soccer, which I continued to play all through college. He taught me how to ride a bike, drive, change a tire. He was one of my best friends when I was a teenager.

And then there's my mom. The sweetest soul you'll ever meet. She makes the best comfort food and gives the tightest hugs. She wouldn't hurt a fly if her life depended on it. I miss them so much, but I hate Texas. I started hating everything about that place once Andrew and Colton left. Damn. I haven't let myself think of that name since my first year of college.

"He wants you to come home, Maya. The doctors are saying he'll be lucky to survive another month or two. He stopped doing treatment. He's refusin' and said his only wish is to spend the last few weeks of his life with both of his kids."

"Andrew…" I sigh into the receiver and grab it with my hand, white-knuckling it. "I can't. You know I can't leave work."

"I get it. I work too, ya know. I had to leave my practice to be here, but I knew I'd regret it if I wasn't here durin' Dad's last days. I promise you'll regret it too." Shit. He's right. I hate when he's right.

"I'll see what I can do. I'm getting married in two months though. I need the money, especially with Claude not working right now."

"Dad offered to help with your weddin'." I swallow hard and try to rid the emotions clogging my throat. My dad won't be there for my wedding. He won't be able to walk me down the aisle. He won't be able to give me away. I've been too busy to even realize that until now.

"I know… I just can't ask him to do that. Especially now after everything he's going through."

"Well, if you aren't gonna let him help you, the least you can do is grant the dyin' man his last wish." If he's trying to make me feel guilty, it's working.

"Alright. I'll figure it out. I'll be there as soon as I can." As busy as I am, I need to see him. I need to hug the man that made me the tough woman I am now.

"Bring that fiancé of yours too, we'd all love to meet him."

"I'll text you when I'm on my way. Have a good night." I hang up before he can respond.

Flopping back in my chair, I wipe the stray tear that tries to escape one of my eyes. *Keep it together, Maya. You see countless people die in horribly gruesome ways every single day.*

You're strong.

You're tough.

You're falling apart.

"I HAVE TO GO, CLAUDE, I'M SORRY." GRABBING A FEW MORE OUTFITS from my closet, I neatly fold them into my suitcase. I don't know how long I'll be there, but I want to make sure I have enough clothes to last me the entire time.

"Ma belle, I do not understand." The nickname makes me grit my teeth. I used to love the endearing name, but now he tends to use it when he wants to get his way.

"My father is dying. He wants to see me. It's that simple."

"So let me come. I want to meet them." Zipping up the luggage, I turn towards the man I am about to marry and try to soften my glare. His dark brown eyes appear emotionless to me lately. The brown hair he used to style perfectly is way too long with messy curls falling into his eyes. His stubble hasn't been shaved in a few days and comes in patchy, complimenting the dirty sweats he always wears.

"It's an immediate family kind of visit, Claude. He's sick. He's not going to want to meet a new face the way he is. Please, if you love me, just let me go alone. I'll be back soon, I promise." I walk over to him and put my arms around his neck, bringing my face close to his. I know if I seduce him, I can get an agreement. He's a man who likes sex, like most French men.

"I do love you. I understand." His hands are now cupping my ass over my tight black pencil skirt. "At least say goodbye the proper way, ma belle." There it is. I knew it was coming. Unable to hold back my smirk, I step up on my toes and press my lips against his. He tastes like chips and stale beer, but the ache inside of me overpowers the immediate disgust I feel. I can't deny my attraction to Claude, even in his worst state. He's a good looking man that any woman would throw themselves at.

"My flight leaves in an hour so you better hur–"

Before I can even finish my sentence, he swoops me up off the ground. My laughter echoes through the room before he throws me on our bed and the clothes I took my time ironing end up in a heap on the floor.

Chapter

TWO

Maya

"It's the driveway on the right." The Uber driver from San Antonio gives me the side eye before pulling over in front of the long dirt driveway with the wooden sign sporting the name, *Magnolia Ranch*. I've been in this car for almost two hours now and I can tell the man driving me is aggravated. He shouldn't be though. I'm paying him double his normal rate to bring me home from the airport.

"My car won't make it down the road. Can you walk from here?" I gape at him, knowing this car would make it just fine down the dry clay and dirt. His face doesn't budge, staring me down, making sure I know the question is rhetorical.

G. L. STRONG

"Thanks for the ride." I glare at him and then step out of the Nissan. The August air hits me like a brick wall. My white button up and black pencil skirt cling to my already sweating body. Moving towards the back of the car, I hear the distinct pop of the trunk right as I reach it. Opening it up, I grab my huge suitcase and drop it to the gravel ground. Thank God it has wheels, otherwise I'd have to carry the thing the entire mile length of the driveway.

The minute the trunk closes the car speeds away with a loud screech. He couldn't get out of here sooner. If I was a spiteful person, I'd leave a shit review for him. But, I'm not. At least I tell myself I'm not. And besides, I've never liked leaving bad reviews. If you have nothing good to say, don't say it. One of the many lessons from my mama.

I look down at my black stilettos and then softly wipe the dirt from my silk top. Time to start walking. Awkwardly, I get the huge suitcase to glide behind me. It's not a smooth ride, since there are countless pebbles and rocks blocking its path.

I can feel my hair sticking to the back of my neck less than a quarter of the way down the long straight driveway. My shirt is damp with sweat and my feet ache from the uneven terrain. The only good thing is I get to stare out at the vast ranch I didn't realize I missed. Dark greens and dusty browns take over my vision. There are trees along the horizon, but flat fields filled with cattle surround me on either side. I forgot how beautiful it was. How serene and relaxing. I spot the huge pond halfway down the driveway to my right and can't help but smile.

Memories hit me harder than I expected them to. Memories of Andrew and my dad teaching me how to swim while my mom watched from the shore. Memories of me tanning on a float with Abby. Memories of sneaking out to watch Andrew and Colton party down there so I could see a certain someone shirtless.

The flush on my face should be explained by the heat, but I know the truth. It's there from the memories of him. From the

20

memories of the boy who treated me better than any man besides my dad ever had. The man I fell in love with at the age of six. The man that left town the minute he turned eighteen and never returned.

I trip on a loose rock and stumble forward, catching myself mid fall. The movement, along with the heat, makes me dizzy and I stop walking. I'm visibly sweating buckets now. It's dripping from every inch of my body. I'm only halfway to the house and I feel like I'm going to pass out.

I park my suitcase at the edge of the driveway and grab onto the wooden fence that separates me from the field. My stilettos puncture the grass under my feet and I try to pull them out, but to no avail. They've become a part of the field for good at this point.

Stepping out of my heels, my toes sink into the soft grass. I keep an eye out for any bulls or longhorn, but none of them are near, so I walk on. Taking each step with care to avoid any patties, I finally make it to the pond right at the edge of the tree line. It looks the same as it did twelve years ago. It's a large pond, almost the size of a football field my dad once told me, but it's quaint and peaceful. The water ripples against the edges and it's clear enough to make out small fish swimming around.

I walk up to the edge and step into it, letting the warm water engulf my sore feet. It feels heavenly. Too good to be true, and better than anything I've felt in a long time.

"Screw this." I reach for my hair and throw it up on top of my head in a twisted bun. I quickly unbutton my shirt before ripping the damp sleeves from my body. Looking around one last time, I unzip my skirt and wiggle out of it before it falls to the dirt floor below. I can't help but laugh when I look down at myself. I'm wearing a matching lace set that costs hundreds of dollars. The thin tan lace is complimented by small white, pink and yellow flowers embroidered into the fabric, intertwined by emerald leaves. It's incredibly detailed and hugs my curves perfectly.

Walking over to the small dock floating in the water, I step out onto the wood beams. The water calls to me, begging the old Maya to come out for just one second. I decide it's only right to let her. Taking one last painfully hot breath, I put my hands above my head and dive head first into the water.

My body is engulfed by warm water, coaxing me to stay under as long as possible. I swim forward, blind to where I'm going or what's in front of me, but not caring. This is what I needed. This feeling of nothing. This dark wet world where all of my worries can disappear and all I have to focus on is holding my breath and surging forward. It's mesmerizing and completely addicting in every way.

After what feels like hours, I resurface and take a deep breath. The air feels less hot now. I feel less like I'm suffocating and more like I'm floating. So that's what I do. I lay on my back and I float, staring up into the bright blue sky. The sun beams down and I can already feel the rays seeping into me, tanning my pale skin. I don't spend a lot of time outside since my life revolves around working in an office or courtroom.

My body bobs up and down softly, ears suspended under the water and cancelling out all of the outside noise. All I hear is a deep hum from the water around my face. I can't hear or think about anything else. I can't think about the fact that my mascara is probably running down my face. I can't think about the fact that I'm here for my dying father that I haven't seen in eight years. I can't think about the fact that I'm about to get married.

The water ripples near my head as if a rock fell into it and I lift my head up to see.

"Excuse me, ma'am? This is private property!" A loud deep voice hits my ears and I search the shore for the culprit. I can't hold back the eye roll at the use of the word ma'am.

"I'm no ma'am, buddy. And this is my—"

My voice cuts out the minute my eyes collide with him. It's like seeing a ghost. I'm thrown back in time to freshman year walking through the halls every morning. Colton Grant stands at the shore line with his hands on his hips. He's unmistakable, even though most everything about him has changed in the last twelve years.

His huge frame is intimidating with each bulking muscle. He's wearing blue jeans and a dark red flannel tucked in with the top few buttons undone. His once clean shaved face is now covered in a thick beard that makes me question my hatred for facial hair. How can I hate something that looks so mouthwatering on him? His hazel eyes bore into me and I find myself shivering in the warm water. The sexiest part is the cowboy hat positioned securely on his head. I've never seen him wear anything like it, but holy shit. Cowboy hats were made for Colton Grant.

"You okay, miss?" He cocks his head at me, not recognizing me at all, and my already dry mouth gets dryer. He's the sexiest man I've ever laid my eyes on. Which I shouldn't be thinking since I'm very much engaged, evident by the diamond on my finger.

"Yeah... I'm fine. I'm coming out now." I shake my head to rid myself of the inappropriate thoughts roaming every cavern of my brain and start the short swim to shore. I feel his eyes on me as my body exits the pond and water drips from my hair and down the rest of my body. I saunter my hips in a way I normally wouldn't if I didn't have such an enticing audience, but don't look into his eyes. A part of me doesn't want him to know who I am, especially since I recognized him right away, after all this time, from such a distance.

"As much as I appreciate the show, darlin', you're not supposed to be here. This is a private ranch." I turn my back to him and reach down to grab my clothes. Slipping the white button down over my arms, I let it hang open and hold my skirt in front of me.

"I have permission to be here. I'm here for Billy Turner. Just took a little detour to the pond." I'm still not looking at him, trying to avoid his eyes until he turns around and leaves, hopefully for good.

"What's your name?" Shit. I don't want to lie but I also don't want Colton to know it's me. This isn't the best first impression.

"I–"

My sentence is cut off by his phone ringing and I take a deep breath as I look out at the pond. "Excuse me, miss." I nod my head in understanding and when I notice him walk off to the tree line, engrossed in his phone call, I book it. I don't calmly leave. No. I run full force through the field like there's a killer chasing me. Except, it's not a killer. It's just my past.

When I find my suitcase, I note Andrew's old beat up chevy truck from high school sitting right next to it. Without thinking, I throw my suitcase in the back and jump into the front seat. Jamming it into drive, I slam on the gas and careen my way down the driveway and away from him.

Should it have occurred to me that he was driving the truck? Yes. Did it? Nope.

PUTTING THE TRUCK IN PARK, I OPEN THE DRIVER'S SIDE DOOR AND hop out of the cabin. My eyes take in the house I grew up in and tears threaten to appear. The white house looks exactly the same. The wrap around porch with a swing and a million pink flowers hanging on every possible hook. The large double pane windows with blue shutters and small candles always shining in each one. The blue double door in the front with one too many chips and cracks that could easily be fixed at any time but never is.

It's perfect. And it's home. A home I haven't thought of in a really long time. At least, that I haven't let myself think of. Grabbing my suitcase, I haul it up the porch steps and reach for the door. The minute my hand grasps the metal handle, it flies open and my mom's angelic face stands before me. My eyes, which match her blue ones perfectly, take her in with unshed tears.

She's aged since I last saw her. Her once blonde hair is now a soft gray color which is tied up in a delicate bun at the nape of her neck. Her smile looks exactly the same, sweet and comforting, but the wrinkles around her mouth and eyes have only intensified. She's astonishingly beautiful with her fit frame and tan skin from working outside on the ranch.

"Mayflower?" The nickname she used to call me makes the first tear fall and I can't hold back the sob that follows suit.

"Mama." I drop my bag and throw myself into her arms, oblivious to the fact that I'm soaked and still showing off my very inappropriate undergarments. Nothing matters in this moment besides my mama's arms around me. Her sugar cookie scent engulfs my nose and her soft hands rub up and down my back like they used to.

"Oh, my sweet girl. You're all grown up. I missed you with my whole heart." I feel her tears hit my shoulder and I pull away from her so I can wipe them away with my hands. I hate when she cries, always have and always will.

"I know Mama, I'm sorry I never came to visit. Life just got the best of me out in the city."

"Oh baby, lost your accent and everythin', huh? We're gonna have to put the Texas back in you before you leave." I can't help but laugh at her words. It feels like just yesterday I was hugging her goodbye at the age of eighteen. "Never mind that, come in, come in. Let's get you somethin' to eat. There's no meat on your bones! Your very wet and naked bones, missy." She raises an eyebrow at me and we both smile at each other.

"I took a dip in the pond. For old time's sake." She simply shakes her head at me and shuffles me into the house once I grab my suitcase. The foyer looks exactly the same. The huge dark wood L-shaped stairs surround the otherwise white room. There are pictures of us covering most of the walls from my first soccer game when I was four, to our family vacations, to both me and Andrew graduating.

"Why don't you go up to your room and get changed and I'll fix y'all somethin' to eat?"

"Thanks, Mama. I can't wait to see Daddy and Drew. I'll be right down." I make my way up the stairs and feel an overwhelming number of memories hit me. Each step brings a new memory.

Me falling down the stairs when I was eight and breaking my foot. Me and Andrew sliding down the steps on a tote cover. Me and Abby running up these stairs to gossip about all of the cute boys we had crushes on. Colton following me up the stairs when I was crying after Taylor called me a boy in front of the entire class. Prom night when I descended these same stairs in my pale blue dress, to the asshole I lost my virginity to, Harrison.

So many memories hit me at once that I feel like my heart is being squeezed by a vice and if it doesn't give some slack soon, I'll collapse on these same steps. Speeding up my pace, I take the stairs two at a time and the minute my foot lands on the top step, the vice loosens and my heart beats at a normal pace again.

My feet move involuntarily to the second door on the right and I turn the brass knob. The same squeaks I memorized as a kid greet my ears and I can't hold back my smile. Nothing's changed. It's like the room was put in a time capsule and preserved until right now. Like they knew, one day, I'd be back.

The stark white walls are covered in posters from Chris Stapleton to Miranda Lambert. I loved country music back then. Something I gave up the minute I started living in New York. The slider door that leads to my own small patio overlooking the ranch still has those gross slimy animal stickers I used to be obsessed with as a kid. My full-size bed has the same gray comforter hanging off it, perfectly made. The white side tables and matching dresser have been dusted regularly and the pictures and trophies on top make me smile.

For a second, I feel like I'm a teenager again, which is bittersweet. After the age of fourteen or fifteen, my teen years turned to shit. I spent most of my time hanging out with Mama and Daddy, which I wouldn't trade for the world, but it made me resent this town. It made me leave. I was the socially awkward, sad girl, who fell in love with an unreachable man who left her without a second glance.

I flop the suitcase onto my bed and unzip it. Grabbing some underwear and a navy short sleeve dress, I take off my wet bra and panties and throw the dry clothes on. I look in the mirror in the corner of my room and tie the fabric belt around the soft material, accentuating my waist. The dress is something I would normally wear on a casual day at the office, but it's still formal, just how I like it.

Running my hands through my wet blonde locks, I fix my middle part and tuck it behind my ears. The freckles covering my skin have already been enhanced by the sun and my cheeks have a light pink tint to them. It's then that I notice the dark black smudged mascara lining my bright blue eyes. I look like a damn racoon. Rummaging through my suitcase, I grab a makeup wipe and my small makeup bag. Once I remove everything from my face, I reapply my concealer, bronzer, blush, and mascara.

With my new face, I build up the courage to go downstairs and face my father. I don't know what to expect, but I know the strong man I left eight years ago won't be staring back at me. I'm expecting the worst, in hopes for the best. The stairs creak as I make my way down them quickly. I try to avoid any memories this time and it works with my quick speed. I turn left at the bottom of the stairs and make my way into the adjoining kitchen and dining room.

The kitchen is expansive with a large middle island that I always sat at as a kid. The cabinets are white and the counters are a dark granite with specks of navy-blue sparkling through. My mom always cooks, so she has the finest appliances my father could afford and they are well used. I turn my attention to the dining room table farther into the room and find a person sitting at it. A person I have missed more than I like to admit.

My brother turns when he hears my feet shuffle across the floor and the minute our eyes collide his face morphs into a huge smile.

"Maya!" He jumps out of his seat and bounds toward me. He looks the same, with his boy next door features: tan skin, blue eyes, and light brown hair. The only difference is now, he has some grays scattered throughout his mane.

Without any warning, he scoops me up into a huge bear hug that lifts me off the ground. I have to close my eyes to keep from getting dizzy as he spins me around the kitchen. Finally, he places me back down on Earth and holds my shoulders to steady me.

"God, you don't look a day over eighteen, baby sis." I smile at his words, thankful for the compliment and open my mouth to respond. "I can't believe you're here! And you're already causin' shit, like always. You stole my truck? You clearly haven't changed at all." He rubs his hand on the top of my head and messes up my hair, earning him a groan.

"Stop, Andrew, you're fucking up my hair." I flatten the scattered pieces and smirk at my older brother before offering him a mischievous wink.

"Actually, you've completely changed." The voice grabs both of our attention and we look over at the bathroom door that branches off the dining room. Colton stands there, resting up against the door frame, taking us in. He doesn't look happy. In fact, when he looks at me, he looks disgusted.

"Nice to see you again too." I try to keep my voice from cracking, but it doesn't work well.

"I think I've seen just a little too much of you already, darlin'. Why don't you scurry on back to where you came from?" He squints his eyes at me before letting his gaze drop down my body in a judging manner. I can't help but cross my arms over my chest at the intensity of it. A small snicker leaves his lips and then he makes his way to the table.

"Last I checked, this is my house, not yours." Andrew and I follow suit and sit at the dining room table, me right across from Colton.

"Actually, May–"

Andrew doesn't get his sentence out before Mama comes into view with enough sandwiches to feed an army. We say thank you before saying grace and then eat in silence for the first few minutes.

"So, where's Daddy?" I take a sip of sweet tea to clear the bread from my throat.

"You'd know if you weren't so selfish." Colt's comment is so quiet I doubt anyone else heard it, but he was staring right into me as he spoke. I heard every word, just like he wanted me to.

"He sleeps most of the day, sweetheart." Mama's soft voice shakes when she speaks. "He's usually up early in the mornin' and then later in the afternoon until bed time. He'll be up in a few hours. He can't wait to see you."

"I can't wait to see him." My smile doesn't reach my eyes when I talk about Daddy. I'm so scared to see what condition he's in.

"That so? Coulda fooled me. Seems you're burnin' daylight." I bring my attention back to the man who used to take up all of the space in my immature brain. The man who treated me like his own sister and friend.

"Hey, man, cut her some slack. She's got a lot goin' on in the big city these days, right baby sis?" Andrew's genuine smile distracts me enough to forget about the brooding mammoth in front of me.

"Uh, yeah. But it's no excuse. I'm sorry I haven't been present. I should have come around these last few years, I just…" I realize I don't have an answer and instead trail off into silence.

"Nonsense, we don't hold grudges against our own. Now, what do you reckon we talk about somethin' happy? Like your engagement?" I wince at the word. I didn't want to talk about that. Somehow, I thought I could avoid it.

"Yeah, where is he anyway? I thought you were gonna bring him along so we could meet him?" Andrew talks through a huge mouthful of sandwich.

"He couldn't come. He, uh, he had some interviews with a few big restaurants that he couldn't pass up. He wanted to be here, but it just didn't work timing wise." I lie straight through my teeth and the steely glare from a certain someone almost makes me admit the truth. The truth that I don't want them to meet him. The truth that I question my decision to get married to him almost every day, but I'm too proud to ever do anything about it.

"That's too bad, we wanted to meet the famous… how do you say his name again?" Mama blinks at me innocently.

"Claude." The word barely sounds like a real name leaving my mouth. I hear Colton's deep snort and grit my teeth in irritation. "What's so funny, CJ?" I use the name he has hated since we were kids and earn myself a tight glare. He doesn't answer my question, instead, focusing on his sandwich and ignoring me completely.

"Well, I can't wait to hear more about him and meet him in a few months." The mention of a few months from now drops the mood. We all know Daddy won't be around then and it doesn't feel right talking about anything positive around that time.

"So, May, what's your plan while you're here?" Andrew's change in subject in graciously welcome.

"I have a big case back home I'm going to have to be on call for at all times, but besides that, I just wanted to hang out with you guys and help around as much as I can. What can I do?"

"Actually, if you're willin' to, we could use your help with the ranch. I've been takin' over some of the chores that Dad can't do anymore, but I have to start headin' back to work a few days a week to make sure everythin's under control. Do you think you can handle a few ranch jobs?"

"Of course." I feel a pang of jealousy that Andrew gets to go back to his Physical Therapy practice and I can't go to work. I know it's not fair of me since he only works an hour from here and I work across the country, but the workaholic in me is screaming. "What do you need help with?"

"She won't be able to do it." This comes from Colton. "Look at her. She'll chip a nail or stain one of her pretty dresses and the whole world will end."

"Oh stop, Colton. She used to help around the ranch and she can do it again. And if not, I know a ranch hand who can help her." Andrew smirks at him as he rolls his eyes and I appear to be the only one in the dark. "You'll be in charge of bottle feedin' some of the calves in the mornin', cleanin' out the barns and stalls, and groomin' the horses. We have a few stallions that need trainin' and a pregnant longhorn that is almost due, but we'll start you off easy for now."

I nod my head in agreement, dreading the manure and flies I'm going to have to deal with but knowing I'd do it every day for the rest of my life if it made my dad feel better during a time like this.

"When do I start?" I finish off the last of my sandwich and tea before pushing my plate away from me.

"Tomorrow mornin' if you can. You can head out to the barn around six if that's not too early."

"Honestly, six is late for me. I'm usually up by four-thirty or five." I sit a bit higher with my admission, proud that I can fit in with the normal ranch lifestyle I haven't been accustomed to in so long.

"Perfect. You'll do just fine then." Andrew and Mama smile at me and I sneak a glance over at Colton. He's miserable. Pure hatred covers his perfect features and I can't help but wonder what bug crawled up his ass. Before I can ask, Mama speaks up.

"Well, your daddy won't be up for another hour or so. Why don't you go get situated in your room and explore a little until then?" The sentence makes me feel like a stranger in my own home. Like I haven't been given the proper tour. I guess after eight years, I practically am a stranger to this place.

"Thank you for lunch, Mama. It was delicious, like always." I stand up and remove my plate from the table before washing it at the sink and placing it on the drying rack.

The entire time, I feel Colton's eyes staring daggers into my side, dissecting me with unknown emotions.

Chapter

THREE

Maya

I've successfully unpacked my entire suitcase into my old drawers and only thought about Colton half the time. Okay, that's a lie. I thought about him the entire time. I can't get his golden, hazel eyes out of my head. I can't stop picturing what his tan skin looks like under that flannel he's wearing. I can't stop imagining him taking all of that raw anger out on me on top of the dining room table or in the pond or in Andrew's old beat up truck. Jesus... I just had sex with Claude this morning and I'm already a horny mess just looking at the ghost from my past.

Guilt consumes me at the thought of my fiancé. He may not be perfect, but we have been through a lot together and I made a promise to love him and follow through with this wedding by wearing this ring on my finger. Looking down at it, I take in the large solitaire cut diamond he gave me before he lost his job. He spent an ungodly amount of money on the four-carat ring. He knew I didn't want a big diamond. He knew I didn't want to waste money on something that doesn't represent love to me, but rather just shows off how much money you have. I hate that aspect of engagement rings. Not to mention this thing is always getting stuck on everything.

Pulling out my phone, I let my guilt get the best of me and click on Claude's name before putting it to my ear.

"Salut." His deep French accent hits my ears and the tone of his voice makes it sound like he doesn't know who's calling even though my name and picture is programmed into his phone.

"Hi, it's me." I tap my foot on the uneven wood floorboards.

"Maya baby, how is… how is uh, how do you say it?" I roll my eyes. He knows exactly how to say it, he just doesn't remember where I am.

"Texas." It comes out as a huff but my charming fiancé doesn't pick up on the irritation.

"Oui, oui, Texas. How is it?"

"It's hot and full of cattle. It's really good to see my mom and brother though. I haven't seen my d–"

"Oh, come on! Tu te trompes petite merde!" His loud shouts interrupt me and I feel tears brim the edge of my eyes. He doesn't care. He's too busy screaming at his video game. "Sorry, ma belle. What were you saying?"

"Nothing, it's been fine. I have to go." My voice hiccups with the last word but he doesn't notice. "I'll talk to you tomorrow." Hanging up, I throw my phone on my bed and use both hands to wipe my eyes. It shouldn't surprise me. He's always like this. He's full of himself and can't seem to acknowledge or notice when anyone else is struggling. The world revolves around Claude

Francois and we're just living in it. I cringe at the thought of my last name changing to Francois.

"Trouble in paradise?" I jump at the voice and spin around towards my door. Colton stands in the doorway, leaning against the frame. He looks like he just took a shower, with his brown locks dripping onto his face. He's wearing a pair of clean blue jeans and a white t-shirt that clings to all of the hard ridges of his body.

"Nope. We're fine." I turn my face away and wipe the tears from my eyes, standing a little straighter.

"Didn't sound so fine. You look like you're eatin' sorrow by the spoonful."

"That's such a stupid saying. And I don't look sad. I'm just worried about Daddy."

"Don't hate on Texas, darlin'. You were like all of us once upon a time. Until you up and left without a second thought." He glares into me and I can't hold back my anger anymore.

"Sounds a bit familiar if you ask me. You and Andrew did the exact same thing. I was here all alone with no one but Mama and Daddy until I left. I was losing my mind in this shit hole of a town. I took a risk and made a life for myself. I'm not going to feel guilty about that."

"You never even call them. You left and acted like the people who raised you didn't exist. You broke your parent's hearts." He walks into the room now, anger radiating off of him. "You are a selfish brat who cares more about her clothes and makeup than things in life that truly matter."

"You have no idea what you're talking about. I bust my ass with my job. If I'm not there, murderers and rapists roam the streets. If I'm not there, innocent children don't get the justice they deserve. You think I want to be surrounded by death and murder every day of my life? You think I wouldn't rather come home and take care of Daddy and say screw it to everything else? I can't! I made a decision to become a prosecutor and if I don't do my job the system goes to shit and people's lives are at stake."

I'm fuming. I didn't realize I walked right up to him during my rant until I feel my chest heave and hit his. We are mere inches apart, face to face. I can smell his deep pine and leather cologne masking the smell of engine grease. It's intoxicating and I find myself inhaling deeper. Every part of me wants to grab his face and kiss him. But, the look in his eyes doesn't reflect my want. Instead, it's filled with hatred and disgust. It makes the once light hazel eyes appear dark and mysterious.

His breath hits my face in a hot puff and fresh mint engulfs my nose. "Well bless your heart, darlin'." He brings his face closer and my breath hitches. We are nose to nose, staring deep into each other's eyes. One small movement and I could feel his plump lips touch my own. One small movement and our bodies would be flush against each other, my hard nipples pressed against his muscles. "Get off your high horse. You don't impress me or anyone else in this town for that matter. If you're lookin' for praise, go back to your fruity fiancé and those hoity-toity city folk. You fit in better with them." He spits each word at me like they will brand me when they hit my skin. Part of me believes they already did. His eyes trace down my dress clad body one more time before looking back into my own. "Nice panties by the way. Really left nothin' to the imagination."

With that, he's gone. He leaves me standing with my knees buckled and my heart hammering. I can't decide if I'm turned on or heart broken. Maybe both. This man can bring me to my knees in more ways than one. He has changed so much since high school that I almost don't remember him being that sweet senior who helped me find my way around school. I picture myself back then and realize I've changed in every way too. I used to be shy, timid, and socially awkward. I used to be a tomboy who always wore her hair back, wore athletic clothes, and cared more about soccer and my family than anything else.

I look down at myself and see the woman I've become now. I wear dresses and skirts. I get a full body wax every two weeks and a blow out every other day. My presence intimidates not only criminals, but also the detectives on the scene. I speak my mind and don't care who's listening. My job comes before everything else, including my family.

I've done a complete 180, and while I love how confident I've become, I hate most everything about myself. I picture Abby and Taylor treating me like shit all through high school. I picture their cute dresses and perfectly done hair and makeup and a part of me cringes, knowing somewhere along the way, I've become the prim and proper bully I hated most of my life.

Making my way down stairs I walk to the right of the foyer and find myself in the living room. The fireplace is lit, crackling fire casting a soft glow on the walls. The sun isn't as high in the sky anymore so the furniture has some shadows covering them. The white sectional is as clean as it was eight years ago. There's a new flat screen tv in the corner of the room and the same huge coffee table.

I move around the room and spot my built-in bookshelf still full of all of my favorite books. I let my fingers glide across each of their spines and feel a smile bubble up at the memory of curling up on the couch with a good book every night. I haven't read anything for my own enjoyment since before law school. Yet another part of me I gave up.

"We couldn't get rid of them. Every time I see them, they remind me of you." Daddy's deep timber hits my ears and I turn toward the sound. He's standing behind me with a cane supporting most of his weight. Tears pool at the sight of him. The once burly man who could scare off anyone is now thin and frail. Even his tall stature looks shorter after all this time. The thick brown hair and beard he used to have is gone, a patchy scruffy beard and bald head taking its place. New wrinkles cover his face, but his eyes are the same. The dark blue color that always shown bright whenever he looked at me, sparkle with love. They are full of life and memories, reminding me of everything I've missed all these years.

"Daddy." The word comes out as a sob and I cautiously make my way towards him. He shakes where he stands, clearly struggling to be on his feet for so long. "Let me help you, let's sit on the couch." I position myself under his shoulder and force him to put most of his weight on me. We walk towards the couch and deposit ourselves on the soft cushion. It's then that I go in for my hug. The hug I so desperately needed, more than I ever expected to.

His deep peppermint and tobacco scent engulf my senses and bring me back to when I was fourteen years old and life was good. When we would ride horses together and race across the fields. When we would star gaze all night and he would show me the constellations. When we would fix Andrew's truck together and then get ice cream afterwards.

"I missed you so much, Daddy."

"I missed you more, squirt." He pulls away from me now and takes in my appearance. "You're all grown up. And you actually look like a girl!" His humor hasn't disappeared with the weight, thank goodness.

"Ha. Ha. Glad to see you're just as funny as always. My style has definitely changed a bit since high school."

"A bit? I was concerned for a while there. When I heard you were engaged, I asked your mama if it was to a lady." A snort leaves my lips and I swat at his arm.

"Hey, I dated guys in high school. Why would you think I was gay?"

"Oh, sweetie, did you see yourself back then?" He chuckles deep and the sound is like music to my ears.

"Okay, good point." I shake my head at my one of a kind father and find myself emotional again. I almost didn't come. I almost stayed in New York and ignored my daddy's wishes. The thought of never seeing him again. Of losing the man I grew up loving with all of my heart. The man who taught me everything. Who I compared every man to for most of my life, knowing no one would be good enough for me because of how perfect my daddy was. The thought of throwing all of that away makes my chest ache like there's a hole spreading throughout my heart.

"Thank you for comin', Maya. I can't tell you how grateful I am to have my babies here with me."

"I wouldn't have missed it for the world, Daddy. I'm sorry I didn't come sooner. I'm sorry I haven't–"

"Nonsense, squirt. Let's not talk about the past. The only thing that matters is that you're here now." I lay my head against his shoulder and inhale deeply, savoring everything about this moment. I need to make up missed time for the last eight years. I need to hold on to every memory and moment that passes so I will have something to look back on when he's gone.

"So, tell me about this fiancé of yours."

Chapter

FOUR

Maya

My phone blares into the quiet night, startling me awake. I jump out of bed and check the clock, noting it's three in the morning. Great.

"This better be important." My voice is groggy and full of sleep.

"Ms. Turner, this is Detective Bronson."

"No shit, Sherlock, why are you calling me at three in the morning?"

"Actually, it's four in the morning–"

"I'm in Texas visiting my sick father. I already told you this. Get what you need to say out before I hang up and block your number."

"Shit, I forgot. I'm sorry. It's about the Wickins case. Apparently, John Wickins has another son. A step son from his first marriage. He's a new suspect in the case. He suffers from schizophrenia and there's a witness saying they saw him near the apartment complex the same night. They're going to push this one, Maya."

"Well, send me everything we have on him. We already have enough evidence to convict John and put him away for life. We'll push harder. Get some sleep, detective." Hanging up, I lay in bed for a few minutes and try to get back to sleep. It doesn't work. Throwing off my covers, I pull myself out of bed. Might as well start my chores early.

Rummaging through my suitcase, I realize I didn't bring anything to wear for ranch work. The closest thing I have is a pair of navy-blue satin dress shorts that tie around my waist and a white short sleeve body suit with a deep V-neck. It will have to do. Throwing them on, I grab my white flats and secure them on my feet. I look like I'm on my way to a meeting, not a barn, but it's the best I can put together right now. I'll have to run into town and go shopping later today.

I make my way through the house quietly, every step creaking under my feet. I know Daddy needs his sleep and if he's anything like he used to be, he's a light sleeper. Opening the front door, I make it out onto the porch and use my flashlight, along with the moon's reflection, to make my way to the barn behind the house. Even the cows and horses are sleeping right now. Everyone but me, thanks to Detective Shit-for-Brains.

The walk to the barn is longer than I remember. The air is cooler on my skin now, but still humid. I turn my head up and my breath catches in my throat, stopping me in my tracks. The stars are on full display. It's like they knew I'd be awake and decided to put on their best show for me. They dance across the sky in sparkling wonder, begging me to play a game of connect the dots with them. I haven't seen stars in years, not with all of the aggressive city lights. Their bright hue always faded out the mystery of the night sky that I've grown to miss.

Making my way towards the barn, I keep my head up to admire the flaming balls in the sky. My body moves from my memory of the many times I made this same walk in the dark to care for the horses. I know where I'm going after all this–

My body hits something hard and I stumble backwards with a yelp. I could have sworn I knew where I was going. Did they change the set up of the horse's stables? I look down and find the thing I hit glaring back at me. I can feel his steely stare through the darkness.

"You've been home for less than twenty-four hours and you're already bumpin' into me like old times, huh baby Turner?" His voice contradicts his glare, sounding almost playful. It reminds me of the old Colt I used to love.

"Only difference is when I bumped into you back then, you smiled at me. Now you try to kill me with a look."

"That's definitely not the only difference, darlin'." His eyes travel down my body like they have so many times since I got here and I feel a shiver travel down to my toes. "What are you doin' awake at this hour?"

"I could be asking you the same thing. What are you even doing here? You stalking the Turner family now? Sneaking around the ranch like a creeper in the night?"

"Somethin' like that." That's the only answer he gives me and I roll my eyes.

"Well, I was woken up by a needy detective and I couldn't fall back asleep."

"Your fiancé know you got men callin' you at three in the mornin'?" He squints his eyes at me in question.

"First off, it's work. And second off, he's not the type to care. Only thing he cares about is him–" I cut myself off before continuing with that sentence. "Never mind."

"Sounds like a real catch. And I don't care if it's work or not, I'm assumin' this detective knows what you look like and his mind isn't thinkin' about work at three am."

"And what exactly do I look like, Colton?"

"You know what you look like, Maya Turner." His voice grows more hoarse with each word and I damn near choke on the air in my lungs.

"I thought you hated the way I look." I glare at him and beg him to answer the way I want. I beg him to say he does like it. That I affect him the way he affects me. That he wants me.

"Gotta say, I liked you better when you were sweet and innocent and had your soft hair tied back in pretty little plaits. But I can appreciate a good lookin' woman." Not exactly what I wanted to hear, but better than nothing.

"You liked me better when I was socially awkward and had no tits?" This earns me a snort from him, but I don't stop there. "Judging by the look in your eyes at the pond, you liked my tits a lot more now than you did back then." I push them up a bit and catch his eyes in the moonlight. He stares longingly at the deep V and I see a flash of danger spark in his hazel pools.

"I'd be careful what you say next, Maya Turner." His eyes haven't left my cleavage and I can feel the heat from their stare spreading across my chest and moving down.

"Why? Maybe I don't want to be careful." I step in closer to him and his shallow breath hits my ears. The confidence I have around Colton Grant is something I've never experienced with him before.

"You're gonna start somethin' an engaged woman shouldn't be startin'." He stares down at the ring on my finger now and it feels like freezing cold water is doused over my entire body. "That's a nice ring, darlin'. Looks real expensive."

With that, he steps away from me and turns his back, heading toward the barn. "Why don't you go back inside and paint your nails or somethin'." His shout travels through the air and slaps me across the face. I stomp after him, refusing to be made a fool by this asshole.

"Fuck you, Colton James Grant. You can't tell me what to do."

"Real naughty mouth on such a pretty lady. You gonna throw a hissy-fit now?" He laughs through his words and I grit my teeth.

"Actually, I'm going to clean out the stables. Why don't you just go home?"

He stops walking, turning towards me abruptly and I almost barrel into him again. "Dressed like that, darlin'?"

"Stop calling me darling. And yes. It's the only thing I have. I wasn't expecting to do ranch work."

"Course you weren't, darlin'." He says the nickname with more exaggeration and I puff out an annoyed breath. More so because I secretly love the name coming from his lips. "Let's get one thing straight. This ranch doesn't need you. We've been doin' just fine without little Maya Turner comin' to save the day."

"Why are you acting like you're a part of this family? You're not! You're not my daddy's son. You're just my brother's best friend from high school who up and left all of us without so much as a phone call! You don't belong here!" I'm yelling at him now, anger rising to the surface.

He just stares at me with a sad smirk on his face. "Looks like we got somethin' in common then."

He turns again and walks towards the barn. I follow him into the stables, ready to keep this fight going. He continues walking forward, towards the other end of the impressively long barn, until we reach a door that I don't remember seeing when I was a teenager. He opens it and walks through, bringing us into a small mudroom with stairs leading up. Since when are there stairs here?

He storms his way up the stairs and like the idiot I am, I follow right behind him. At the top, there's a door that leads into a large apartment. The apartment is the length of the barn. There's wood everywhere, giving it a cabin feel, with concrete countertops in the kitchen and upgraded appliances. The kitchen opens up into a living room with a black sofa and a small tv. A little farther down there is a queen size bed facing huge windows overlooking the field that the horses always graze in.

The place is spotless, but there are small additions that prove someone lives here. That Colton lives here. His football trophies along with his bull riding belts. A basket of his laundry sitting in the corner. Pictures of his family. Pictures of Andrew and him. Pictures... pictures of me. I walk towards them, taking in the few pictures he has of me playing soccer when I was fourteen. Of me and Andrew sticking our tongues out at him when he tried to take a picture of us. Of me after he left for college, winning our last game senior year, my hands thrown up in the air, mouth open in an excited shout.

"I don't understand." The words come out so quiet I doubt he heard them.

"I've been livin' here for the last two years. I spent a few years in Houston, workin' a corporate job behind a desk every day of the week. I hated it. So, when my ma and pa got in the accident two years ago, I moved back home and Billy let me move in here."

My stomach drops at the words I just heard. "Your... I had... Colt, I'm so sorry. I had no idea about your parents. Are they..." I can't finish the sentence, refusing to say the words out loud. Tears threaten to escape and I curse myself for becoming so sensitive since arriving here.

"They didn't make it. Semi-truck hit them and they were in their old Chevy with broken seat belts. The one they refused to give up for the last ten years." He shakes his head with a sad smile plastered on his face. "They died on impact, so they didn't suffer. Everyone kept callin' them lucky." His laugh startles me. "Imagine that? Bein' called lucky for dyin'?"

A single tear cascades down my cheek and I try to sniffle away the rest of the emotion. There's no way Colton is going to take my tears the right way. He'll think I'm pitying him or trying to make it about me in some way.

I turn my head to look away from him, hiding the tears that refuse to stay put, where they belong. His warm hand touches my shoulder and I flinch from the sensation. His hand turns me so I'm facing him and instead of the annoyed glare I've been getting since I showed up here, his eyes stare into me with another look entirely.

A look of curiosity, confusion, and deep down, maybe even love. The love he used to have for me when we were younger. His eyes dart between my own and calculate me like he's never seen someone cry before. Like this is the strangest thing he's ever seen and he's trying to figure out how to handle it.

I watch, my breath caught in my throat, as his hand reaches up slowly and wipes the tear from my cheek. The small contact leaves tingles in its wake, a constant reminder of the sweet gesture.

"Don't waste your tears on me, darlin'." I stare into him and see something deep within that I hadn't seen before. That I've never seen in Colton Grant. Loneliness. A feeling I know all too well, due to my own actions. I ran away from the only people that ever truly cared about me because I was heartbroken and self-conscious. I isolated myself and focused on work, ruining all of my relationships until I found someone so obsessed with himself, he forgot I even existed.

"It's not a waste, Colton." I step towards him and dare touch the beast in front of me. If anyone can tame this wild stallion, why not be the one person who loved him whole-heartedly for half of her life? The person who feels just as alone in this world and needs to feel something again. Anything at all.

"What are you doin'?" His voice comes out breathy and quiet as he stares into my soul.

"Something I should have done the minute I saw you." I cautiously bring my arms out to wrap around his huge frame. I move slow so I don't spook the beast. So he doesn't run away and hide from me. I press my cheek against his chest and hold onto him, my arms wrapped around him tightly. He stands there rigid at first, unable to comprehend the proper response to this. I wait, patiently, for him to do something. For him to push me away or hug me back.

What I don't expect is for his hands to grab under my thighs and lift me off the floor until my legs are wrapped around his midsection. I don't expect him to wrap his arms around me so tight that I can barely take a deep breath. I don't expect his hand to find my hair and hold my head against his shoulder, caging me in so the only thing I know is Colton Grant.

He breathes deep against me, our chests moving as one. So many emotions flow around us in the small room. Emotions I can't name, or maybe I refuse to decipher. We stay like this, consumed by each other, for what feels like hours, days even. My tears soak into his white t-shirt, but it doesn't seem to bother him.

"I missed you, Colt. I missed you so fucking much." I let the admission sit between us in the air, not expecting a reply. I know the feelings I had for him back then weren't reciprocated. I know my love for him has always been different than his love for me. He loves me like a sibling, like his best friend's little sister.

"I missed you too, Mayo." I laugh at the nickname, having not heard it since my freshman year of high school.

"You promised you wouldn't call me that anymore." I pull my face away from his shoulder and look down at him, still suspended in his arms. His hazel eyes appear green in the dim light of his apartment. There are gold flecks splattered throughout the iris, giving him an ethereal look. His tan skin looks like porcelain and the beard covering his chin looks soft and supple. My hands beg to grab onto it, my face begs to be scratched by it. I notice the cowboy hat on his head and decide I love the way he looks in it.

"I promised I'd only call you that if we were alone." My mouth goes dry from his voice. My core suddenly very aware that it's pressed up against Colton's hard abs. "We're alone right now, Mayo."

The atmosphere around us changes. Suddenly the air feels thicker as it enters my body. The light seems dimmer, casting a sexy glow on us both. The air smells only of Colton, filling my lungs with him.

"Yeah. We are." The three words come out in a heavy breath. I look down at him, darting between his eyes and lips. I watch as his tongue slips out and licks his bottom lip, wetting it slightly, and my insides clench. I don't mean to squeeze my thighs around him, but I do, and the sexiest groan I've ever heard leaves his mouth.

"Maya. Tell me you want to leave." He's staring at my lips now, walking forward. He takes each step at the same time my chest heaves up and down. One breath for every step. Five breaths go by before my back hits something hard and cold. I turn my head just slightly and find myself pressed between Colton and the wall of windows.

"Maya. Tell me. Or you won't be able to." The threat sounds more like a promise and I squeeze my thighs again, letting my mouth fall open in a silent moan.

"No. I don't want to leave."

I watch something in his eyes flicker. Like he flipped the switch, turning off all signs of his humanity.

"Wrong answer." He doesn't give me time to register his words before I feel his lips crash into mine. It isn't soft and gentle. It's exactly what we both need. Full of pain and suffering. Full of feeling and passion. It feels like every nerve in my body has moved into my lips, making the sensation of his more intense. I grab onto the back of his head and hold onto his hair tight, preventing him moving and ending this before it even started.

His tongue glides against my lips and I open up for him, desperate for his taste. Desperate to memorize every outline of his mouth. He tastes like spearmint and I moan into him, savoring the feel of him against me. It's the most intoxicating kiss I've ever experienced. My mind feels like mush as we collide, devouring each other in a way that can't be described by mere kissing.

We are living for each other. Breathing in the other's oxygen. Sucking each other's souls out and keeping them captive so ours won't be completely alone anymore.

"God, you're even sweeter than I thought you'd be." His mouth moves against my own with his words and I grab his bottom lip in mine to keep him from talking before sucking it into my mouth and biting it softly. That small gesture takes away any taming I did to this beast and he unleashes everything he has on me.

He pushes me harder into the window, placing both of my hands above my head. His lips move away from my mouth and he trails his tongue down my chin before finding my neck. He sucks it with such ferocity that I cry out from the stimulation. It's all too much and somehow not enough.

"You drive me crazy, Maya Turner." His growl vibrates against my skin and I can't keep the gasp from escaping me. "Just one time. That's all I need." I don't grasp his words, too filled with lust. Instead, I find myself nodding my head, agreeing to anything this man says.

He moves us over to his bed and I watch as he removes his hat and shirt. My veins pulse at the sight of him shirtless before me. His body is made of hard ridges and dips that shouldn't be real. He has the physique of a man who spends all day outside, working on a ranch. When he moves towards the bed, bending down towards me, his biceps ripple and flex, showing off the impressive muscles under his tan skin. My finger's itch to touch him. To feel his warmth seep into me.

"Will you let me, Maya? Will you let me taste you?" My brain has shut off. I can't form proper words. If I try to speak, it will be a jumble of letters that don't fit together. Part of me thinks I'm still in my bed, dreaming the best dream I've ever had in my life. That would be such a cruel trick.

I nod my head yes, staring down at him near my feet. Goosebumps cover every inch of my body, anticipating what this man is about to do to me. I've touched myself more times than I can count thinking about this exact moment through the years.

His hands reach for my shoes first, keeping eye contact with me the entire time. Once they are properly thrown on the floor, I watch him crawl up the bed slowly, dipping his head down low when he reaches my knees. His mouth barely grazes against the flesh on the inside of my thigh and I have to fist my hands in the sheets and bite my tongue to keep from making embarrassing sounds. Wet heat lights up on my skin wherever he kisses and when he gets close enough to undo my pants, he rips them off in one swift movement, leaving me in my body suit.

"Too many fuckin' layers, darlin'." He looks up at me through hooded eyes before bringing his head down and nipping at the crease where my thigh ends. He stares into me the entire time and I whimper where I lay, my back arching off the bed.

"Please, Colt." I somehow form the two words. As much as I want his mouth on me, I want him in me more. I want us moving together in perfect unison. I want to feel him against my walls, rubbing me until we both come undone.

"Please what, baby girl?" The endearment makes me whimper again and I pick my hips up off the bed, desperate for him. "Tell me what you want."

I bring my hands down to where my body suit connects and snap the buttons open, before peeling the tight fabric off my body and over my head. I now lay completely naked in front of him, since I had foregone a bra and panties with the bodysuit.

"Fuck." His guttural groan rings through my ears and I heat up at the look in his eyes when he stares down at my body. I never thought Colton Grant would ever look at me like this. Ever touch me like this.

"I want you inside of me, Colt. Right now. Please. Please just fuck me." He clearly didn't expect me to say that. He seems surprised at first, staring down at me with feral eyes. He moves to remove his pants in one quick movement and I watch intently as his black boxers fall to the floor as well. We are now both completely bare, staring at each other's bodies with such lust, it makes the air thick.

The dark happy trail down his abs leads to his impressive length. He's so big, and so hard, that I can't help my mouth from watering at the sight of him. I want to taste him, but I can't risk us missing this connection. Not if it's the one and only time I ever get with Colton Grant.

"You want me to fuck you, Maya?" He crawls on top of me, bringing his face close to mine. "You want me to shove my dick into your tight little pussy?" My vision goes blurry, so blurry that I can barely see him. I feel drunk with lust. Drunk from the intensity of this man and the need I have for him.

"Yes. Fuck me, Colton. I want you deep inside of—"

"Ahhhh!" My sentence is cut off by him thrusting his hips forward and filling me up completely. It's so painfully glorious I have to squeeze my eyes shut to keep from floating off into the atmosphere.

"Look at me. I want you staring into my eyes when you come on my dick." His dirty words almost make me come right then, but I take deep breaths and focus on the color of his irises. He hasn't even moved yet and I'm already this far gone.

His hips slowly pull back and then sink into me again. It's a slow, torturous movement that sends my nerves buzzing into oblivion. I feel him everywhere. In my toes, my fingers, my ears. Colton Grant has taken up every inch of my body.

"You're so fuckin' tight, baby girl." He speaks through gritted teeth and it sounds more like a growl. He continues his slow movements, driving me mad.

"Harder. Please, Colt, fuck me harder." I grab onto his ass with both hands and pull him into me. He braces himself against the bed near my head and starts driving in, hard. His dick shoves into me at such a harsh speed, I feel like I'm going to be ripped apart from the inside out. My screams can't be muffled. When he throws his hand over my mouth, it only intensifies the pleasure.

"I'm gonna..." I can't get the words out. I'm cresting the top of the mountain, about to reach the peak. I feel tunnel vision taking over and right when I'm about to fade into oblivion, Colt pulls out of me. He pulls out completely, leaving me thrashing and begging on the bed.

"That's for leavin'." He grabs my waist and flips us over, positioning me so I'm sitting on top of him. I look down at the jerk I'm craving more than I crave air and bring my hands to his chest. Dragging them down, I scratch his skin hard, leaving red marks.

"That's for leaving first." My response makes his groan echo through the room. He lifts me off of him and then drops my body down hard onto his rock hard length. He gets deeper at this angle and I have to hold my breath through the pain of adjusting to him. After a few seconds, I grind my hips forward, using his toned midsection to intensify my pleasure by rubbing against it. I know he wants me to move up and down, but I'm going to torture him a little now.

I bring my hands up to my boobs and squeeze them, making my nipples even harder than they already were. Looking down at him, he has his hands behind his head, staring up at me like he's the king of the world. I keep moving, bringing myself dangerously close to the edge again, and this time, instead of making me stop, he brings his hand down between us and rubs me with his callused fingers.

"Go ahead and come now, darlin'. I won't make you stop this time."

"Oh God." I moan the words and throw my head back, my climax exploding through me like a stick of dynamite going off. I feel his hands reach for my hips and then suddenly I'm lifted partially in the air before he starts thrusting his hips forward and fucking me hard. I hear myself screaming, climaxing harder than I ever have in my entire life. His punishing thrusts extend the orgasm and make me spasm around his dick, drawing sounds out of me that have never existed before now.

"Fuck, baby girl. I'm gonna come." He pumps into me three more times before his deep groan lights up the room with sparks and flames so hot, I think we might burn to death. He pulls me to him, chest to chest, as I feel his release fill my body, his dick pulsating deep inside of me. I never want this feeling to end. I never want this memory to leave. It's the most amazing moment of my life.

Our deep breaths are the only sound that fill the room. We lie here, connected still, for at least ten minutes. His hand brushes through my hair and my palms rest comfortably on his hot chest, occasionally stroking the hard muscle underneath.

"Are you…" he fumbles on his words and starts to pull away from me. "Are you on birth control?"

I almost laugh at the question. "A little late for that question, don't you think?" The joke doesn't get a laugh in response. Instead, awkward silence greets me. "Yeah, I'm on the pill. No need to worry about that." I pull myself away from him and slide my way across the bed until I'm at the edge. Standing, I look back at him and find him avoiding my eyes at all cost. He doesn't so much as look my way.

"Alright. This was fun. Thanks for the orgasm, buddy." I roll my eyes and grab the clothes off the floor before making my way through the house.

"Maya." His voice stops me in my tracks. My heart pounds for some sort of reassurance. It pounds for an apology, for an admission to something. Anything. "Can we keep this between us? I think it's best if we just…" He cuts off, so I finish his sentence.

"Pretend this never happened? Already done. I'm about to get married, remember? This was a stupid lapse of judgement. A mistake. We were both sad and lonely and our emotions got the best of us. Consider it wiped from my memory." The mention of my marriage sobers me and I feel my stomach drop into my feet. I just cheated on my fiancé. I've never cheated on anyone. That's not who I am. I'm loyal and trustworthy. At least, I used to be.

My walls start crashing in around me and I have to leave this apartment before I break down in front of him. I dart for the door, hyperventilating, ignoring my name being called behind me. I make my way down the stairs and throw myself into the barn. It's only when I'm standing among the horses that I remember I'm still completely naked. Colt's cum sticks to my thighs and reminds me of the sin I just committed.

I grab my navy shorts and wipe myself clean before throwing my white bodysuit back on. I frantically search the barn until my eyes make contact with one horse in particular. He's staring right at me, with soft understanding eyes. Jax. The horse I trained as a teenager. The black stallion that wouldn't listen to anyone else. He was such a stubborn animal, but once I got through to him, he followed me around the ranch like a dog. He's my horse. Always has been and always will be.

Walking towards him, he starts to huff loudly and his feet prance against the ground. He nays for me, reaching his neck across the gate to reach me. My hands graze his soft nose and up towards his eyes. He's as handsome as I remember. His beauty almost distracts me from what I just did. From the horrifying act I just committed with a man who doesn't care about me. A man who couldn't even look me in the eyes after he came inside of me. Fuck Colton Grant.

Grabbing a saddle off the wall, I throw on a pair of my mom's extra boots in the corner of the barn and throw the saddle over Jax. Within minutes, I'm securely placed on top of him, petting his mane.

"That's a good boy. I missed you baby. I'm sorry I left you." I talk into Jax's ear and he rewards me with a shake of his head. "Wanna go for a ride?" His nay is loud through the barn and I can't hold back my laugh.

"Maya!" His voice echoes across the barn and the minute I hear it, I kick into Jax's side and he shoves us off into the night, leaving Colton in our wake.

Chapter

FIVE

Maya

Jax stops past the tree line, in the overgrown field that means so much to me. So much to my family. It was the place he always brought me when I was sad or angry. When Abby and Taylor laughed at me in the halls or I felt extra lonely. The lone tree in the middle of the field casts shadows across the grass. I can barely make out the flowers blooming above, but the intoxicating scent of magnolias fill my nose.

He stops near the tree, nibbling on the overgrown grass. The sun is just starting to rise, casting a soft orange glow on the world around us. I watch the tall grass surrounding us sway in the soft breeze and find myself wishing I was a strand being kissed by the wind, exactly where I'm supposed to be. It's mesmerizing. It looks like something out of a picture book, not real life.

Kissing Jax's mane, I hop off and walk over to the tree. I look up at the winding branches and memories of us laughing and climbing our way through the maze of bark take over. Andrew never wanted me to come out here with them, but Colton always made him. One of the many spots we loved to play, just like the pond. My grandparents planted this magnolia tree when they started this ranch. They built a life while this tree grew and grew. I wish trees could talk. I'd love to hear the stories this one has.

Sitting down with my back against the bark, I let my brain beat me down. I let it tell me how pathetic I am. I let it tell me that I'm a horrible person who is going to hell. That I'm a monster who destroyed not only my life, but Claude's as well. All over a man who never saw me as more than a kid. I forced myself on him during a sad, vulnerable moment, and he caved. Who wouldn't want to feel something good after thinking about such a horrible memory? It meant nothing to him and I turned it into one of the most important moments in my life.

I let myself wallow in self-hatred and self-pity for what feels like hours. It might have been, since the sun has completely risen and the birds are chirping loud. I know I have to get back to the ranch. I know I have to start working and forget about everything that happened in the last few hours. Daddy needs me, whether I feel up to ranch work near Colton or not. I need to be a big girl and pull my weight on the ranch.

"Ready, big guy? It's time to go home." The word sounds bittersweet coming out of my mouth. Part of me feels a twinge of hope when I say home and another part feels dread, knowing I'm only pretending. My real home is in New York... isn't it? Where my job is and my fiancé who probably won't be my fiancé much longer lives.

JAX TROTS INTO THE BARN AND I THROW MY LEG OFF OF HIM AND HOP down. Giving him one last kiss on his nose, I turn around to start my chores. *His* large frame stands inches away, blocking me in the stable.

"Move." I don't meet his eyes. I look straight at his chest and clench my teeth.

"Are you fuckin' crazy? You coulda been killed! Jax doesn't let anyone ride him." His voice sounds crazed and angry but I can't help but snort.

"Won't let anyone but me, cowboy. Relax. And move. I have chores to do." I put my hands on his chest and try to push him away but he doesn't budge.

"You're gonna act out cause, what? We didn't cuddle? You wanna go cuddle, Mayo? Let's go. Walk up those stairs and I'll spoon the shit out of you." He's mocking me. I gave him all of me and in return, he's making fun of my emotions.

"Fuck you, Colton."

"Already did that, darlin'. What's next?" My hand reaches out and slaps him before I can stop myself. The loud sound echoes against the walls and Jax snorts behind me.

"From this point on, we are nothing more than acquaintances, got it? I'm not Mayo. I'm not baby girl. What happened a few hours ago didn't happen. We have to be here for the next few weeks together and I don't need all of this." I throw my hands in the air. "To distract me from taking care of Daddy. I'm your best friend's baby sister. Nothing more, nothing less."

I finally allow myself to look up at him and the depths of his eyes threaten to drag me back down. Every word I speak is a lie, but it's a lie I need to convince myself of.

"You've always been more than just my best friend's sister, Maya." My heart squeezes and pounds. "But, you're right. We can't risk anythin' hurtin' your dad in anyway. From this point forward, I'll help you with your ranch duties, we'll be friendly around the house, and we'll forget about what just happened between us."

"And then in a few weeks, I'll be gone and we'll never have to see each other again." My sentence sits between us. I feel dread creep up inside of me like a shadow threatening to remove all of the light from my life.

Instead of answering, he just shakes his head and walks away, slamming the door leading to his apartment hard enough to make the walls in the barn shake. I hold my breath for a few seconds, squeezing my eyes shut, trying desperately not to break down. I haven't seen Colton Grant in twelve years and he's already grabbed hold of my heart in his callused hands. He's already squeezing it and trying to make it explode in his cold grasp.

I feel Jax's nose nuzzle up against my back and turn towards him. "Thanks, baby. I'm okay. I love you too." I place a kiss on his snout before walking out of the barn. I spot Andrew walking towards me with a concerned look on his face.

"What the hell you two doin' out here? That door slammin' was loud enough to wake the entire ranch."

"Nothing. He has a stick up his ass like always." I turn my head towards the barn and look into the top level of windows I hadn't noticed before. The windows my body was pressed up against mere hours ago. I can feel his eyes on me even though I can't see him through the glass.

"You guys better start gettin' along. You have to spend the next few weeks together and if you're takin' over my jobs, you'll be spendin' a lot of time together." Great. Just what I need. More time with the man who sends my emotions into overdrive. I audibly groan and Andrew squints his eyes at me.

"What's your problem with him? You guys used to get along so well when we were kids. I used to get jealous cause he was my best friend but he seemed to like you more." The chuckle that comes from his mouth is accompanied by a slow shake of his head.

"Yeah, that was more so out of pity than anything else. He always felt bad for me because I was a loser with no friends. Now, he doesn't have to pretend to like me." The admission hurts more than I thought it would.

"You weren't a loser and you had friends. You and Abby were attached at the hip."

"Yeah, until high school. After freshman year she ditched me. She took over Taylor's job of making fun of me when she graduated. I think she called me a boy almost every day until graduation."

"Damn. Why didn't I know that?" He looks genuinely surprised which only irritates me more.

"You went off to college. You were so focused on partying and school. I only ever saw you on holidays and it was only for a few days. You and Colton left me behind and I isolated myself."

"I'm sorry Maya, I had no idea. Why didn't you tell me?"

"I didn't really tell anyone. I guess I was upset with you and Colton." I don't know why I'm telling him this right now, but I can't seem to stop myself. "You barely came home and Colton never came over a single time after you went off to college."

"I don't know why he didn't. Somethin' changed in him after we left. He came home with me the first time but he refused to come over. He didn't even come see Mom and Dad until a year after you left for college."

"It doesn't matter. He's clearly changed and I have no interest in being his friend, so don't push it please." I feel the walls around my heart lift into place. They hold strong and provide a small layer of protection around the vulnerable organ.

"Alright little sis, I won't push it. But please try not to kill each other while you're here. For Dad's sake."

"No promises, but I'll try not to kill him. Maybe just put him in a coma for a little while?" I give him a lopsided smirk and we both start laughing, ridding the air of the awkward tension.

"I have to head out to work. I already fed the calves so now you just have to clean out the stables, and transfer the horses to their other pasture. Mama might need help weedin'." Andrew's eyes travel down and he starts laughing hysterically. "What the fuck are you wearin'?" I look down at my white bodysuit which is now dirty and mama's brown work boots that hit my knees. I look insane.

"Oh, shut up. I'm going to run to the store to grab some work clothes now, okay? Can I take the truck?"

"That truck is technically Colt's so you're gonna have to ask him. I've gotta run, love you, Maya."

"Love you too." Screw Colton. I'm not asking him shit. Making my way into the house, I throw on a tan short sleeve dress and brush through my hair. It's now almost eight in the morning which means I'll get to the small Apparel n All, one of the few stores in Evergreen, right when they open.

There's no sign of Mama or Daddy so I leave a note on the dining room table saying I ran into town. I speed walk to the truck parked out near the barn and hop into the front seat. Pulling the visor down, I catch the keys right before they fall into my lap. Starting the engine, I put the truck in reverse and open the windows. Turning the volume knob on the radio all the way up, Lynyrd Skynyrd's *Sweet Home Alabama* blasts through the cabin. I can't hold back my smile as I put on the aviator glasses sitting on the dashboard. I know they're Colton's and that thought only makes my grin widen.

"Hey! Maya what the hell are you doin'?" His yell can be heard over the music, just barely. I ignore him and back the truck up, a little too fast. The dirt road swirls up around me in a tornado of brown, blocking him from view. He's running out of the barn, towards the truck, but he's too far away. I throw the truck into drive and press the gas pedal hard, spinning the tires and flinging dry dirt and dust towards the man himself.

The smile stays plastered on my face the entire fifteen-minute drive into town. I'm so focused on the look on Colton's face when I sped out of the driveway in his truck, that I don't even realize I get to town until I'm pulling into the small plaza. I got here based off my memory after eight years.

I make my way into the log building filled with everything from ATVs to bras, and rush to the women's section. There's a section of flannels that I start at. Finding four different flannels in my size, I grab them and throw them in my cart. Next, I grab some white tank tops and a few plain t-shirts.

Searching for anything other than blue jeans, I stumble across the only shorts they have. They can barely be described as shorts. The jean material is torn in a few spots, including on the ass, and there's no way they are going to cover everything they are meant to cover. I grab three pairs, all in different shades of blue and throw them in the cart. They'll have to do.

My last stop is the shoe section. I grab a pair of flips flops and a pair of brown and black cowboy boots, along with a short pair of Muck boots. I turn to make my way to the cash register when I spot the bathing suit section. My mind wanders back to the way Colton looked at me in my lace underwear and I visibly shiver at the way his eyes scorched my skin. I definitely need a bathing suit if I want to go swimming again. I'm not sure what I'll do if I see that look in his eyes again.

The section is bare, leaving me very few choices. Grabbing the American flag bikini, I can't hold back the snort at the thought of Claude seeing me in this. He'd hate it. Which makes me want it even more.

Happy with my decisions, I start the short walk to the cash register. "All set, sugar?" the cashier's voice slurs slightly with her overly sweet tone. I remove all of my items and place them on the conveyer belt, ignoring the clearly intoxicated woman.

"Well I'll be. Maya Turner?" My name on her lips makes me look up at her in dread. The eyes of my ex best friend stare back at me. Only, they appear glazed over and the body they are attached to share no resemblance to the girl I used to know. Her once small frame is now swollen and puffy. Her brown hair looks wiery and thin and there are wrinkles covering her face. When she smiles at me, her teeth look like they are about to rot out of her head. It's obvious she's been doing drugs, and I feel a pang of guilt fill my stomach.

"Abby? Wow it's been a long time." I offer her a nice smile but I know it doesn't reach my eyes.

"Look at you. All fancy and dolled up. You look so different." I feel my eye twitch at the way her eyes travel down my body. The tone in her voice proves she's trying to belittle me, even now, after all of these years.

"Thanks. I have to dress like this for my job. Just came to grab a few things that I can wear around the ranch."

"What do you do now? Are you home for good?" She continues to stare at me rather than ring me up. I huff in annoyance but answer her questions.

"Oh God no. I'm just here visiting my daddy. I'm a prosecutor in New York City."

"A what?" She stares at me like I just spoke a different language and I have to bite my tongue to keep from laughing.

"I'm a lawyer who fights to put the bad guys in jail." I dumb it up a little and when her eyes go wide, I can't hold back my genuine smile.

"That's a big job for such a…" She doesn't finish her sentence.

"Such a what, Abby?"

"Such a pretty little thing, is all. I just wouldn't picture someone like you havin' such an important job. Gotta be scary dealin' with criminals."

"Aw, bless your heart. Don't worry about me. I'm doing just fine. Would you mind ringing me up so I can go back to helping my daddy? Thanks, sweetheart." My old accent comes shining through when I speak and I feel a bubble of pride rise up inside of me.

"Course. Heard Colton Grant was livin' on your families ranch these days. That true?" She starts ringing up my clothes and I find myself standing a little straighter with the mention of Colt. She always knew I had a crush on him. She was the only person who knew I was in love with him as a kid.

"Yes, he's working as a ranch hand for Daddy. He's been very helpful the last few years."

"I saw him round town a few weeks back. He's as delicious as always. You two ever…?" I gawk at her, in awe that she would be so forward with someone she hasn't seen in eight years.

"Um, that's frankly none of your business, Abigail."

"Poor thing. I know you always did have a thing for that boy. Shame he never saw you that way. You're missin' out." She fans her face with her fingers and I note the faded tattoos on her arms. Everything about her reeks cheap and dirty.

I ignore the insinuation in her voice even though it hits me hard. The way she said it makes it sound like her and Colton have been together. The thought makes me sick for more than one reason. Paying with my card and reaching for my bags, I try to leave without saying anything else. The minute my hand makes contact with the bag, I feel her grimy fingers grasp onto my hand. I try to pull it away but she holds on tight and brings the hand closer to her face.

"Now that's a rock. Looks like little Maya knows a thing or two about how to trap a man after all. Congrats." The word slithers out of her filthy mouth like a viper trying to strike me. I rip my hand from hers and offer her a fake smile.

"Have a great life, Abigail." I don't give her time to answer before I walk out of the store. The interaction turned my mood sour and when I hop into the truck and find the maintenance light beaming up at me, I slam my hands on the steering wheel and curse this town.

That girl ruined my high school experience and even now, after I've made a life for myself, she somehow gets to me. The comment about me missing out with Colt sits in my brain. I refuse to bring it up to him, since it's none of my business who he screws, but it doesn't stop me from thinking about it. Would Colton really fuck the girl he thought was my best friend? I can't picture the old Colt doing that, but this version of him would probably do it just to spite me.

Throwing the truck in drive, I make my way back to the ranch. I park the car next to the house and run upstairs to change. It's sweltering out today, so I forego the flannel and stick with the shorts and a white tank top. The shorts show off the bottom of my ass, which is not a look I regularly sport, and the waist is too big. Searching the room, I find one of the only things I left when I packed all of my clothes eight years ago. My brown leather belt with the big silver buckle. It somehow still fits after all this time, and I slip my new matching brown cowboy boots on before looking in the mirror.

I don't look like myself. I almost look like the old me, only older and with bigger boobs. I grab my blonde hair and throw the long strands up into a high ponytail, a few of my layers escape the hair tie and fall down, framing my face.

"Time to go fix a truck," I say to my own reflection and then head down the stairs. "Hey, Mama." I find her tidying up the kitchen and she gives me a big smile.

"Look at you, Mayflower. You look like a real Texas girl now." She walks over to me and places a soft kiss on my cheek. "Where are you off to? Do you want some breakfast?"

"The truck's maintenance light is on. I'm gonna go check it out. I'm good on breakfast but I'll come back inside for a cup of coffee if you have any."

"One coffee comin' right up." Her eyes gleam with unshed tears and I pull her into my arms without thinking.

"What's wrong, Mama? Please don't cry." I rub her back with my hands and she sniffles against my shoulder.

"I'm okay. It's just so nice havin' my baby home. I missed you so much."

"I missed you too, Mama. It's good to be back." I mean it whole heartedly. It's good to see my family and be back on this ranch. Without the lingering dread of the people in this town, I can actually enjoy life here. I missed the horses, the open fields, the stars.

"Go, don't let your sappy mama keep you from gettin' work done. I'll have coffee ready for you when you're done." She pulls away and walks back into the kitchen without another word.

"GOD DAMNIT." OIL SPITS OUT AND LANDS ON MY FACE AND CHEST. My once white tank top is now covered in the disgusting thick liquid. I move the pan under the oil pouring out and wipe my face with the back of my hand.

"You steal my truck and then break it?" His voice scares me and I jump under the truck, banging my head. The sound is loud and my hiss afterward can't be missed. "Get the fuck out from under there before you knock yourself out."

I pull myself out from under the truck and stand up, searching for the asshole himself. He's leaning against the driver side door, looking out into the field. I take in his cowboy hat and open blue flannel that exposes his wash board abs and try not to salivate. Why does he have to be so attractive?

"Your oil needed to be changed. I was doing just fine until you scared me." I glare at him until he turns my way. His eyes widen at the sight of me and crawl their way down my body. He lets them sit on my oil covered chest, the small exposed strip of skin on my waist, and my legs. I watch as heat flashes across his eyes and my knees almost buckle under me. It's too hot out here already without of the flames in his stare burning my skin.

"New clothes, huh?" His eyes don't meet mine. He continues to stare at the barely there shorts covering my sweaty body.

"Hence why I needed the truck. I'd ask you what you thought but it's pretty obvious." My ever growing smirk is impossible to hide. I watch as he moves in closer to me and the heat he was already throwing my way turns into a wild fire that threatens to burn me up from the inside out. He stands only a few inches from me, his head dropped down to stare into my fluttering eyes.

"I know the last time you were on this ranch you were a teenager, but that doesn't mean you have to shop in the children's section still." His words assault my ears in a husky whisper. I'm so turned on by his presence that I almost miss the insult. By the time I realize what he said, he is walking away from me.

"Actually." His voice is behind me now, closer than I thought he would be. "I take that back. I love these damn shorts, darlin'." His growl makes me take a deep breath, and when a hard slap hits my almost bare ass, I choke on the air in my lungs. I spin around to yell at him for being so inappropriate, but his back is already to me, walking to the barn. I can feel the smirk on his face even though I can't see it.

I squeeze my hands to prevent myself from exploding. I feel so much irritation for the man rise up inside of me that it's almost too much to bear. It bubbles up and threatens to boil over, burning me in the process.

So why am I smiling?

Chapter

SIX

Maya

"Tell us about New York," my mom's chipper voice makes me jump from across the dinner table. This is the first dinner we have had all together since I arrived a few days ago. Even Daddy managed to stay up to join us. I look over at his thin frame and my heart tugs. How can someone change so much? Thinking about the amount of pain and suffering he has had to go through makes me lose my appetite.

"You guys would hate it." I look down at my near empty plate while I talk. "There's always traffic, everyone is always in a rush. Instead of grass there's cement everywhere, it smells like grease and garbage half the time. You can't even see the stars. I haven't seen stars in years until coming back here. That's probably the worst part. Well, that and the water. The water is shit." I watch my fork roll around the peas sitting on my plate. The mac and cheese and short ribs are long gone, happily residing in my full stomach. I missed my mom's cooking more than I thought.

The silence suddenly gets to me and I look up from my plate to find four sets of eyes staring at me. Andrew has an amused grin, Colton looks indifferent with his bored glare, and Mama and Daddy both look worried.

"What?" My eyes dart between the four of them, waiting for an answer.

"If you hate it so much, why are you there?" Daddy has his hands clasped in front of him on the table.

"It's not all bad. I love my job and the city gives me so many opportunities there. The shopping and gyms are convenient. There are a million restaurants with all kinds of cuisines to choose from."

"What about your fiancé?" Colton's clipped tone grates at my ears. My eyes drag through the room until they land on him. His tan skin is red from exertion and the sun. He has small specks of dirt on his cheeks and forehead that he missed while cleaning up for dinner. His hazel eyes stare into mine, unknown emotions dancing across them.

"What about him?"

"You didn't include him in the list of things you like about the city." The bored glare turns into a smug expression and I find myself wanting to punch the expression right off his face.

"Well, that's a given, isn't it? He's my fiancé after all." I watch as one single brow raises and his hand rubs over his manicured beard. He's looking at me like he knows something I don't.

"Oh sweetie, when are we going to meet him? I want to meet the man that stole our baby girl's heart." Mama's voice steals my attention from the gorgeous jerk sitting across from me.

Before I can answer, Daddy's voice chimes in. "Yeah, I'd like to meet him at least once. You know, before I'm dead."

"Oh, good heaven, Billy. Don't talk like that." I watch as Mama shakes her head and looks down, avoiding the amused smirk on my dad's face. He jokes to make light of the situation, but I can tell how much it kills Mama to think about it.

"He's just busy right now. I'll try my hardest to get him to come back here with me soon." It's a complete lie. I never want Claude here. He'd taint this place somehow.

Colton's snort echoes off the walls and I can't help but glare at him. He thinks he knows so much, but he has no idea.

"Colton Grant, don't snort at the dinner table." Mama's firm scold brings a smile to my face and I find myself raising an eyebrow at him now.

"Sorry, ma'am." The way he says it brings me right back to when I was thirteen and we sat at this exact same table all together. Colton's sweet smile staring back at me, Daddy's boisterous laugh filling the room. Things were so different back then. We were all so happy, so oblivious of the shit life can serve you.

"Thank you, sweetheart." She brings her attention back to me now. "Are you gonna let your poor Mama help you plan your weddin?"

"Honestly, I haven't made any plans yet myself. Works been busy and I have a huge case I'm dealing with that's been taking up all of my time."

"Aren't you gettin' married in a few months? How do you expect to get everythin' done in such a short amount of time?" Andrew's voice is hard to understand through the food he's shoveling into his mouth.

"I don't want a big wedding. I don't have a lot of friends in the city, so I was planning on doing something small. I don't care about the big white wedding like most girls." That's the second lie

I've told tonight. I have always dreamed about my wedding day. The only problem is I can't imagine planning it next to Claude.

"Loser." Andrew coughs out the word and I flip him off.

"You two better knock it off before I make you eat outside like the rest of the animals." Mama can't hold back the laugh even though she's scolding us. "Either way, I'd love to help you plan it. You're the only daughter I have."

"Okay, Mama. I'd love if you helped plan it." I give her my best smile and watch as she looks at Daddy with a mixture of sadness and love in her eyes. I know what she's thinking. She wants him to be there. She wants him to walk me down the aisle. It's the same thing I'm thinking right now. The same thing I have refused to let myself think about until this moment. Because if I think about it, I won't ever stop crying. If I think about it, I'll fall into a hole that I won't be able to dig myself out of.

The feeling of being watched distracts me from the morbid thought and I turn towards the eyes staring me down. He's looking at me with the same confusing look on his face. The look that is full of emotion, each one impossible to identify. All I want is to climb into Colton's brain and figure out what he's thinking. Figure out what he sees when he looks at me. Figure out what secrets he's holding and what secrets he thinks he knows about me.

"What about you, Colton?" I grab my iced tea and take a big chug of it, my eyes never leaving his.

"What about me, little Turner?"

"Back in the day, I thought you would have been married by now." The quickest flash of sadness sparks in his eyes, but it's gone as fast as it comes.

"Oh, he's married to his job," Mama answers before he can. "We've been tryin to get him to settle down with a young lady, but he has no interest."

"That so? Why's that, Colt?"

He shrugs his shoulders before answering. "Haven't found the right girl. Every time I find someone I like, they end up showin their true colors." Something in the way he's looking at me makes a chill travel down my spine. It feels like he's talking to me and only me. Like we are the only two people in the room. To avoid his intensity, I take another sip of my drink. I wish the brown liquid was whiskey instead of sweet tea.

"You've always been so picky, Colton Grant. Even in high school, it seemed like the only girl you ever liked was our Maya." Mama's comment makes the tea go down the wrong pipe and I find myself coughing up a fit in front of everyone.

"I was just busy is all. Maya just happened to always be around. Couldn't seem to get rid of her." He smiles through his words, making it sound like a joke. So why does my heart feel like it's crumbling in my chest? I used to have this overwhelming fear that Colton always pretended to like me. That I was just the annoying little sister.

"Oh, that's bull. You always wanted her around," Andrew chimes in and hits Colton on the shoulder. "I couldn't get rid of her because you couldn't get enough of her."

"That sounds more accurate. I was always happy you were around to take care of our little girl. She needed a big brother to protect her since the actual brother she had was a selfish dufus." Daddy's joke makes the table erupt into laughter. That is, from everyone but me and Colton. We just stare at each other from across the table. Our eyes stay glued to each other, calculating and dissecting. I feel our past flowing between them, the memories of our friendship. The small globes in our heads hold onto every single one, replaying them as if they were projectors spinning on a constant reel.

"I was not a selfish dufus, I just didn't want my kid sister followin' me around everywhere I went."

73

"She was definitely your little shadow. I like to think she just looked up to you." I can't hold back the snort that escapes at my mom's words.

"Sorry Mama, but that definitely wasn't it. You remember Andrew when he was in high school, right?"

"Hey! What's that supposed to mean?" The smirk on Andrew's face makes it hard for me not to smile back.

"How do I put this nicely? You were a lazy, dumb, horny teenager." Colton's loud laugh surprises me and I find myself laughing along with him. His eyes shine with humor when he looks at me and it's the most beautiful sight I've ever seen.

"Great, you two are gettin' along again. I'm havin' PTSD already from my childhood when you two left me out constantly." The minute Andrew makes the joke, Colton's demeanor changes completely. The once humor filled look he was throwing my way is now replaced by sharp daggers that slice through me and make me wince.

"Thank you for dinner, Mrs. Turner." Colt's chair screeches against the floor when he stands. Without another word, he walks out of the house.

"What bug just crawled up his ass?" I don't answer Andrew out loud, in fact, no one does. But I know the answer. That bug is me.

Chapter

SEVEN

Colton

"Hey there Margo baby, how you feelin today?" I walk up to my favorite Longhorn and brush my hand against her nose. The horns on this animal could kill you with one swing, but she wouldn't hurt a fly. At least, not on purpose. There have been countless times she has accidentally swung her head a little too hard and come close to skewering me like a shish-ka-bob. I don't hold it against her though.

Margo is due any day now and I swear she gets bigger every time I see her. She's getting pretty hostile with the impending due date and over the course of a week, she's wandered off the ranch and into neighboring land countless times. The worst part is, most of the herd tends to follow her when she wanders. They stick together, which makes my life a lot harder. Luckily, they are very food motivated, which means I just have to shake a bag of grain or corn and they usually follow me back home.

Grabbing the knife from my back pocket, I cut the apple in my hand into four pieces and feed them to her one at a time. While she eats, I admire her unique pelt. She's a mix of white, brown, and black, and the design on her reminds me of paint being splattered on a canvas.

"So, what do you think of the new help, Margo?" I nod my head over to the other field, where Maya is brushing one of the horses. She's been here for five days now and I've barely spoken a word to her since dinner two nights ago. She gets under my skin like no one else. It's been that way since we were kids. Except back then, I thought she was the sweetest girl in the world. I wanted to protect her from everyone and everything. Turns out, she didn't need protecting, she was as cruel and ruthless as the rest of them.

Margo's loud moo rings through my ears and I can't hold back my laugh. Patting her on the head, I watch Maya as she works. "She drives me crazy too, pretty girl." My eyes land on the shorts she's wearing and I grit my teeth. She's trying to torture me, I'm sure of it. It should be a sin to wear shorts like that on a body like hers. I've seen pictures of her from Andrew and Mr. and Mrs. Turner, but for some reason I still pictured her like the tomboy from years ago. When I saw her for the first time the other day, with her soft features, long blonde hair, and curves that went on for miles, I damn near lost my mind.

I think back to our experience the other morning. I reacted like a horse's ass after it happened and she called it a mistake. I hate to admit how much that hurt. Hurt like damn hell. But, if she can be civil and act like that morning never happened, so can I… kind of. Lord knows she doesn't care about me like I once thought she did. She outgrew all of us, and now she's moved on to bigger and better things. Like putting people behind bars. The thought of her working so closely to criminals makes my blood boil. I'd go crazy with worry if I was her fiancé.

Fuck. Her fiancé. The French pussy she cheated on with me. The loser who can't get off the couch long enough to find another job. I looked into him, as much as I begged myself not to, and I wasn't impressed. The cocky prick was a well-known chef once upon a time, but now he's nothing more than a pompous loser who thinks the world owes him something. He's not good enough for Maya Turner. Not the Maya Turner I used to know at least. I don't know this Maya.

"Woah, boy. It's okay." Her worried voice along with an aggravated nay flows through the hot air. Looking over at where she is, I find her standing with her hands up next to one of the new stallions, who is currently up on its hind legs. One of the new stallions that we keep separate from the other horses since he's aggressive.

I don't think. I just run. I run faster than I've ever ran in my life. Hopping over the fence separating the two fields, I feel my heart racing out of my chest. Maya's scared face takes up every inch of my mind. My ears ring with the sound of Maya's worried voice. Watching, I see her walk towards the horse, calmly, thinking that will work.

"Maya, don't!" I yell towards her, still ten yards away. My voice startles the horse and he kicks back up on his hind legs, catching Maya in the shoulder on its way up. The world stops spinning as I see her fall to the ground. She falls in slow motion, her arms reaching out to catch something, her legs giving out under her, her head hitting the ground first followed by the rest of her fragile frame. She turns and cowers into the ground, protecting her face and vital organs from the possibility of being trampled.

The horse runs away at the same time I make it to Maya. I fall to the ground and grab for her shaking body, my own replicating her movements from the fear coursing through me. She's shaking so hard from her sobs, I dread seeing how bad her shoulder is. The thought of it broken, ripped open, or worse, makes my vision go blurry.

"Baby girl, I'm going to flip you over, okay?" I don't give her time to answer, not that she could through the sobs anyway. I grab her waist and flip her over, pulling her onto my lap. I take a deep breath and then look down at her, preparing for the worst. I find her white shirt scuffed and stained with dirt, but it isn't ripped open. There's no blood stains covering the bright fabric either.

Chancing a look at her face, I furrow my brows at the sight. The shaking wasn't coming from her sobs. It was coming from her hysterical laughter. Her perfect lips are turned up in a gorgeous smile as her eyes crinkle at the sides. She's laughing so hard that no sound is coming out and I find myself staring at her like she's lost her mind. Maybe she has.

"You should see your face right now." The words are barely audible through her cackles. Alright, she's definitely lost it. Maybe the horse hit her head, not her shoulder, after all.

"You could have gotten yourself killed." I glare down at her but the gesture holds no real anger. I'm fighting back the smile that wants to escape when I look at her huge grin and sparkling eyes.

"You're the one that screamed near a scared horse!" She swats at my chest and I finally let myself laugh. She's right. I've been around horses all my life and somehow, I managed to do one of the worst things you could in that situation.

"I thought he was going to kill you! Sorry I panicked." I reach for her sides and pinch her softly, bringing out the cutest squeal I've ever heard from her plush lips. The sound is so addicting I keep tickling her, desperate to hear it again. She thrashes and pulls away from me, her intoxicating laugh echoing through the air. She pulls herself off of me and onto the grass, but I don't let her get away that easy. Moving fast, I position myself on top of her and let my weight crush her into the soft dirt, keeping her trapped.

Her giggling cuts out, but the smile stays plastered on her face as she looks up at me. Her eyes are wide and shining, staring straight into me in a way no one else ever has. A way that scares me and entices me all at the same time. Like she knows my every fear, want, hope in life. Like I'm an open book for her to dissect with her piercing blue eyes.

"So, he has a heart after all." It comes out as a joke, but I hear the serious tone behind her words. She thinks I hate her. If only she knew the truth.

"I just didn't want to have to clean up the mess. I'm not big on blood." I can't hide my smirk when her eyes roll. She looks like the old Maya right now. The innocent little girl who always smiled and joked with me. Who looked up at me with the biggest sparkling eyes and was able to melt my heart with a single word.

"So, Colton Grant is afraid of a little blood? Maybe you aren't as tough as I thought."

"Oh darlin', don't you go playin' with fire. You're gonna get burnt before you even realize you touched the flame." I don't know why I'm flirting, but the southern drawl in my voice comes out thicker and more husky. I'm the one playing with fire here.

"Is that a threat, cowboy?" The lopsided grin staring back at me is impossible to ignore. I feel entranced by it, completely fixated on the way the soft pink flesh curves up at a slight angle. The way her cupid's bow dips down forming a slight v in her top lip. The way one of her dimples shines through with the crooked slant of her mouth.

"Threats are meant to inflict pain, baby girl. You're not gonna feel pain." I'm crossing a line. A line I know I shouldn't be crossing again. A line I promised myself I would stay far, far away from after our last encounter. She's dangerous. She's addictive and her presence alone makes me second guess everything in my life.

"I like a little pain, Colt." My groan fills the air and I drop my head, ripping my eyes from hers. I'm two seconds away from grinding into her and taking her plump lips in my mouth right here in the field.

"Colton?" Andrew's voice breaks me from my trance and I practically throw my body off of Maya's before standing. Looking at the intruder, I find Andrew sauntering towards us in the field. "You better not be tryin' to kill my sister." His voice is coated in humor, but if he knew what I was thinking, he'd kill me. If he knew I was two seconds away from ripping the tiny white t-shirt off of Maya and sucking on her nipples. If he knew how painful my rock hard cock was pushing up against the zipper of my jeans. If he knew I came inside of his sister just days ago, right here on his family's ranch. I grit my teeth at the memory, desperately trying to rid her soft moans and naked body from my mind.

"She's got that part covered herself. Caught her tryin' to train Trigger over here."

"Trigger?" I look over at her raised brows when she says the name.

"Yeah. if you even try to touch him, he goes off. Hence why I was so worried." She nods her head in understanding but shrugs a shoulder as if it wasn't a big deal after all.

"Well, he seemed lonely and I wanted to give him a chance. I was fine until you screamed." She sucks her bottom lip into her mouth before biting down on the pillowy flesh. Her eyes blink at me in innocence and I glare back, knowing exactly what she's trying to do.

"You screamed near Trigger? Have you lost your damn mind?" Andrew finally reaches us, bringing his hand down hard on the back of my shoulder.

"Fuck off, I have a lot on my mind."

"Sounds like you need a night off then. How bout it?" Andrew waits, eagerly, for me to agree. As much as I don't want to go out, I could use a stiff drink or five to forget about the pain in the ass sitting in the field in front of me.

"Yeah, a night off sounds good."

"Can I come?" Maya's excited voice flows through my ears and I whip my head in her direction, watching her stand.

I'm about to answer, telling her no way in hell, when Andrew beats me to it. "Hell yeah. I think it's about time my baby sis and I have a legal drink together. Especially since you're five years over legal drinking age already."

"You sure that's a good idea? How would your fiancé feel about his girl goin' out to bars without him?" I say a silent prayer that the fake judgement in my voice makes her feel guilty and she agrees that she shouldn't come.

"Oh, he's fine. Besides, there's a lot I've done since being on this ranch that my fiancé wouldn't agree with." Her insinuation isn't missed and I grit my teeth. She's trying to get to me and it's working. Andrew's laugh interrupts my thoughts and I look over at him again.

"Yeah, he doesn't seem like the type to get down and dirty on a ranch, huh?"

"Not at all." Her suggestive eyes stare straight into mine. "He couldn't handle how dirty I've gotten since being here." She licks her lips and I have to look away. If I don't, Andrew's going to bear witness to the many dirty things we are both thinking right now.

"It's nice seeing you working out here, Maya. I know it's different from your usual work load, but I think a little ranch work is good for the soul." How Andrew doesn't pick up on the sexual tension radiating off of us is almost comical. He's oblivious to the double meaning of her words and I find myself wishing I was too.

"I agree. Alright, I'm gonna go take a shower. What time are we leaving?"

"Let's meet at the truck in an hour and a half?" Andrew answers her question as she starts to walk off.

"Great. I'll meet y'all there." The accent she used to have shines through in her voice and I hate how sexy it sounds. I force myself not to look at her as she walks away, but I'm slowly realizing that I'm a weak man. Her heart shaped ass practically spills out of her tight jean shorts. She sways her hips as she walks, torturing me with the movement.

"She'll be the old Texas Maya before we know it." Andrew's loud voice makes me jump and I look away from the mesmerizing view. Clearing my throat, I chance a look at him, hoping he didn't notice the way his best friend was ogling his younger sister.

"I don't know about that. She's a city girl through and through now." I spit the words out like they're sour.

"What happened between the two of you?" His question makes my mouth go dry. Does he know? Did Maya tell him what we did?

"What do you mean?" I tread lightly, not wanting to give anything away.

"You used to be so close. Now you talk about her like you don't know her." We start walking through the field, towards the barn.

"I don't know her, Drew. Not anymore at least. Yeah, we were close when we were kids. She was family to me too, but after twelve years, people change."

"Oh, that's bullshit. People don't change. Yeah, her life is different now, but she's still the same sweet Maya she used to be when we were kids."

"I wouldn't be so sure about that one." I think back to the day that changed everything for me. The day I found out the truth about how Maya actually felt. What she said.

"Well, at least try to be nice to her tonight." He bumps his shoulder into mine before walking off ahead of me. I take a deep breath and try to think of anything but Maya Turner. The girl who meant so much to me and ruined me for it.

The girl who hides behind a mask of innocence and lies.

Chapter

EIGHT

Maya

Normally, if I were to go out to a bar in the city, I'd wear my work clothes. Something consisting of a nice dress, a pencil skirt, or fitted dress pants. But, knowing the places we are going to be stopping at will be a bit closer to honky-tonk dive bars rather than night clubs, I dressed accordingly.

I take one last look in the mirror and admire my appearance. I'm wearing my white deep V-neck body suit, tucked into a pair of the shorts I haven't worn yet. These ones have extra holes and tears, and are a darker blue denim. They hit high on my thigh, and even higher on my ass. The dark gray flannel falling off one shoulder and my new cowboy boots tie the entire look together.

I curled my long blonde hair so it falls down my back in loose waves and added a light gray smokey eye to match my flannel and make my eyes pop. The crimson stain on my lips promises to stay put all night, no matter how many drinks I have. I look like a completely different person. I don't look like the old Maya or the new Maya. I don't look like Maya at all. Which is exactly who I want it to be tonight.

Making my way downstairs, I find Andrew and Mama in the kitchen. Mama's cooking on the stove and Andrew is sitting at the island, talking to her about work. Something about the sight brings tears to my eyes. With Daddy sleeping in his room, I can't help but picture this scenario happening when he's gone. If Andrew doesn't stay here to keep her company, she's going to be completely alone when the time comes. She'll be standing in this kitchen making dinner for herself, with silence surrounding her.

I think about Colton living outside and say a silent prayer that he continues to live on the ranch. I know it's a hopeless prayer. One day Colton will find someone and he'll get married and move into his own house. One day he'll outgrow the ranch work he's doing for my parents. And then, Mama will be on her own, living on a huge farm with no one but the animals and memories to keep her company. I can't let that happen. I refuse to.

"Hey Mama." I walk up behind her and place a soft kiss against her cheek.

"Hi Mayflower. You look beautiful." Her eyes shine as she looks at me and it only makes me want to cry harder. She's such a strong woman. The love my parents have for each other is something I always wanted. Memories of Daddy coming up behind her and whisking her away from the stove to dance in the middle of the kitchen even though there was never any music playing flash across my mind. Memories of them sitting out on the front porch, under a blanket, staring up at the stars until well past bedtime. Memories of them looking at each other from across the dining room table every night, their entire lives together reflecting in their eyes. Their hard work, their friendship, and their love that brought them to where they are now.

I was too young to truly appreciate that about them. I was too caught up in my own misery to acknowledge everything they went through together. And now, it's being ripped out from under them. The only man my mother has ever loved is being taken all too soon. Yet, when I stare into her light blue eyes, I still see the reflection of their lives together dancing across her irises. She still smiles and laughs.

"I love you, Mama." The words come out choked. I watch as her eyebrows furrow with worry and she drops her wooden spoon to pull me into a tight embrace.

"Oh, Maya. I love you so much more. Please don't cry."

"I'm sorry," I sniffle through my words. "I just… I don't know why I'm crying."

"It's an emotional time for all of us, sweetheart. We're all overwhelmed. I'm just happy we are able to be together during it." Her sniffle rings through my ears and I hate myself for making her cry. I need to be stronger. I need to be more like her.

"Me too, Mama." I wipe my eyes and pull away from her, letting her get back to cooking.

"You walk in here and a two seconds later you're making Mama cry. You ought a be ashamed of yourself." Andrew shakes his head at me, while pulling himself off of his chair. He puts his arms around me and squeezes tight. "It's okay to cry, baby sis," he whispers the words so only I hear them.

"Should we get going?" I sniffle away the last of my emotion and pull myself together.

"Just waitin on Colton." I turn to look at my brother and take in his outfit. He's wearing a blue t-shirt and a pair of dirty jeans.

"This is your going out attire? You're never going to find a woman if you don't try to look a little nicer."

"I'm doin' just fine in the lady department thank you very much. I just don't want to settle down yet."

"Don't get your brother started. I've been beggin him for grandkids for the last four years. At least I have you to supply me with lots of those now." Her voice sounds so excited but the words make my stomach drop. The thought of kids with Claude sounds like a version of my own personal hell.

"Uh, yeah, definitely Mama." I give her my best forced smile and then turn towards the door of the kitchen to leave. Colton's glare makes me stop in my tracks. He looks mouthwatering with a black button up, his dark gray jeans, and his cowboy hat placed on his head. His beard is perfectly manicured and his light hazel eyes pierce into my soul.

"Have somethin' you forgot to mention?" He overheard the conversation, and if looks could kill, I'd be dead. "That why all your clothes barely fit ya?"

"Shut up. I'm not—"

"So, it's a shotgun weddin' then? It's all makin sense now. Congrats little Turner." He gives me a disgusted smirk and I can't stop my hands from balling into fists at my side.

"I'm not pregnant." I glare daggers into the man who keeps giving me whiplash with his emotions towards me. One minute he looks at me like he'd kill for me, and the next he looks like he wants to kill me.

"But hopefully after the weddin you will be soon, Mayflower! That's what honeymoons are for after all." Mama's excited voice echoes through the silent room and I cringe at her words. Colton's jaw ticks but he schools the rest of his emotions with a dangerous smile on his face.

"I'm ready for a drink. We leavin or what?" Colton walks over to Mama and gives her a kiss on her cheek before walking out of the house without another word.

"That boy has been through so much." Mama's head shakes slowly, her lip wobbling slightly. "I pray every night that he finds someone to give him a family of his own. He deserves love." Her words aren't said to anyone in particular, so neither one of us answer as we kiss her goodbye and head out.

I can't help but think of her words as we make our way to the truck. She's right, he has been through a lot. He has no family left, besides my family. I'm surprised he hasn't found someone to settle down with yet, honestly. With how handsome and hardworking he is, I figured women would be throwing themselves at him and begging him to impregnate them. The thought alone makes me sick with jealousy.

"You sit in the middle." Andrew opens the passenger door for me and waits for me to get in.

"Why can't you sit in the middle?" I cross my arms over my chest and stand up straight.

"Because the middle seat has no leg room and you are almost a foot shorter than both me and Colt. Get in before I throw you in." He moves like he's about to grab me and I yelp, jumping back.

"Okay, fine, I'll get in!" I jump into the truck to avoid him picking me up and slide in faster than I mean to. Colliding right into Colt's hard body, he puts his hand out to stop me and it lands right on my tit. My very braless tit under the shirt I'm wearing. The small contact makes my nipples stand at attention and Colt's eyes drop right to them which only makes them pebble even more. Clearing his throat, he averts his eyes and I sit up straight, making sure I'm positioned half in the passenger seat and half in the middle seat. I don't want any part of my body touching Colt, for both of our sakes.

"Scooch your ass over. Colt won't bite. He promised me." Andrew pushes me with his ass and makes me move into the middle. My thigh rubs up against Colton's and I have no way of moving it. Everywhere we touch feels like it's on fire. Andrew's words repeat in my head and I gulp down at the thought of him doing exactly that. Biting me in all the right places.

"Alright, let's get wasted!" I couldn't agree with my brother more.

IT TAKES THREE SHOTS OF JAMESON TO FINALLY LOOSEN ME UP. Andrew took the first two with me but now he's off dancing with some girl. Colton on the other hand, disappeared the minute we showed up a half hour ago. The bar we are at is called Wet Whistle. The walls are covered in American flags and longhorn heads and the speakers are blasting loud country music. It was pretty empty when we got here, but it's slowly filling up with people.

Sitting in my seat at the bar, I signal for the bartender to come over. He comes over quick, giving me a smirk. He's good looking enough, but he's a lot cockier than he should be. He has dirty blonde hair, a sharp square face with brown eyes, and a bulky body under the red flannel he's wearing.

"What can I get ya now, sweetheart?" His voice booms out over the loud music. He leans against the bar, getting closer so he can hear me. His eyes dart right to my cleavage and stay put, waiting for my answer. Rolling my eyes, I shift in my seat so my tits aren't in his line of sight any longer.

"Can I do a double Jack and coke please?"

"You got it." He winks at me once before walking off to make my drink. Pulling out my phone, I click on Claude's name and scroll through our messages. I've texted him every day since being here, but he barely gives me the time of day. If he takes the time to text me back, it's a quick, 'Have fun, miss you!' I get it though, he's super busy trying to get the high score on his stupid soccer videogame.

"Here ya go. This one's covered, sweetheart." I look up at the bartender and give him a sweet smile.

"Thank you, but you don't have to do that." I pull out my wallet to start my own tab since Andrew bought the shots.

"No reason to thank me. That guy over there wanted to buy you the drink." He nods his head to the right and I follow its movement. Sitting at the bar is an attractive man with very familiar features. I stare at his light blue eyes and jet-black hair that's pulled back into a messy bun, a few pieces falling around his face. When his eyes make contact with mine and a dimpled smile greets me, I realize exactly who it is. Standing from my seat, I grab my drink and walk over to the man from my past. The man who took my virginity.

"Holy shit. Harrison Leary?" I watch as he stands from his seat and take him in with a quick drag of my eyes. He got a lot bigger since high school. His bulky frame is covered in black skinny jeans, a black t-shirt, and a distressed jean jacket. He looks like your typical hipster, but it suits him well.

"I thought that was you, Maya Turner. I could pick out those blue eyes anywhere." We give each other a quick hug and then I sit down in the seat next to his. He was a player back in high school, but I could use a familiar face tonight.

"Thank you for the drink. How've you been?" I'm genuinely curious what he ended up doing after high school.

"Really good actually. I opened up my own tattoo shop in town a few years ago."

"I had no idea you were into art! That's amazing, Harry. I've always wanted to get a tattoo." The liquor is making my lips a lot looser than they normally are. I have always wanted a tattoo, but that's not something I tend to tell people.

"Well, how long are you in town? Maybe I can be another one of your firsts." He winks at me and my giggle slips out into the air.

"Hopefully the first tattoo is better than the other first was." My eyes widen at the joke I meant to say in my head. Jameson is not my friend. "Uh, sorry that was…"

"A low blow, but very true. I had a huge crush on you all through high school and I was a little drunk after prom. Not the best combination, apparently."

"It wouldn't have been good either way. Losing your virginity is never fun." I take another big chug of my drink and answer his earlier question. "I'm here for a few weeks, I'm not sure exactly how long yet though."

"I heard about your dad. I'm sorry to hear that, Maya. Can I do anything?" He puts his hand over mine in a comforting way and I smile back at him.

"Thank you. We're just taking it day by day at this point. Trying to keep him as pain free and happy as possible, you know?"

"He's lucky to have all of you guys. I heard you were a hot shot lawyer out in New York?" His hand squeezes mine and it's at that moment I realize we are still touching hands. I gently remove mine from his and nod my head with a smile.

"Hot shot, no. But Lawyer in New York, yes." I grab my drink again and take another big sip. Harry's low whistle pulls my eyes to his and I find him staring at my hand.

"That's quite the ring. Who's the lucky man?" He smiles genuinely at me. He doesn't seem upset that I'm not single, in fact, he almost seems relieved.

"Just some guy I met in the city."

"That's all I get? No name? No love story? Just some guy?" His laugh hits my ears but the alcohol in my stomach turns sour. I called him some guy? The man I'm supposed to marry in a few months can only be described as some guy? I try to think of our love story but nothing beautiful or romantic comes to mind. We have no story.

"Um, yeah. Sorry. His name is Claude. He's a chef, er, he was a chef." I grit my teeth at the thought of him. The longer I'm away from Claude, the more I'm realizing how much I can't stand him. How easy it is to live without him.

"Claude, huh? So, you're into French men?" His shoulder bumps into mine and I roll my eyes at him. His phone starts ringing and I watch him pull it out before grinning at the name on the screen. "I'll be right back."

I stare down at my drink and play with the straw, my mind racing. I try to think of positive memories. I try to think of the qualities I love about Claude, but nothing comes. All I can remember are bad memories. Memories of being let down and disappointed. Memories of being forgotten and ignored.

The sound of my phone binging breaks me from my thoughts and I look down at the text I just received. It's a number I don't recognize.

Unknown: Stop trying to make me jealous.

My first thought is Claude, but that doesn't make sense since he's in New York. Not only that, but he would have to stop thinking about himself long enough to actually care about what I'm doing.

Me: Who is this?

Unknown: Keep your hands off of him, Maya. I'm warning you.

The text makes my heart skip a beat, from both fear and exhilaration. I have a feeling I know who this is, or who I want it to be.

Me: Or what?

Unknown: Or I'll haul you out to the truck and punish you.

Unknown: I don't give a shit that your brother is here. Not right now.

Me: How did you get my number, Colton?

Colt: I can't get you out of my fucking head. What did you do to me, Maya?

Me: You're drunk, Colt.

Colt: Because of you.

Colt: I've been losing my mind trying not to look at you.

Colt: Trying not to touch you.

Colt: Trying not to fuck you.

Jesus. My stomach flips with his dirty words and sweat gathers at the nape of my neck. My good friends Jameson and

Jack convince me to play along. They make me forget why this is so wrong.

Me: Then stop trying.

Me: I wanted you to kiss me back in the field.

Me: I wanted you to touch me so bad in the truck, even though Andrew was right there.

Me: I can't stop thinking about how it felt… how you felt inside of me. I want more, Colt.

Colt: Fuck.

Colt: Don't push me, Maya.

Colt: I'm close to my breaking point.

Me: What happens when you break?

Colt: Oh, baby girl. You couldn't handle what happens when I break.

The typing bubbles appear and then disappear two times before his next message steals my breath and halts my racing heart.

Colt: When I break, you break.

"Sorry about that. Where were we?" Harry's voice makes me jump and I throw my phone down on the bar. My face is clearly flushed, but he doesn't comment on it.

"Um, I don't… I don't remember."

"Oh, we were talking about Claude." Hearing his name makes me cringe. I don't want to talk about him. Especially after texting Colton.

"Enough about him. Do you have a girlfriend?" His laugh startles me. I watch with furrowed brows as he shakes his head. "What's so funny about that?"

"No, Maya, I don't have a girlfriend. I'm, uh… I'm gay." My mouth falls open on its own accord and I find myself speechless. Harrison is gay? How did I not pick up on that? "Close your mouth Maya, you're gonna catch flies."

My face turns redder than it already was and I avert my eyes from him. "I'm sorry, I just… I had no idea." I finish the rest of my drink, still avoiding his eyes. "Do you have a boyfriend?"

"Yeah, I do. His name is Dan and we've been together for the last three years. He's actually an artist at my shop." I turn towards him and take in his huge grin. He looks like a lovesick puppy. I see the same look in his eyes that my parents have for each other and find myself jealous.

"Wow. I'm so happy for you, Harry." My heart feels like it's about to leap out of my chest. I signal for the bartender to get me another drink and when it arrives, I chug the entire thing down. What am I doing? I can't marry Claude. I don't love him. At least, not like I should. Not like Harry loves Dan. Not like Mama loves Daddy. I want that kind of love. I want heart stopping, butterfly inducing, soul mate kind of love. I want can't keep our hands off of each other, stare into each other's eyes for hours kind of passion.

The realization makes my breath turn shallow. I feel the beginning stages of a panic attack setting in and try to calm myself down, but I can't. I can't control my breathing, I can't slow my heart. The need to throw up suddenly consumes me and I stand from my seat, wobbling on my shaky legs. Excusing myself, I make my way to the bathroom as fast as I can.

I'm just about to get to the door at the back of the bar when I feel someone's hand grip my arm. I'm spun around so fast, my vision goes blurry and the alcohol in my stomach threatens to come up.

"Where do you think—"

He stops talking when he sees my face and suddenly, we are moving through a door. We are now locked in the small one toilet bathroom, mere inches away, with my back pressed against the door.

"Maya, what happened? Are you okay?" His eyes shine with a layer of intoxication but everything about him is steady and focused. Focused solely on me.

"I'm fine… I'm." The first tear falls down my cheek. It doesn't make it far before Colt's warm fingers wipe it clean off my face.

"I'm just drunk." I blame it on the alcohol even though I'm only buzzed.

"Why are you cryin'? Did that guy–" His voice cuts out and I see red flash across his eyes. "What. Did. He. Do?"

"No, Colt, he didn't do anything. It wasn't Harrison." I shake my head and grab onto his hands that are still resting on my cheeks. My thumbs rub up against his callused skin in a reassuring way. I'm the one crying and all I want to do is make him feel better. Make him stop worrying. Make him smile.

I stare into his hazel eyes, getting lost in their watery depths, and feel something move in my stomach. I feel butterflies let loose, trying to fly up my throat and out into the air. I feel them slowly rising, making their way higher and higher until–

I just barely make it to the toilet before my stomach unleashes something that is definitely not a bunch of flapping butterflies. Instead, Jack and Jameson wave goodbye to me as they land in the toilet. The hair curtaining my face is pulled back and a strong hand rubs up and down on my back. It's the most comforting contact I've had in a long time and it makes more tears fall, mixing in with the bile in the bowl.

"I'm sorry. I just drank too much. I'm just–"

"No, you didn't, Maya. Don't lie to me. This isn't from the alcohol. What happened?" I sit on the dirty floor and spin around so I can look at him. He brings himself to my level and sits cross legged, right in front of me, so our knees touch.

"I just… I guess I." Closing my eyes, I take a leap and say the words out loud. "I just realized I don't love Claude." The room is completely silent besides the loud country music being muffled by the door.

"Well, no shit. I could have told you that before you even showed up here." I peel my eyes open and stare at him in awe.

"What?" I blink three times before he answers me.

"I know it's been a while since we've seen each other, but I know you. At least… I know the old you. I knew this guy wasn't good enough for Maya Turner. I knew you were settlin' for what was easy. And… I don't know how to explain it. Your eyes almost go dull whenever his name is brought up."

His words bring more tears to my eyes. I know exactly what he means by that. It's exactly why I freaked out at the bar. Because instead of a dancing reflection of the man I'm supposed to be in love with, it's a dull reflection of the man I could live without. The man I am happier without.

"What am I supposed to do? I am supposed to marry him in a few months. We live together. I built a life around him." I almost don't say the last sentence, but something about the golden flecks in Colt's eyes pulls the truth out of me. "I have no one else."

"Don't you ever fuckin' say that again, you hear me?" I look down at the floor until his hand grips my chin and pulls my gaze back to his. "You, Maya Turner, will never be alone. You have your family no matter what. You have… you have me." It almost comes out as a question, like he's asking himself if it's the truth or a lie he's telling both of us.

"Wh… what happened? Why do you hate me, Colt? We used to be so close and now… I feel like you can't even stand looking at me, let alone talking to me." My bravery surprises both of us judging by the look on his face.

Now he's the one dropping his eyes to the floor. "I could never hate you, Maya. Trust me, I tried. And the problem is I can't stop lookin' at you. No matter how hard I try to stay away, I can't get you out of my mind."

"Why did you try to hate me? You were my best friend… you were." I stop myself before I confess my love for him.

"I was what?" His eyes meet mine and I get lost counting the specks in his irises again. They sparkle and shine in the fluorescent light and beg me to tell him my secrets.

"No. Answer my question first and then I'll tell you." I stand strong, even though that small coat of armor is slowly slipping with every blink of his mesmerizing eyes.

His defeated sigh fills the air before he starts talking. "Remember the first time Andrew came home from college to visit?" I think back to almost twelve years ago, nodding my head in answer. "I came with him. I hadn't planned on comin' home, but I couldn't stop thinkin' about your family. About you. I missed you guys so much. I was so worried about you, but I didn't have your number and felt like it was inappropriate to call your parents to talk to you or ask Andrew for your number. I was such a stupid, worried kid and didn't want to risk my relationship with Andrew.

"Anyway, I figured I'd surprise you. We got to town on Friday night and Andrew dragged me to some high school party. It was the last thing I wanted to do, but he was my ride and I didn't want to piss him off. So, we went and I ran into your friend, Abby. She confided in me about a lot of things. She told me how much you had changed. She told me you constantly called her names and made her life a livin' hell. I didn't believe it at first, but then she started talkin' about things you said about me. About us."

My teeth are clenched so tight with anger right now that I swear they are going to crack. "And? What did she say about us?"

"She told me you couldn't wait for me to leave. She said you complained about me always bein' around and told her I was." He stops and thinks for a second. "Clingy and creepy? I think those were the words she used. She knew things that I had only ever told you and your brother. She knew about my father's drinkin' problem. She knew that I hated playin' football. She knew about the time I cried with you because one of my favorite horses on your ranch died. She told me you mocked everythin' I did."

He looks like the Colton from my childhood right now. Like the sweet, caring boy that was always there for me. The boy who was sensitive and had a heart too big for this world. Meanwhile,

I'm sitting here with steam coming out of my ears. I feel like I'm about to boil over with rage at any moment and it's all because of Abby. The piece of shit who ruined my life in more ways than one.

"You really believe I would say any of that?" My voice comes out angry and accusatory. I try to contain it, but my irritation for that woman is being thrown straight at Colt.

"I didn't know what to believe. I was immature and hurt. Then, when I came back home after college, you were gone. Abby's story fit together perfectly and I had no choice but to believe it all of these years."

"You did have a choice. You could have come and talked to me. Instead, you believed that bitch and deserted me." I shake my head at him, annoyed that my past is bombarding my brain at full force.

"So, you're sayin' none of it's true? That your best friend lied to me back then?" One of his brows raises and I glare straight into his soul.

"First off, Abby was not my best friend. The minute we stepped foot in high school she decided I was a loser who dressed like a boy and made my life a living hell. Second off, I would never tell anyone anything that you told me in confidence. I have never talked to a single soul about the way I feel for you."

"Feel for me?"

"I said felt. The way I felt. I can assure you, I never mocked you. I never made fun of you. I never wanted you to leave. I hated life after you left."

"So then, how did you feel, Maya?" His eyes search mine, darting between them like they are telling him the answer I'm scared to say out loud. His earlier text replays in my mind.

If I break, you break.

I use his own words to describe it. "I... I wanted you to break. I wanted you to break me. I wanted all of you no matter what the consequences were. No matter how much it destroyed us both."

"And now?" His eyes no longer look glazed over from alcohol. He looks straight into me with such intensity that it takes my breath away. Like he's scared if he blinks, he'll miss something important. Something that could change his life forever.

I simply nod my head at him. The small gesture speaking a million words. I still feel the same way, even if I can't say it out loud. Even if I haven't seen him in twelve years. Even if our lives don't match up anymore. Even if he hates me. "Does it really matter how I feel though?"

"Maya," my name comes out breathy and it sends a shiver down my spine. "I spent every single day thinkin' about the beautiful, blue-eyed girl that was off limits. Not just because you were my best friend's sister, but because of our age difference. You were there for me more than anyone else ever was and I woke up every mornin' excited to see you and fell asleep every night hopin' I'd dream about you." He stops when he sees a tear fall down my cheek again. His fingers brush it away. "All I'm sayin' is, I'm already broken. You broke me years ago. You left me breathless and beggin'. Time can't change a broken man. So, you better be sure. There's no takin' it back. There's no puttin' us back together. If you break for me, I'm never lettin' you go." He sounds so sure, so ready.

"You're just drunk." My hiccups and sobs make it hard to talk. Hearing the words from him doesn't feel real. I've dreamt about this moment all of my life and somehow, it's happening in a dingy dive bar bathroom with the taste of vomit in my mouth.

"I'm not that drunk. I promise you... in the mornin' my thoughts will be the same. I'm sorry I doubted you all of these years. I'm sorry I pushed you away and thought the worst of you. I'm sorry we wasted so much of our lives thousands of miles away."

"We have so much going against us. There's so much we would need to figure out." I look down at the ring on my finger. "I'm engaged." The two words sit in the air until my laugh breaks through. I don't know why I'm laughing, but I can't stop. The thought that I'm sitting here confessing my feelings for another man while the fiancé that I can't stand is thousands of miles away shouldn't be funny, but it is.

After a few seconds Colt's laugh joins in and I relish in the sound of it. I could listen to his deep laugh forever. I could stare into his eyes for the rest of my life and never get bored. I see my reflection in them and see someone I haven't seen in a long time. Someone happy.

"You never make anythin' easy, that's for sure, Maya Turner." He gives me a genuine smile and I can't help but match it. "We will figure everythin' out together, I promise. I won't give up on this."

I laugh and sob at the same time while shaking my head. "Okay, let's do this. No holding back." I put my hand out as if I'm about to close a business deal and when his hand engulfs mine, he pulls me forward. I crash into his arms and breathe in his addicting scent. I'm grateful he doesn't try to kiss me yet, since I still reek of throw up. But this embrace is everything I could ever need and more.

"I'm sorry for shuttin' you out after we had sex. I was overwhelmed and mad at you. I thought I could push you away, but I'm losin' my mind trying to and it's only been a few days. I wouldn't have lasted much longer. I miss my Mayo."

"I don't miss that nickname, that's for sure. But I missed you so much. And I'm still the same... Mayo... I just dress a little nicer and have a bit more confidence."

"I'll take you however I can get you, baby girl. You're perfect either way." His lips brush against my forehead when he pulls away and tingles rain down my face. "What do you say we get out of here? Andrew already left."

"What? He seriously left me with you? He knows we were minutes away from killing each other." I smirk up at him as he pulls me to my feet.

"I was minutes away from doin' somethin' to you, darlin', but it wasn't killin'."

"What was it then?" I bring myself close to him, our chests just barely touching.

"If we get out of here, I can show you. I'll show you all night long." The southern drawl in his voice rumbles through my body and makes me feel him everywhere.

"Lead the way, cowboy." I reach up and grab the hat on his head before placing it on my own.

His low growl lights something deep inside of me. "Damn, you look sexy in my hat. We better hurry or the people at this bar are gonna get one hell of a show." I don't get a chance to answer before he whisks me out the bathroom door.

WE BARELY MAKE IT TO THE BARN BEFORE OUR HANDS ARE ON EACH other. His hands scoop me up under my ass and I find myself suspended in the air, being carried through the stables.

"These shorts," his voice growls against my lips. "They should be illegal. Every man in that fucking bar was staring at your ass. I wanted to rip all of their eyes out." He makes his way up the stairs, both of our heavy breaths mingling in the small space between our mouths.

"I only wanted you to look. Even when you glared at me, I wanted you to look at me."

"Maya, those glares were full of lust. Every time I glared at you, I was picturin' your tight fuckin' body under me. I was hearin' your little moans over and over again in my head." His tongue darts out and runs down my neck, drinking me in and sending currents of want through my body. His mouth moves dangerously close to my ear before he speaks again. "I've fucked myself every night since you've been here, thinkin' about comin' deep inside of you again." I can't hold back my moan anymore. I let the guttural sound leave me as my head falls back. His voice is toe curling to begin with, but hearing him talk so dirty is too much to handle.

"Colton." His name comes out in a breath.

"Fuck yeah, baby girl. I love hearin' you say my name like that." At this point, we are already in his apartment and moving fast across the floor. Within seconds I feel my back pressed up against his mattress.

"I'm gonna take my time with you tonight, baby girl." The only response I can give him is a whimper. A whimper of desperate want and need. Of so many feelings I've never felt before. At least, not until him. His hands grab at the shorts around my waist and within seconds they are on the floor. "I'm startin' to hate this fuckin' body suit."

He lowers himself and places his head near the buttons at the bottom of the white material. His deep inhale fuels the fire inside of me. "Are you wet for me, Maya?" His nose nudges the thin material covering me and I have to stop myself from grinding against his face. "Fuck yes. You're soakin' through the fabric for me." I squeeze my eyes shut from the deep vibration of his voice against me.

Wet heat engulfs me when his tongue moves flat against the body suit, making the already damp fabric even wetter. His hands grab at my legs and push them apart, trapping them open in his harsh grasp.

"I'm gonna devour you until you scream my name. Until the only name you can ever scream again is mine." I can't answer. My voice is lodged somewhere in my body. It's stuck with all of the butterflies, desperate to be released and set free from the fire blazing inside of me.

His teeth grab at the snaps and I hear the distinct sound of one snap popping open. I wait for the next to echo through the air and it feels like I'm going to die waiting. I hold my breath, refusing to fill my lungs until I hear it.

Pop.

The second snap releases, leaving one more before I'm completely bare for him. I look down at him and find his hazel eyes staring straight into mine. I watch as he opens his mouth, about to grab onto the last snap with his teeth and set me free. He grabs onto the snap, letting his bottom lip and tongue touch my bare skin, and the glorious sound graces my ears.

Pop.

The last snap comes undone and I finally take a deep breath. I let the air fill my lungs up to full capacity and as I let it back out I feel the first sweep of his tongue against me. He licks me from bottom to top before placing his tongue firmly on my clit.

"You taste so fuckin' good." He growls the words against me and I grind my hips at the feeling. "That's it baby, ride my face. Do whatever you want with me. Don't be shy." He takes my clit into his mouth and sucks before biting down lightly. My head arches against the bed with a deep moan and I move my hips against him, just like he asked.

He continues to devour me, bringing me right to the edge before backing off over and over again. The buildup is so intense I fear I might explode from the pressure deep inside of me.

"Please, Colt," I pant out the words, his tongue darting into me before traveling back to the sensitive bud and circling it. "I need–"

"I know what you need, baby girl. I need it just as much as you. I need to feel you come on my tongue." The minute he finishes his sentence, he shoves two fingers inside of me and fucks me with them hard. His beard rubs against my soft skin as his tongue circles my clit again and I can't stop myself from grabbing onto his head. I hold onto the soft locks and push him into me deeper, desperate for more. His deep groan rubs against me and I feel the pressure reach the top of the peak.

"I'm gonna..." He moves his fingers into me even faster, curling them until they reach the sensitive spot inside of me. "Aghh, Colton!" I scream his name when I come. I scream it so loud it hurts my ears. The pressure moves like a wave through my body. It consumes every inch of me, taking me away from this moment and suspending me into a blissful heaven that I never want to leave. It lasts for what feels like hours, almost too intense for my body to handle. A body isn't built to feel this type of euphoria. It doesn't know what to do with the almost painful pleasure. Where to put it. When to end it. What to do when it's over.

But like all good things, it must come to an end. I feel myself come down from the high even though Colt's magical tongue is still moving against me. He's drinking me in, the greedy man he is, until there's nothing left. My body goes limp against the bed and I look down at him, his face finally coming out from between my legs. The soft glow of the light in the kitchen shines against his face. His nose and mouth glisten from my climax and he brings his tongue out and licks some of it away.

"So fuckin' sweet. I knew you'd taste good, baby girl, but damn. Your pussy is the best thing I've ever put in my mouth." He crawls up my body until we are face to face. My eyes dart along his perfection, desperate to memorize every detail of him. The small freckles that dot his cheeks and nose, barely visible if you don't look for them. The soft curve of his lips. The thick eyelashes that flutter when he closes his eyes.

"You're so beautiful." I don't mean to say it out loud, but the whisper slips through. Something flashes across his eyes when he looks at me.

"I'm supposed to say that to you, darlin'." His hands reach for my body suit and he pulls it over my head. I watch him remove his shirt before working on his jeans and then he's back on top of me, his hot skin pressing against my naked body.

"You, Maya Turner, are perfection. I want to kiss every inch of you. I want to memorize every curve, every dip, every freckle." His eyes stare into mine and I see my own eyes reflecting back in his glossy color. I can't stop the tears from forming in my eyes. One slips out and Colton leans down and kisses it away.

"I'm sorry, I'm just…"

"I know, baby girl. I feel it too." His lips graze against mine and I close my eyes, two more tears falling. "I wish I was your first. I wish we could have felt this." He thrusts his hips forward, filling me up inch by inch, torturously slow. "This feelin' for all of those missed years." He goes still when he is completely inside of me. He doesn't move a muscle, his body weight crushing down on me, while the feel of him inside of me takes my breath away.

"God, I wish I was your first." He finally moves, bringing his hips back until he slips out of my completely. I whimper at the loss, still staring into his eyes. He slides his dick against my wetness, rubbing the head against my clit. I buck underneath him and gasp at the sensation. "But I will be your last." When he says the word last, he fills me to the hilt with one sharp thrust. I cry out but he doesn't give me time to adjust before he drills into me, hard and fast.

"That's it. That's a good girl." His mouth is near my ear now and the hoarseness of his low voice pulls more moans out of me. "Take every inch. Take me in all the way."

"You're so…" I try to get the words out through his harsh movements. "You're so fucking deep."

"I'm gonna ruin you for anyone else. No matter what it takes." Another deep thrust. "Every part of you is mine. Your dirty little mouth." Thrust. "Your perfect fucking tits." Thrust. "This tight little pussy." He grabs my hands and puts them above my head, never stopping his movements inside of me. "All of you is going to be mine. Got it?"

I can't answer. I'm so overwhelmed by the sensations coursing through my body and mind. Everywhere he touches feels like sparks of lightening and fire tickling my skin.

"Answer me." His rough tone matches the thrusts he's gloriously punishing me with.

"Yes." It comes out shaky and I can see in Colt's eyes that it's not enough. He looks like a wild animal right now. He looks like he wants to destroy me.

"Say it. Tell me you'll be mine." His movements stop and he stares into me, unmoving. "Say it if you want me to keep fuckin' you."

"I'm going to be yours, Colton Grant." The growl that escapes him with my admission can only be described as carnal. He brings his lips down to mine while his hips move forward. He drives into me with such force that I feel my legs shaking. The rhythmic movement pushes me towards the edge again and the desperation I feel to fall off the cliff becomes all encompassing.

"I can feel you squeezin' my cock baby. Fuck. It's gonna make me come." He drills me harder with each word and I close my eyes with my impending orgasm. "No. Open your eyes. Look down. Watch me fuck you." I look down and watch as his thickness pulls out of me only to slam back in over and over again. "Fuck yeah. Watch my cock drive into you. You like that don't you, dirty girl?" I moan out his name as my orgasm starts to take over. I keep my eyes open and convulse under him. "Oh God. I'm gonna come. Watch me fill you up."

He drives in two more times before his loud groan fills the air. I watch, my own orgasm coursing through me, as he pulls out enough for us both to watch him empty himself inside of me. He pulses and thrusts his hips forward just slightly with each milk of his cock. I feel warmth spread through me and when he's completely empty, he pushes all the way in again and falls on top of me.

Our heavy breaths mingle as one, along with our racing hearts. The sound is hypnotic and my eyes start to feel heavy. I close them for a second and relish in the feel of Colton on top of me. This is where I'm meant to be. Right here, being protected and cherished by this amazing man. By my first love. The man who knows more about me than anyone else.

I feel the bed move after what feels like a few seconds and realize I no longer feel Colton on top of me. Opening my now groggy eyes, I find him pulling himself under the covers, where I already am.

"You fell asleep, baby girl. I cleaned you up and put you under the covers. There's water on the bedside table if you need it." The simple act makes my heart skip a beat. No one has ever taken care of me. No one has ever thought about what I might want or need. Pulling myself into his warm chest, I curl into him and let him consume me every part of me.

"Thank you for taking care of me," I whisper the words against his burning skin.

"I will always take care of you." I feel him kiss the top of my head as his arms wrap around me. My eyes start to close again and I feel myself fading when I hear him say one last thing. "I take care of what's mine."

Chapter

NINE

Colton

My eyes don't want to open even though the sun is shining against my lids. I feel like I'm sleeping on a cloud. A warm, soft, vanilla scented cloud. I pry them open and look down at the reason I slept better than I ever have in my life. She's curled up next to me, with her back pressed against my front. One of my arms is trapped under her head, keeping me in this position. Not that I'd dare move if it wasn't stuck. If I could stay in this moment forever, I would.

Her blonde hair is curtained over her soft features, so I gently pull it behind her ear to get a view of her profile. The soft curve of her button nose, her puffy, swollen lips, the light eyelashes surrounding her closed eyes. She's perfect in every way. Always has been and always will be. The slight blush covering her cheeks and the tip of her nose brings a smile to my face and I can't stop myself from leaning down to place a kiss on the side of her head.

I hate myself for being such a dick to her. I hate myself for ditching her and missing out on half a lifetime with this woman. I hate myself for believing the lies Abby told me. My mind wanders back to that night and I feel my teeth clench at the memory. She tricked me into thinking she was a sweet girl. She cried with me and I comforted her. So much so that we exchanged numbers and continued talking. Talking randomly, every now and then… for three years.

Until she told me she was accepted to the same college. Memories of what we did when she started her freshman year… how many times we did it... My stomach flips upside down with the thought. I need to tell Maya. I need to tell her that not only did I believe everything Abby told me, but I was also with her. I slept with the girl that succeeded in tearing us apart.

She stirs next to me before turning until her face is only mere inches from mine. I wait for her eyes to open, and when they do, the light blue color sucks me in. I can't look away. I can't think of anything else but those eyes. The eyes I have dreamt of countless times whether I liked it or not.

"Hi." Her sweet voice is loud in the quiet room. I dart my eyes between her own and the only thing that pulls my attention from them is the smile that takes over her face. Her white teeth shine in the morning light and it damn near steals my breath.

"Hi." I feel my lips curve up into a smile as I look at her. "How do you look so beautiful first thing in the mornin'?"

She half laughs, half groans while whipping her head back on the pillow. "God, that was cheesy."

"Cheesy, but true, you little shit." I grab at her sides and tickle her until she's squealing and begging for mercy. When I finally give it up, I grab her and place her on top of me. "Promise me I can wake up like this for the rest of my life." I don't know why I say it. The minute it leaves my mouth I feel a pang of fear that she doesn't feel the same way. That last night was all a drunken lie.

She stares down at me with emotions I can't name. She's not smiling. She's not sad. She's calculating. Staring into me and thinking things I want so desperately to know. After what feels like an eternity, the smallest smile appears on her face.

"Yes, Colton. I promise." Before I can so much as breathe a sigh of relief, her mouth is on mine. Her lips melt into me, so soft and addicting. She caresses every arch of my lips, somehow pouring all of her feelings and thoughts into me.

And those feelings and thoughts? They're the most beautiful thing I've ever felt.

"WHAT ARE YOUR PLANS FOR TONIGHT?" I GRAB AT HER ASS WHILE she brushes one of the horses next to me. She swats my hand away and shakes her head, trying to hide her smirk.

"I'm going to watch Top Gun with Daddy this afternoon but I don't have any plans after. Why, what are you thinking?"

"Tellin' you would ruin all the fun, darlin'. Just meet me out here at eight, got it?" I continue shoveling up the hay in one of the stables even though her eyes are glued to me in curiosity. All morning I made sure we were working right next to each other.

"I don't like surprises, Colton Grant."

"I know you don't, Maya Turner, but you'll like this one. Trust me."

"I'm gonna like it, huh? Okay, let me guess… I'm gonna meet you out here and you're gonna bring me up to your bedroom and screw my brains out for the second time today?"

"To be fair, you were the one ridin' me this mornin', so technically you screwed me." I look over at her with a lopsided grin. Her blonde hair is pulled up in a high ponytail and she's wearing another pair of those damn shorts and a blue flannel that's tied in the front, revealing a sliver of her creamy skin. It should be a sin for someone as distracting as her to exist. It makes life for all of us a lot harder. Well, she makes a lot of things a lot harder…

"I didn't hear you complaining."

"Oh, baby girl, I will never complain about watchin' your tight little body bouncin' on top of my cock." Her hands falter with the brush, surprised by my forwardness. A light blush covers her cheeks and the desire swirling in her eyes is directed straight at me. "Keep lookin' at me like that and these horses are gonna get a view of it."

She shakes her head and laughs awkwardly. "You're a horndog."

"Only with you, Maya Turner. I swear I've spent the last week hard as a rock." Her eyes dart down to the front of my jeans and I groan at the way my dick stirs from just her gaze. I need to change the subject or we are going to end up with hay in places hay should never be.

"The surprise has nothin' to do with you in my bed, but don't think you're gettin' out of that. You will be in my bed at the end of the night and you will be wakin' up in it tomorrow mornin'. And every mornin' after that."

"Alright, cowboy, if you insist." She gives me a smile but it doesn't quite reach her eyes. She's stressed out. She's worried about life outside of the two of us. I don't blame her, but all I can do is try to be her rock right now. With the coming events, she's going to need it. We both are.

I watch her as she puts the brush down, eyebrows furrowed. "Come here, baby girl." I meet her halfway before pulling her into my arms. She melts into me, the stress and worry radiating off of her and into me. I try my hardest to absorb as much of it as I can and refuse to give it back. "It's all gonna be okay. I'm right here."

Each word I speak makes her physically relax into me more. After a few minutes, she pulls away slightly and looks up at me with a relaxed smile.

"Thank you, I needed that. I just keep getting stuck in my own head."

"No need to explain, baby girl. You have a lot goin' on. Why don't you go take a hot bath and I'll finish your ranch work for the day." I give her a soft peck on her lips and force myself to pull away. "Don't forget about tonight. Out here at eight."

I admire her grateful smile and wish I could take a snap shot of it in my brain so I could look at it forever. "Thank you, Colt. I'll see you tonight."

She pulls away and makes her way out of the barn, leaving me alone with my thoughts. My plans for tonight keep circulating in my head, making it almost impossible to focus on work. There's a tree in the middle of one of the empty fields that we used to climb as kids. It's the same tree her grandparents planted when they started this ranch. The same tree that both her grandparents and her parents got married under. The same tree she told me, almost fourteen years ago, that she wanted to get married under one day. She was twelve at the time, but I saw the look in her eyes.

After that day I made sure she always came with me and Andrew when we went to play in the tree. I saw how much she loved it, how much she admired it, and I wanted to see that look as many times as I could. I prayed one day I could witness her get married in that exact spot. Deep down, I prayed I would be standing next to her, looking into those mesmerizing eyes, but that seemed like an impossible hope.

Until right now. In this moment, I feel like anything is possible. I feel like us ending up together isn't just a pipe dream anymore, but something that is meant to happen.

Something that, dare I say, almost feels like fate.

Chapter

TEN

Maya

"**Y**ou look really happy, squirt." My dad's voice breaks me away from the screen in front of us. Top Gun is my dad's favorite movie, and I've gotta say, I don't mind looking at young Tom Cruise. To my surprise, Daddy is staring at me instead of the movie. He has a gleam in his eye, almost as if he is about to cry.

"I am happy." It's the most honest I've been in a while. Since last night, I have been happier than I have been in years. Colt's admission and our plan to try this out has made me feel things I never thought I would ever feel. I can't stop thinking about him. I can't stop thinking about the life we could potentially have together. For him, I would move back to Texas in a heartbeat. For

G. L. STRONG

him, I would quit my job and shovel cow manure for the rest of my life. The thought makes me smile.

"All I could ever ask for is my little girl bein' happy and taken care of when I'm gone. I'm so relieved that's true." He thinks I'm happy because of Claude. He thinks the fiancé that can't even remember our anniversary or my birthday is going to take care of me like he would want. The thought almost makes me laugh.

"About that, I want to talk to—"

"Ahh." My dad's pained groan interrupts me from my admission and I feel my heart stop in my chest. His hands clench at his sides and his eyes squeeze shut.

"Daddy? Are you okay?" I move on the couch until I'm right next to him, reaching out to him without actually knowing what to do. "What is it?"

"My stomach. I'm okay, it's just—"

He can't even finish his sentence. His face now drips with sweat and his skin has gone even paler than it normally is. "Mama! Andrew!" I shout their names and hold onto Daddy's hand. I hear feet running across the hardwood floor and then both of them show up, worry covering their faces.

"What's wrong?" Mama comes over to his other side and grabs his arm, looking at him with fear.

"He said it's his stomach. He's in a lot of pain." My voice is so fast and frantic I doubt they can understand what I'm saying.

"Andrew, call Dr. Stanley. Tell him it's happening again. Maya, stay with him and hold his hand, I'm going to go get the Ibuprofen." She's back in less than a minute with pills and a glass of water.

"NSAIDS don't feel like the answer. He doesn't have anything stronger? He's in so much pain!"

"The stubborn man refuses to take anything stronger. It's like he's trying to torture himself." She seems so calm. Truthfully, so does Andrew. I feel like I'm about to throw up and my heart is going to rip out of my chest. "Sweetheart, don't cry. This is just a symptom of the cancer. It's normal." I don't realize I'm crying until she says that. Wiping my tears away, I look anywhere but at them.

"I'm sorry, I just… I got scared."

"You haven't witnessed his bad days yet, it's okay. I reacted the same way at first." Mama doesn't look at me when she talks, instead plopping the pills into daddy's mouth and bringing the water up to his mouth. I watch him swallow down the pain meds and take a deep shaky breath.

"I'm sorry, squirt. I should have warned you." His voice cuts out again with his shallow breathing. "That tends to happen a lot lately."

I nod my head in understanding, but I don't understand. Why isn't he doing treatment? He has so much to live for. My mom, his kids, future grandkids. Guilt hits me hard and I realize I pushed them away so much that I stopped being a part of the list of things to live for. How can you want to live for someone you haven't seen in eight years? Someone who left you behind and started a life somewhere else?

I missed so many Thanksgivings. So many Christmases. So many birthdays. I didn't even come home when they called me about Daddy's diagnoses. I was so selfish and work focused that the most important people in my life were left behind, in the dark shadows of my new life. Forgotten.

My throat starts to close up as my breathing gets shallower. I feel like I'm seconds away from screaming or crying… maybe both. My ears feel like there is watering clogging them, muffling the sounds of Mama and Daddy's worried voices. I see them talking, looking at me with matching expressions.

I feel my head nodding still, unable to control the movement. I don't say a word, I simply can't get them out through my closed throat. Air can barely slip through, let alone words. The second panic attack in the last twenty-hours sweeps through me and I do exactly what I always do. I run.

Without looking back, I run out of the living room and through the front door. I can barely see a few feet in front of me. I can't hear the birds chirping or the cows mooing. I feel like the world is fading away from me and I don't know what to do. I just barely make out the dirt road under my feet. I'm running, or stumbling, down the driveway. I don't know where I'm going. I'm just searching for air. For something to stop this panic attack from taking over.

My stumbling gets worse as the tunnel vision takes over. Darkness creeps and crawls inward until the only vision I have available is through a small pinhole. I feel my feet trip over themselves and the feeling of my body hitting the hard ground barely registers. I blink once, twice, three times, until finally, the darkness consumes me.

WARMTH ENGULFS ME AS I WALK FORWARD. ONLY, I DON'T FEEL LIKE I'm walking. I feel the movement from each step. I feel myself moving forward. But I don't feel my body moving on its own. I cringe at the feeling of my eyelids trying to open. I pry them with all of my might, until finally, the light outside graces my sore eyeballs.

"There you are, baby girl." His voice sounds like a soft melody when it hits my ears. I can't control the whimper that escapes me. "You're okay, I've gotcha." I finally get my eyes to stay open for more than a second and look up at the man carrying me. His worried hazel eyes stare into mine.

"Wh... what happened?" My voice comes out hoarse and cracked.

"Well, I was just gettin' ready to come in for dinner when I heard Andrew and your mama screamin' your name. When

I reached the porch, I saw you runnin' down the driveway and Andrew runnin' out the front door with a phone pressed against his ear. I told him I'd handle it and booked it after you before he could answer me." I pull myself tighter into his chest and let the sound of his heartbeat calm my own racing one.

"I'm sorry."

"No need to apologize, I was just scared shitless for a second. You wanna tell me what happened?" I feel the memories of Daddy's episode spin around in my brain. All of the horrible thoughts I was thinking come barreling back and I feel my breath hitch in my throat again. I tense up with the onslaught of self-hatred filling me up.

"Hey, baby girl, it's okay. Take a deep breath for me, okay?" I do as I'm told and feel my lungs fill up with the fresh air surrounding us. I hold onto it and close my eyes, willing the thoughts to leave. "You forget how to breathe properly? Damn, darlin', now let it go!" His joking voice makes me laugh and I instantly feel lighter.

"That's my girl. Best damn sound in this world." I can't help but blush, completely enthralled by the sweet tone of his voice. We stop moving and Colton brings us both down until he is sitting and I'm lying on his lap. I look around for the first time and find us sitting on the dock of the pond where we first saw each other a week ago. When my life somehow fell apart and put itself back together at the same time.

"It was about my dad," I say the words quietly and almost hope he doesn't hear them.

"I figured it had to do with him." His thumb rubs up and down on my bicep, hypnotizing me with the movement.

"I just... I don't know why he isn't doing treatment anymore. I started thinking about everything he's going to miss out on... And that made me think about everything I missed out on. I forgot about the most important people in my life. I ignored their pleas to come home for holidays. I didn't even think about visiting when

Daddy was diagnosed. I was so selfish and missed out on the last few years Daddy had before everything changed. Before he lost so much of himself. I missed out on so much because my priorities were somewhere else."

It's silent for a second and I let my eyes dart across the calm water below us. "I hate myself, Colt. I hate myself so fucking much." I let the admission sit between us, feeling lighter for being able to say it out loud.

His huge hands grab at my face and pull my attention to him. With both hands clasped around my cheeks, he stares into my eyes with such an intense need, it takes my breath away.

"Never."

His eyes flash with anger.

"Say."

His mouth ticks with each word he says.

"That."

His hands grab onto me even harder.

"Again."

It's a command, so bold and stern that I swear the world ripples with the command. It's like those words were etched into me, each harsh word cutting into my flesh and leaving its scar so I will never forget.

"You're amazing in every way. You were focused on getting your career going. You were a hard worker and put your job first, that doesn't make you a bad person. You are allowed to be a little selfish. You're allowed to want things and have dreams. You can't sit here and think about what could have been. You have to focus on now and do what you think is best for you and the people you love. That's it. It's that simple."

"But Daddy is going to die. He's in so much pain. It's not fair… it shouldn't be him. Why is it him?" My tears pour out hard and I try to stop the sobs from escaping but there's no use. It's like a river flowing down my cheeks.

118

"Life isn't always fair, baby girl. That's not a reason to stop fightin'. That's not a reason to give up and let the despair and regret take over."

"So then why is Daddy done fighting? He's giving up and letting the cancer win." His callused fingers wipe away the stray tears that keep trying to make an appearance. He sighs while I can practically see the gears working in his head, trying to figure out how to answer.

"He has fought harder than any person I have ever met. But it got to be too much for your mama. Every appointment she would get her hopes up. She was convinced the treatment was gonna fix everythin'. Billy knew it was a matter of livin' for another year or another few months. He knew if he prolonged it and let your mama get her hopes up every week, it would kill her in the end. He made the decision to save her from more heartache."

"But… seeing him like this. Seeing him deteriorate before her eyes. Dealing with the pain he's going through. How can that save her from more heartache?" His fingers brush a stray hair behind my ear, eyes darting between mine. Full of emotion. Full of knowledge. Full of shadows.

"Sometimes it's better to deal with the pain of the inevitable, than with the hope of the impossible." His words hit me hard in the chest. The words are beautiful and heartbreaking. I say them over and over in my head to try to memorize them. Turning my body so I'm completely facing him, I put my hands up on his neck and brush against the stubble residing there. Our eyes meet and the sadness deep inside of them breaks my heart all over again. He blinks a few times, the gleam in his eye proving how much this conversation is affecting him.

"I'm so sorry I wasn't here for you during your parent's accident." I don't know why I say it, but now that I have, I can't stop myself from continuing. "You deserved to have someone tell you everything you just said to me. You deserved to have someone grab you and hold you tight until the last of your tears dried up. You deserved to have someone to pour your pain into and help you cope with your loss. It should have been me."

His silence scares me. Maybe I shouldn't have said that. Maybe I just brought up horrible memories that he wasn't already thinking about. Maybe I read everything wrong. I'm about to backtrack when I see the glimpse of a tear in the corner of his perfect eyes. Right before it falls, I bring my finger up to the corner of his eye and wipe it away.

"I didn't get it before." His hoarse voice pauses and I look at him in confusion. I'm about to ask him what he didn't get, when he continues on. "There are billions of people in this world. Billions of women. And somehow, after twelve years, I could never get you out of my head. It always came down to you, and I never understood why." I wait for him to continue, breath held deep in my lungs. "It's because you were never just in my head. I tried so hard to get you out, but the entire time, you were takin' up every corner of my heart. You are lodged so deep that I can't shake you. You make me forget all of the horrible in this world just by bein' you. You say you wish you were here for me when they died, but... you were. My memories of you, the pictures of you, the idea of you bein' out there... it helped me get through the toughest time in my life whether I wanted to admit it or not."

I'm completely speechless. How do you respond to that kind of admission? I know exactly how. But I don't think either one of us is ready to say it out loud yet. Not when I'm still engaged. Not when we still have so much to figure out.

The hard truth is that I have loved him my entire life. I've been in love with Colton Grant since I was barely six years old. I didn't think it was possible to love him more than I did, but every day I spend with him as an adult, the harder I fall. I'm at the point where I've fallen so far, I could never dig myself out of this hole.

I've far surpassed six feet under and managed to lodge myself hundreds of feet down.

Since I can't tell him what I so desperately want to say out loud, I grab his face and show him instead. My lips just barely graze his before he's grabbing at the back of my head and slamming our lips together. Like all of the other kisses we have shared, it's full of passion and desperation. Like this is the last time we will ever get to feel this magnetic pull and collide together.

After what feels like hours of exploring each other's mouths and pouring our souls into each other, we pull apart with labored breaths. "As much as I want to rip these pants off of you and shove myself deep inside of you, we should probably go back to the house before your mom and brother come searchin' for us."

"I guess you're right. I don't think either one of them would like seeing you fuck me on the dock." His deep groan vibrates through my body when he brings his head down to rest on my chest in defeat.

"You're tryin' to kill me. Or get me killed." I laugh before placing a kiss against the top of his head. "Are you gonna be okay, baby girl?"

"Yes, because of you. Thank you for helping me get through that."

"Anytime you feel another panic attack comin' on, you find me. I'll help you through it before it makes you pass out next time." He lifts me off of his lap effortlessly before standing and pulling me up with him.

"I don't usually have panic attacks... I had a few when I moved to the city myself but I haven't had them in years until now." We walk forward through the field, hand in hand. "It's actually funny that you brought me to the pond because that's how I used to stop them when I was younger. I'd fill up the bath or just get in the shower and let the silence from the water surround me. I don't know why I started doing it but it works."

His silence greets me and a small squeeze of my hand makes me look over at him. His face is looking straight ahead, taking in the Longhorns scattered throughout the field. "I know. I brought you to the pond because I knew that would work if you had another."

My eyebrows furrow in confusion. "How?" His head turns towards me now and his soft features form a smile.

"I taught you that. When my dad first started drinkin', I had a lot of panic attacks. I would jump into the pond and sit under the water, pretendin' nothin' else in the world existed but me and the water. You asked me what I was doin' one day and I told you that any time you felt overwhelmed to the point where you couldn't breathe and your heart was pumpin' out of your chest, to sit under the water and let it melt all of your problems away."

For the second time in the last few minutes, I'm rendered speechless. Colton taught me that? All of the times I was alone and terrified in the city when I was younger, I had Colton right there with me without even knowing it. He saved me from so many panic attacks. It almost feels like he was there with me, sitting under that water and reassuring me that everything was going to be okay.

"How do I not remember that?"

His laugh fills the air. "I mean I was eight when my dad first started drinkin'. Which means you were four. I don't remember much when I was four, that's for sure. But clearly, deep down, you remembered it."

I can't respond, too overcome with so many emotions. How did I last so long without Colton Grant by my side? How did I manage every day not seeing his face and hearing his voice for twelve years?

Because right now, I truly feel like I can't breathe without him by my side.

Chapter

ELEVEN

Colton

The fear I felt when I saw Maya pass out in the driveway is like nothing I've ever felt before. It was in that moment that I realized how deeply fucked I am. She owns my heart, and she has since we were kids. Hearing her say she hated herself, that she wishes she could change the past, is bittersweet. The anger from her words was palpable, but the relief I felt that she wanted to be with her family, be with me, was like a wave moving through my body.

When we got back to the house, Maya hugged her family before I brought her into the bathroom and cleaned up the scrapes and cuts on her knees and hands. Even through the sting of the alcohol brushing against her wounds, she smiled down at me from the counter top, making my insides feel all warm and mushy. Something I've never experienced before her.

Now, we are just finishing up dinner and I'm anxiously waiting for everyone to excuse themselves. It's almost eight and I can't stop thinking about getting Maya alone. I've never been one for sentimental shit. I've never been one to cuddle and just enjoy each other's company. But, right now, that's all I want. That's all I can think about sitting at this table, sitting across from her.

I keep getting weird looks from Andrew and I can't tell if I'm being paranoid or not. To be honest, both Mrs. Turner and Andrew are acting weird. They keep exchanging long glances and Mrs. Turner has a weird smile on her face. After everything that just happened with Maya and her dad, I figured no one would be smiling.

Luckily, the pain in Billy's stomach subsided and now he's just resting in his room. The doctor said he was going to send a prescription for something stronger just in case it happens again, or gets worse.

Finally, everyone gets up and starts clearing the table. I jump to my feet and grab as many dishes as I possibly can, feeling like a giddy kid excited for dessert. Except the dessert is Maya, in more ways than one. The thought brings a smile to my face and Maya sees it, giving me a curious look. I simply wink at her, promising her answers later.

When I pass by her, I whisper as discreetly as possible. "Make an excuse to go put on some warm, comfy clothes and then meet me outside." I make sure no one's looking and pinch her ass, which earns me a small squeal. My deep chuckle makes Andrew turn towards me but I'm already at least five feet from Maya. That doesn't stop him from raising a brow at me, to which I simply shrug my shoulder and look away. Kissing Mrs. Turner on the cheek, I head out of the house and towards my apartment.

I quickly change into an old football hoodie and a clean pair of jeans before heading back down to the stables. My girl is already waiting there for me when I get there, and what she's wearing makes me stop in my tracks.

"God damnit, baby girl. What are you wearing?" I take in the long silk pants and matching shirt that cling to her curves. The black material contrasts against her pale skin and light hair and all I want to do is rip it off of her.

"You said warm and comfy... I don't have any sweats or jeans so I figured this was the best bet. It's comfy and I'm warm enough." She shivers against the slight chill in the air now that the sun has gone down and I itch to grab her and warm her up in a very fun way that involves a lot less clothes.

"You like testing my control, Maya Turner, that's for sure." I turn around quick and run back into the small mudroom below my apartment, grabbing one of my flannel jackets hanging on a hook. When I reach her again, I drape the jacket over her shoulders and place a kiss against her forehead.

"Let's go before it gets too dark."

My heart is racing by the time we reach the tree line that leads into the overgrown field we don't use anymore. Well, the mostly overgrown field. I bring us to the small clearing I made earlier today and look at her face when we are able to see the mowed path. Her breath hitches and her eyes widen when she sees what I did.

The mowed path leads straight to the lone magnolia tree sitting in the middle of the field. Lining the cleared path are small led lanterns on either side, lighting up the way with a soft golden hue. She stares at the twinkling lights glistening among the pink flowers and branches while I stare at her, just as mesmerized as she is.

"Colt... this is..." She finally turns to look at me and I know all of my hard work today was worth it just by the look in her eyes. "No one has ever done anything like this for me... Why?"

"Baby girl, that's not the question you should be asking. The question is, why not? Why hasn't anyone done somethin' like this for you? You deserve to have this everyday of your life. You deserve to feel relaxed and look at somethin' almost as beautiful as you. And when I say almost, I mean not even close." Her soft laugh flows through the crisp air. "You deserve to be taken care of and worshiped every day for the rest of your life. You deserve the world. I don't know if I can give you that, but I can do everythin' in my power to try."

She doesn't say anything, instead staring into my eyes for what feels like an eternity. Even in the darkness, I can see the one emotion in her eyes when they capture my own. It's the same one I know mine reflect right back into hers.

"Let's go, the surprise isn't over yet." I pull her along with me before either of us can let the admission I know we both feel slip through our mouths and out into the air. I want to say it, it's something I think we've both felt most of our lives, but not like this. Not when there is so much happening outside of our little bubble. Not when she is wearing another man's ring on her finger.

The thought makes me look down at her hand clasped in mine. I turn it over and find the gaudy ring gone, leaving the smallest tan line in its place from the hot Texas sun. I feel my lips curve up in a devilish grin. A grin I couldn't hide even if I wanted to.

"Didn't feel right wearing it anymore. Especially not with you." I can hear the guilt in her voice and I pull her hand up to my mouth to place a soft kiss against her ring finger.

"No guilt. Not right now. Not tonight. We will deal with everythin' when we need to. Don't feel guilty for followin' your heart and finally lettin' yourself be truly happy."

"You know, you've gotten a little too smart for your own good. And maybe a bit too poetic for a cowboy." Her lopsided grin is illuminated by the twinkling lights and moonlight.

"Hey, who said cowboys aren't poetic? Just to name a few… George Strait, Toby Keith, Willie Nel—"

"Alright, alright. Like I said, a little too smart for you own good. I stand corrected, cowboys are very poetic."

I grab the hat off my head and place it on hers, loving the way it looks. "Damn straight we are."

We reach the open clearing of the tree and I walk us over to the blanket set out. Small LED candles and magnolia petals are scattered across the checkered fabric and I set out an array of desserts from chocolate cake to gummy candies and there's a bottle of red wine sitting in an ice bucket. Music flows from the small Bluetooth speaker I bought this morning. I spent a small fortune on everything for tonight and I'm so grateful I did.

"Baby…" The nickname comes out so naturally. "This is amazing… no, amazing doesn't even begin to cover it. This is… this is."

"This is what you deserve." I twirl her as I speak, before bringing her in close to me. Right on que, Alan Jackson's deep voice dances through the air, singing *Remember When*.

"I love this song," she says it like I don't already know.

"I remember. You used to blast this in your room over and over again. Andrew hated it so much." I chuckle at the memory of Andrew banging on her door to tell her to turn off the depressing music and her screaming back to shut up. "Every time I hear this song, I think of you. And every time I listen to the lyrics… I can't help but think of us. Or I guess… hope for us. To have a story this beautiful one day. To be able to look back on our life and say, remember when."

I can't believe the words that are coming out of my mouth right now. I've never said anything like this, never thought anything like this. It's like Maya Turner has put me in a trance since she admitted her feelings for me. Since I found out I threw away so many years over lies. We continue to sway under the tree that I have so many hopes and dreams for until the song ends.

When another song starts playing, she pulls away from me and places her hand on my heart. The organ beats frantically against the warm touch.

"I have since we were kids and I haven't stopped since." The look in her eyes proves what she means. Those three words we can't say yet.

"I have too. I may not have known what it was back then, but I have and I always will." I kiss the lips I've become obsessed with in every way. The way they mold to mine. The way they move so slowly and deliberately like they are practicing a perfectly choreographed dance with my own. The way the taste so sweet like they are coated in a layer of sugar.

"Let's sit down, it's about to start." I take her hand again and bring her over to the blanket I set up.

"What is?" She admires the desserts in front of us and I suppress my chuckle at how cute she is. Grabbing a fork, I pass it to her and she smiles at me like I just gave her the best gift she's ever received.

"You'll see, baby girl." Pouring some wine in the plastic cups, I watch her dig into the chocolate cake. She brings the fork up to her mouth and when she sucks the chocolate clean off of it, letting a quiet moan of approval slip through. I swallow down my own and look away.

"Lay down with me?" I ask the question even though it's rhetorical. She doesn't have the option to say no as I bring her down with me, bring one of my arms behind her head as she finishes her bite of cake.

"I missed the stars so much," she says it with so much awe in her voice that I can't help but snicker.

"That's nothin' baby." The minute I say that, the first star shoots across the sky. If you blinked, you'd miss it, until the next one soars through the air, following the first. Suddenly, what seems like hundreds of shooting stars stream across the navy blue sky, begging us to make a wish, to remember them.

"Oh my gosh..." Her soft voice cuts out and I can feel the pure joy radiating off of her. Not only can I feel it, I swear I can see it. As bright as the stars above us, I see her skin, her blonde hair, her blue eyes, reflecting off the dark sky. She glows with more happiness than I have ever seen from another human being. Her smile radiates astonishment. Her eyes reflect each glistening ball of fire above us.

"I thought you'd like it." I can't help but comment, proud of the fact that I put this giddy smile on her face.

"Like it? I fucking love it!" She practically screams into the air, knowing no one can hear us. "God, don't you just wish you were up there with them? Away from all the stressful shit life throws at us?"

"The only way I would ever go up there is if you came with me. Otherwise, I'm happy down here with all of the stressful shit life throws my way..." I stop before correcting myself, looking straight into her eyes. "Throws our way."

"I missed you more than the stars, Colton Grant." Somehow the admission feels like the biggest accomplishment of my life. Like until now, I was merely residing on this planet rather than actually living on it.

"If you could make one wish." I grab her hand while I continue on. "One wish, on one shootin' star, what would it be?"

"If I told you, it wouldn't come true." Her voice is full of sarcasm and flirtation.

"Humor me, darlin'. One wish." She's silent for a while, staring up at the lit sky above us. I can't keep my eyes off her, watching the stars refection gleam in the clear blue of her irises.

"One wish, huh?" I nod my head even though she can't see me. I watch as she closes her eyes and the sweetest smile graces her lips. "I'd wish for a life full of dancing. Dancing reflections... dancing stars... dancing in the kitchen..." A small giggle escapes her. "I don't know, just... never ending dancing. With the man I love. With the man that I could live anywhere with and be happy. With the man I would be proud to call the father of my babies. With the man I could compare to my father."

"You want what your parents have," I say it matter of factly, knowing exactly what she means. After all of these years, it would be impossible not to see the magic of their love. The uniqueness. The once in a lifetime kind of emotion coursing through both of their veins. It's something I have always dreamt of for myself. Dreamt of for both Andrew and Maya. Something my parents unfortunately never possessed. They loved each other but the fighting never stopped. The drinking took over and they lost each other. They lost each other long before the accident happened.

"It's like nothing I've ever seen before. The fact that Daddy is about to leave her forever. The fact that that kind of love is going to leave this Earth forever once he takes his last breath. It almost feels like the world is going to become a worse place without it. Like their love somehow counteracts all of the shit in life."

"Just because your dad won't physically be here anymore doesn't mean their love will cease to exist. Love like that doesn't just disappear if one of them passes away. Love like that exceeds death. It exceeds everything else."

"How do you know?" I can hear the shakiness in her voice, proving this conversation isn't going where I wanted it to. I want to make her smile tonight, not cry.

Grabbing onto her tighter, I pull her into my arms and wrap myself around her small frame. "Because, baby girl, God wouldn't let somethin' that beautiful fade away. Their love is like a diamond. It lives on forever and never fades or gets dull because it's so magnificent. Because it took so much work to get it to be so perfect. Just like your parents love."

"I hope you're right." Her voice cuts out and then she turns her body so she is facing me, both of us lying on our sides. "What's your one wish?"

I almost forgot that this conversation started because I asked her to tell me her wish. I pretend to contemplate it. I pretend to have to think long and hard about what I could possibly want. But it's not a question. It's not a difficult thing to answer. I know exactly what I would wish for the minute she asks the question.

"A family of my own." It sounds so sad in the quiet air surrounding us. I think about everything that comes with my own family and smile, staring right into her eyes. "I want a wife and kids and a dog and a house. Hell, I'd even take a cat even though I hate those little shits." This earns me a giggle and I relish in the bubbly sound.

"I want that too. More than I ever thought I did." The sadness in her voice is misplaced. It sounds like she doesn't think it's possible. Like a family and a house of her own isn't in the cards for her. Oh, how wrong she is. Not if I have anything to do with it.

"How many kids do you want?" My arm fits snugly under her head, serving as a pillow for her. My other arm is flung across her hip, my hand drawing circles along her silk clad back.

"Honestly for a while I stopped wanting kids. I couldn't imagine having them with…" She doesn't even say his name which makes the cave man inside of me pound on its chest in triumph. "But I used to want a huge family. Like six kids huge."

"Damn, baby girl. You'd almost have enough for your own football team." Her eyes crinkle at the sides with her huge grin. "How many do you want now?"

"I don't really have an answer. All I know is I want kids. I definitely want kids. It would depend on how many my future husband would want too."

"Well, I want at least two or three if that helps," I say it with confidence and she shakes her head at me, thinking I'm joking around. I'm not. At all. "Do you want to live in the city forever?" It's a question I've been wondering for a while. I hated working in the city. I hated the people, the smells, the lack of any fresh air.

"You're pulling out the tough questions today, huh?" I simply raise an eyebrow at her with a cock of my lips. "I guess I don't necessarily want to live in the city forever. I just want to be able to work and the city is the best place for me with my job. I can't imagine raising kids in the city though. It's a little... aggressive there."

"So where do you want to raise kids?" Please say Texas. Please say Texas.

"In a perfect world, I'd live somewhere like this and be able to commute for work to a close big city. That would be my dream. To come home to my own little sanctuary off the beaten path but still be able to make the world a better place."

"You know that's possible, right? You just have to find the right place. It's out there. I promise you that much." I make another promise internally. A promise to find her exactly that. A sanctuary to call home that lets her follow her dreams in her career as well. "What's your dream house?"

"Good lord you're full of questions." She pushes my chest lightly before bringing her finger up to her chin and tapping on it like she's deep in thought. It makes her look even more adorable than she already does. "Hmmm... I guess I'd want something similar to Mama and Daddy's house. A big farmhouse with a wrap around porch. Black shudders and distressed wood everywhere.

"I'd want there to be a huge pond in the front of the house that I could jump in after work. And two swings. One on the front porch and one near the pond. And a stream that ran through the property with a little wooden bridge to cross it. I'd want magnolia trees everywhere and a huge garden. But there would have to be enough open land to be able to see the sky at night."

I whistle low, my eyes wide. "That it?"

"Well... if it was a perfect world I'd have a barn and a few open fields so I could take Jax with me... and maybe a few other horses. Because my kids should learn how to ride horses and take care of them, you know? And... if you have horses, you might as well get a few cows too." She looks up at the sky for a second. "Oh! And a separate shed or guest house with room for a private office so I could work from home some days! And maybe a workout room attached to it with an area for the kids to play."

I wait before I talk, making sure I don't interrupt another dream of hers. She sounds just like eight year old Maya dreaming about her life as a cowgirl. She never wanted to be a princess or a ballerina like most girls. She wanted to be a cowgirl. She said she wanted to spend every day on a horse, getting rid of the bad guys and making the world a better place. I guess she followed one part of that dream becoming a prosecutor.

"Okay, baby girl." That's all I say. That's all that needs to be said. On the inside I'm saying every wish of hers over and over again so I don't forget it. On the inside I'm making plans to start my search for her sanctuary. But I don't let her know that.

"Okay? You make me rattle off all of that and all you can say is, okay?" Her laugh breaks through her words and I just shrug my shoulders.

"I didn't tell you to go on and on for hours. I almost started snorin' halfway through that damn story." My joke earns me a punch on the arm and before she can take her hand away, I grab it, holding it still. "I loved every second of hearing your dreams. Somehow you get more and more perfect with every word you say." I pull at her arm and she slides toward me on the blanket. A shiver runs through her body and I know it's not from the chill in the air.

"Well…" Her voice fades out as her eyes look down at my lips, mere inches from hers. "What would your dream house be?"

"I don't care what my house looks like, baby girl. As long as you're who I'm comin' home to." I don't give her a chance to register my words before I crash my lips to hers and steal any semblance of a response from her.

The stars are long forgotten.

Chapter

TWELVE

Maya

A bird chirping wakes me up. I open my eyes and bright pink magnolias are the first thing I see above me. The chill of the morning air slips through the blanket on top of us, but Colt's body wrapped tightly around mine keeps me warm. I should be waking up sore and groggy from sleeping outside on the ground, but instead, I feel lighter and more refreshed than I ever have.

Last night's events flash across my mind on replay. The things I admitted to. The hopes for my future I never let myself think about. Hearing Colton say he wants to come home to me one day. It feels like a dream. A dream I want to start living in right now.

"Colton, wake up." I shake the arm that's resting on top of me. The huge arm that looks like a damn tree branch. "Wake up, baby." I turn my head and place a soft kiss on his lips. The small gesture makes him groan in his sleep before I'm being pulled closer to him. His hips grind forward and the thick length of his morning wood rubs up against my bare ass. No matter how many times we have sex, I can't get enough of him. My stomach dips and tingles at the feel of him behind me.

He grinds into my backside and it takes all of my power not to moan and give in to this gorgeous man. "Mmmm baby girl. I love wakin' up with you ready for me." I gulp down my lust. Focus. Focus on what you wanted to say.

"Colt, wait." I try to pull away from him but somehow, he pulls me in closer still. He's so much stronger than me and suddenly, my body is being flipped and maneuvered until I'm on top of him in the matter of seconds.

"What were you sayin'?" His voice is coated in sleep and it somehow makes him even more irresistible.

"Wait, I wanna tell you some—"

Before I can finish my sentence Colton's hips thrust up and he enters me in one swift movement. I gasp at the fullness and grab onto him for stability.

"Get on with it, darlin'. Keep talkin'." He grabs my hips and guides me just the way he wants me. He lifts me up before dropping me back down torturously slow, drawing out the sensation of him sliding back into me.

"Oh God." My head falls back and I stare up into the blue sky overhead. He continues to move me, deliciously slow, making the stretch of him inside of me even more intense.

"Tell me what you were gonna say, Maya." I look down at him and find him staring at where we connect like an animal watching its prey. The look alone is enough to send me over the edge. I feel my impending climax bubbling to the surface before it spills over and my body grips him tight. "That's it. Squeeze it baby. Fuck yeah."

Each dirty word adds fuel to the fire inside and my orgasm pulses through me for an ungodly amount of time. When I come down, I stare into his eyes, trying to contain myself against the rhythmic movement that still coaxes against me. "I'm going to call Claude and end it today. No more waiting."

My admission halts his movements and his eyes widen for a split second. He blinks at me once, twice, three times before the biggest, most devilish smile I have ever seen takes over his handsome face. He moves us fast, until I'm lying on my back and he's above me, staring down into my soul.

He doesn't give me a second to breathe before he drives into me so hard and possessive, I see stars in the morning sky. His body weight crushes me with each damaging thrust. It's the most intense feeling I've ever experienced, like he's making sure he leaves his mark.

"There's no turnin' back now, Maya Turner." Another punishing thrust rattles through my body,

"You're."

Thrust.

"All."

Thrust.

"Mine."

Thrust.

"Say it. Now." He doesn't slow down. He doesn't hold back.

I whimper through each one of his movements, practically crying from the buildup of both pain and pleasure. "I'm…" I gasp when he hits that spot deep inside over and over again. "I'm yours. I've always been yours."

He drives into me three more times before his loud groan assaults the air. He fills me to the hilt with one last pounding thrust. I feel his release course through me and my own follows suit at the mere sight of him emptying himself inside of me. His body collapses on top of mine and I hold onto him, loving how perfectly we fit together. Loving the way his body feels on top of mine. Loving the way he feels inside of me. Loving him.

"Thank you, baby girl." He kisses me passionately and I hold onto it tight, trying to savor the feeling forever.

"I'm ready to start living. To start the next chapter of my life… our life."

WE WALK BACK HAND IN HAND. I OFFERED TO BRING EVERYTHING with us but Colton said he was going to come back later with a four-wheeler and grab everything. When we reach the barn, he pulls me towards him and gives me a hug before placing a soft peck on my lips.

"Do you want me to be there when you call him?" I shake my head in answer.

"I should do it myself. I'll be fine. Thank you." My hands shake with nerves. I don't like the idea of hurting Claude, but I can't keep this up. I can't pretend to be in love with him when my heart belongs to another. I can't let him sit at home oblivious to what I've been doing.

"I'm gonna go get some chores done and then get showered. I'll be over by the time you're done talkin' to him, sound good?" He kisses my forehead now and I nod in agreement.

When he lets go of me, I start my walk back to the house. I find myself walking slower than normal and realize my body is trying to push this off for as long as possible. He's going to scream at me in French. He's going to call me every name in the book. He's going to hate me. But it's all worth it if I can be with Colt.

I hear laughter coming from inside when I reach the front porch. Opening the door, the laughter gets louder and I hear something sizzling on the stove.

"Thank you for makin' breakfast. It's so nice havin' someone else cook for once since no one in this family can so much as boil water." Mama's voice comes from the kitchen and I follow the noise.

"Hey, I can cook!" Andrew throws the comment at her and I can practically see the eye roll she's no doubt giving him.

"Mayflower is gonna be so happy when she sees you!" That's the last thing I hear Mama say before I round the corner and find out who she's talking to. My mouth drops to the floor and the dreams inside of my head come to a screeching halt.

I'd recognize his shaggy brown hair anywhere. He's standing there, back to me, cooking something in my family's kitchen. In Texas. Right in front of me.

"Um... Claude?" My voice comes out squeakier than it ever has. At the sound of it, he turns around and his face looks like a ghost to me. Like an old memory I want to let go of. His brown eyes look stale and lifeless. His curly hair looks wiery and thin. His skin looks pale and greasy. The once muscular frame I used to admire looks lacking now.

"Ma belle." I cringe at his voice. He puts his spatula down and comes over to my stunned body, engulfing me in an uncomfortable hug. "I missed you."

I don't say a word. I'm speechless and stuck in my own head. Wondering if this is some nightmare I haven't woken up from. If this is some sick joke. He finally let's go of me and places a kiss against my forehead. The same way Colton did just minutes earlier. Except, when Claude does it, it makes my stomach flip. It makes the butterflies fluttering around in my stomach shrivel up and die.

"What... what are you doing here?" I barely get the words out.

"We wanted to surprise you! And that's not the only surprise..." Mama's voice chimes in and Claude walks back to the stove. I glare at his back, disgusted that he's cooking for my family. He hasn't cooked a meal in months. He's been too busy eating take out and sitting on the couch all day.

"Um…" I can't find any other word to say. I don't think I've blinked since I walked into the kitchen.

"We're havin' the weddin' here! In two weeks! Isn't that just amazin'?" She clasps her hands together while I stare at her in awe. What did she just say? No. I must have heard that wrong. She couldn't have said–

"Your daddy and I were talkin' about you gettin' married and he said how much he hopes and prays he'll be around for it. I got to thinkin' and why risk it when all of your family is here now and we could do it on the ranch! So, I snuck into your phone the other day and contacted Claude and he agreed! It was meant to be, sweetheart. I'm just so happy!" She pulls me into a hug and I can't move my arms to hug her back. I can't feel them. I can't feel anything. My heart feels like it crawled out of my body and found somewhere better to hide.

"Um…"

"Oh, Mayflower, you're speechless. I know, it's just so exciting!" She takes my lack of words in the wrong way.

"Mama, can I talk to you?" I don't know if I can walk since I can't feel my legs, but I chance it. I need to get out of the same room as Claude. I manage to make it out the front door and onto the front porch without falling and when I close the door behind us, Mama does something that surprises me.

She bursts into tears. Not the soft tears I have seen once or twice since being here, but full on gut wrenching sobs. "Oh, Maya. I can't tell you how happy this makes me. This is all your daddy has been talkin' about. He looks at pictures of you when you were ten and dressin' up in my old weddin' dress, every night and he cries and cries. I've been heartbroken over it for weeks.

"This is the best thing that could ever happen to him, Maya. He actually gets to walk his only daughter down the aisle. He gets to give you away to the man you love. He gets to see his little girl say I do." More sobs crash through her and hit me like a truck, head on. Guilt and utter heartbreak sit deep in my soul.

My daddy's one wish is to see me get married and my mama planned everything to make that happen. My dying daddy who isn't going to make it much longer wants to give me away, his only daughter, and I can give that to him. Except, I don't love Claude. I love Colton. I want Colton.

I picture telling Mama and Daddy that I am breaking it off with Claude and the worst case scenarios pop into my head. Images of Daddy having a heart attack. Images of Mama crying her eyes out and telling me I broke her heart. And then I picture their reaction to me and Colton wanting to be together. The man that's practically my brother. The man that has been Andrew's best friend since they could walk. Andrew would kill him. Andrew would hate us both. Daddy would threaten his life for taking advantage of his daughter and ruining her engagement.

Suddenly, all of my hopes and dreams scatter like ashes in the wind. They fly out of me so fast that I physically wince at the painful hole they leave. I can't end my engagement. I can't ruin Daddy's one hope before he dies. I have to go through with this wedding. For him.

The realization brings tears to my eyes. I let them fall, one by one, while I grab onto Mama for support. Each tear that falls feels like a memory of my time with Colton slipping away. Each tear feels like a dream for the future we had falling down to the ground and splattering on the porch.

"I know, Mama. It's going to be perfect. Thank you." The lie tastes like bile in my mouth. I want to throw up. Or scream. Or hit something. Maybe all three.

But I don't. Because I can't be selfish anymore. I was selfish and left, breaking my family's hearts in the process. I've thrown them away and deserted them too many times in my life. That ends today.

I'm going to do this for Daddy. I'm going to marry Claude in two weeks.

Chapter

THIRTEEN

Colton

Have I become the sappiest mother fucker that's ever existed? The handpicked flowers sitting in my hand confirm that I have. I walk fast towards the farmhouse, desperate to see her again. It's been an hour since I left her this morning and it somehow felt like a lifetime. How did this happen? Two days ago, I was trying to stay as far away from her as possible and now I feel like I can't breathe unless she's right by my side.

I wrote down everything she told me last night. I wrote it on a post-it note and stuck it in my wallet, so I would always have her dreams on hand no matter where I went. I don't care how long it takes. If I have to build the damn place from the ground up myself,

I will. She will have her perfect life. She will have her perfect home full of kids and a husband that loves everything about her.

I have a feeling she's going to be upset when I see her, but I'll be right by her side. I'll hold her until she feels better for as long as it takes. And once we have that taken care of, we will tackle telling her family. I know her parents won't be mad. Her mom and dad love me like their own, but Andrew worries me. He tends to have a temper and Maya is his little sister. He can get overprotective when it comes to her.

Climbing the steps two at a time, I make my way to the front door with a smile on my face. Right before I reach the door to open it, it swings open and Maya runs out with, eyes wide like she just saw a ghost. I reach for her, flowers long forgotten as the slip from my hand and fall to the floor.

"Maya, what's wrong?" I try to pull her into a hug but she pushes me away, staring up at me with the worst expression I've ever seen on her face. "Is it your dad? Is he okay?"

Her head shakes before she answers. "Please, just try to understand. I'm so sorry Colton."

I see someone come into view in the corner of my eye, but don't look away from Maya. What is she sorry for? Why is she talking like this? Why isn't she letting me touch her?

"Ma belle, are you ready?" The voice hits me like a whip, digging deep into my skin. I furrow my brows at Maya before turning my attention to the man I've never met but hate so much. He walks up to Maya and puts an arm around her waist, pulling her into him. I fist my hands at my sides and suppress a possessive growl. He looks like a preppy douche bag with his black blazer and tight skinny jeans.

None of us speak. I glare daggers into him while he stares at the phone in his hand. I feel Maya's eyes on me and turn my attention back to her. She looks disgusted and devastated, but she lets the fucker keep his hand on her. I look down at the tight black dress she now wears and when my eyes drag down her body, something sparkles halfway down. The gleam of her diamond ring nestled perfectly on her finger assaults my eyes. The chuckle that comes out sounds cold and menacing. It's the only thing I can do to keep from either tearing the world apart or falling into a heap at her feet.

"Who is this, Maya?" He finally looks up at me and while his eyes size me up, he gives me a real smile. He has no idea who I am. He has no idea his fiancé is in love with me. He has no idea I was just inside of her an hour ago.

"This is…" her voice cracks and fades out before she can finish. She sniffles once and I force myself not to look at her.

"Colton Grant. I've known Maya here since she was on her hands and knees." His face scrunches into a hideous expression, confusion swirling through his eyes. Maya's gasp is so quiet, I doubt this idiot heard it. But I did. I always do. "Since she was crawlin'."

He laughs awkwardly and then pulls Maya in tighter to him. She stumbles with the movement, but steadies herself quickly. I watch as his slimy hand snakes down her waist and rests on the curve of her ass. I'm seconds away from beating his face in. From throwing him off this porch and grabbing onto Maya. She's mine. Not his.

"Nice to uh, meet you. I'm Claude. Maya's fiancé."

"That so?" I look down at Maya, aiming the question at her. She's not looking at me. She's avoiding eye contact completely by looking out at the field. She's shutting me out. "And what's the *fiancé* doin' in Texas?" I exaggerate the word, raising one brow at her when she finally makes eye contact with me.

"Mama and Daddy surprised me by flying him down. They planned the whole thing. He's, um… he's here to—"

The fact that she can't finish the sentence proves to me exactly why he's here. I feel my heart crack with each second of silence that goes by. It cracks once, twice, three times before someone says something.

"We're having the wedding here in two weeks, right ma belle?" I almost wish it stayed silent. The silence was only making hair line fractures. But those words hit my heart like a hammer. The cracks are turning into caverns and holes.

"Yes." That's all it takes. The one word that used to have no meaning to me breaks my heart into a million pieces. It crumbles and explodes until there is nothing left. My teeth are clenched so tight, I can feel them trying to burrow back into my gums. I take a few deep breaths, trying to calm the overwhelming rage coursing through my blood.

"Well, I'll be. Congrats to the happy fuckin' couple." I don't wait for them to answer. I give Maya one last look, letting all of my emotions pour from my irises, straight into hers. I let her feel the anger, the misery, the disgust, the pure heartbreak. I let her feel everything and then I turn my back and walk away.

I jump into my truck and back out while the tears cloud my vision.

They fall down my cheeks when I fly down the dirt driveway.

They fall for the life I prayed I'd have one day that just got ripped out from under me.

They fall for the only girl I've ever loved, picking someone else.

Maya

I NEED TO TALK TO HIM. WATCHING HIM WALK AWAY FROM ME WAS the hardest thing I've ever had to do. I swear when he looked me in the eyes, he stuck his hand straight into my chest and ripped my heart out before taking it with him. Now, sitting here in the car next to Claude, I feel like an empty shell of a person. I know he's talking, but I can't hear him. I can't hear anything but the sound of Colton's heartbroken voice over and over again.

How can this be the right thing if it feels so wrong? How am I going to survive without Colton by my side? I know I did it for half of my life, but now that I've had him, had him completely, I can't imagine going on without him.

"Maya, are you listening?" His voice breaks through my thoughts when he touches my arm. I jump from the contact and the wheel jerks to the side. I'm driving my brother's car, since Claude doesn't like to drive. We are on our way to same convenient store I went to a week ago to get my clothes. Claude demanded he needed the full Texas experience.

"What?" I turn to look at him and can't hide the annoyance covering my features.

"I had an interview two days ago." I can't help it when my brows shoot up into my hairline. That was the last thing I expected him to say.

"And?"

"They mock me with the money they offer. I was the head chef of a Michelin star restaurant and they practically spit in my face." I squeeze the steering wheel tight, telling myself not to start a fight.

"So you turned them down?"

"Oui, of course, ma belle. I will not be taken advantage of." The snort that leaves me can't be stopped. The fact that he's saying he won't be taken advantage of is too ironic. He's been taking advantage of me for the last six months while he sat on his ass and spent my money on takeout and videogames.

I don't answer. I just nod my head and then flip the radio on. Turning the knob up all the way, I let Lee Brice's voice drown the French man sitting next to me completely out. After five more minutes of blaring music, we pull into the small plaza and I get out of the car without another word. He follows me in and I tell him I have to use the bathroom before veering off to the back of the store on my own.

I feel like my whole body was hit by a truck. My head is pounding, my heart is weeping, my legs are numb. Nothing feels right. Nothing's going to feel right until I talk to Colton and explain. I hate that he hates me right now. Grabbing my phone out of my pocket, I pull up his number, trying not to look at our previous conversation from the bar.

Me: *Colt, please let me explain. I'm begging you.*

I continue walking until I find the small hallway that leads to the bathroom. There's a bench in the hall so I plop myself down on top of it and stare at the phone in my hands, my knee bouncing frantically.

Me: *Colton, please.*

Colton: *There's nothing left to say. I got the message loud and clear.*

Me: *No. There's so much I need to say. Please, just let me explain tonight. Can I meet you in the barn when everyone goes to bed?*

Colton: *Gonna sneak away from your soon to be husband so you can fuck me one more time? He's a lucky guy.*

Me: *Don't you dare try to hurt me. I promise you'll understand if you just let me explain.*

Colton: *I can try all I want, but I will never hurt you the way you have completely destroyed me, Maya Turner.*

The typing bubbles disappear before reappearing seconds later. I wait for another message to come in for what feels like hours.

Colton: *I'll give you five minutes. Barn at ten o'clock.*

I didn't realize I was holding my breath until I finally let the breath out in relief. He's going to talk to me. He'll understand. He has to. Shooting off a quick thank you, I stand up and head back out into the store. Before I even pass the exit of the small hallway, Abby stops me in my tracks. She is standing in the doorway, blocking me in.

"Hey, you!" She gives me a sickeningly sweet smile and I don't even attempt to give one back. I'm tired of pretending.

"Get out of my way, Abigail."

"Uh oh, someone woke up on the wrong side of the bed, huh?" She folds her arms over her chest. "I met your fiancé. He's nice on the eyes. Not as nice as Colton, but a close second that's for sure." The mention of his name sends a spark of anger through me.

"Don't talk to me about Colt. Go fuck yourself." Her hand moves over her heart and she pretends to be offended.

"Does your fiancé know you were in love with him? It was really quite pathetic Maya. I didn't know how bad it was until I read that diary of yours. Never laughed so hard in my life." The minute she says it, everything clicks. That's how she knew about Colton's dad and every other secret she spewed to him. I wrote everything in that stupid fucking book. She had all the ammo she would ever need.

"What are we in high school still? Grow up. You're working at a fucking department store. You barely have any teeth left and the cheap ass tattoos on your arms are doing a terrible job at hiding those track marks. I see the real you and, baby doll, it's not getting any better for you. You reached your peak in high school and from this point on, you're just going to keep going downhill."

I shove past her and start walking away when her next sentence makes me trip over my feet. "Actually, I'd say I peaked in college. When I was fuckin' Colton Grant."

I turn around slowly, my heart hammering in my chest. "You're lying." I don't know why I'm even acknowledging what she said, but I can't seem to stop myself. I feel like I've been slapped across the face.

"I guess you're right. That is kind of a lie. It wasn't just fuckin'. We were datin'. We talked all through high school and then he practically begged me to go to the same school as him. I got bored of him after a year but I think he was in love with me. Isn't it funny how the boy you were obsessed with ended up bein' obsessed with me?"

I don't know what comes over me when I do it. I'm not the type who stoops so low. I don't do violence. But the minute my fist makes contact with her fat nose, joy spreads through my body like a wildfire. It wasn't a hard punch, but it was enough to make her nose bleed and her mouth fall open in awe.

"Shut that disgusting fucking mouth of yours." My heart is pounding in my chest. I feel like I'm seconds away from crying but I make sure I don't.

"Holy shit…" Her voice sounds nasally and full of pain. "You're still in love with him." I don't answer. Which is answer enough. Instead, I give her a sweet smile and turn my back on her. I walk forward until the floor below me changes from ugly linoleum to hot black tar. When I'm in the parking lot, next to the car, I let myself cry.

The betrayal sits deep in my chest and pounds along with my heart beat. He lied to me. He found out how horrible Abby was to me and still didn't tell me about their past together. Him being in love with her. Them fucking. My stomach flips and without warning, I throw up on the pavement, spilling my guts out. Each heave feels like a piece of me is leaving my body.

But they aren't pieces of me. They're pieces of Colton Grant that made their way in. Each heave ejects a memory. A hope. A dream. Until, suddenly, the heaving stops and every last piece of Colton is lying in a pile on the pavement. Because the Colton I was about to change my life for wasn't Colton at all. He was a liar who knew the right things to say. He was a man who hated me so much, the love he showed me felt that much more extravagant.

I hear Claude's voice echo through the air and find him walking towards me, engrossed in a conversation on the phone. He doesn't look my way once before slipping into the passenger side. Wiping my mouth, I open the front door and gracefully slip into the car. Taking one last deep breath, I turn the key and drive away from the betrayal lying on the ground beside me.

I drive away from the last pieces of Colton Grant I will ever let slip through the cracks.

Chapter

FOURTEEN

Colton

I'm wasted. I know I shouldn't be, since Maya is going to be here to talk in the next ten minutes, but I couldn't stop myself. The tears just kept coming and I was getting fed up. I don't cry. I don't plan romantic starry nights or pick flowers. I don't do any of the shit I've been doing for Maya Turner. And the only thing that seems to keep me from doing any of that is drinking. So that's what I'm doing.

The bottle of bourbon in my hand is nearly empty at this point. Walking forward, I stumble on my own feet and the liquid in the bottle sloshes, threatening to spill over.

"Not today, fuckerrr." I stare into the bottle, making sure it knows I mean business. We aren't wasting a drop of this liquid gold tonight. I feel the horse's eyes on me and I glare at them. "What are you guys lookin at, huh? Mind your damn business." I kick my foot against the dirt ground for emphasis, bringing a cloud of dust up around me.

Rather than going upstairs, I walk out of the barn and sit down so my back is leaning against the open door. Taking another chug of my drink, I look up at the glistening sky and wait.

And wait.

And wait.

And wait.

My eyes feel heavy after what feels like an hour. I let them close, my head falling forward, when the sound of someone walking towards me wakes me up. Stumbling on my own feet, I stand up and stare into the dark night, desperate to see her gorgeous face even though I'm so mad at her.

Andrew's tall frame makes my heart fall to my feet. He's not the Turner I was hoping for. Sitting back down in defeat, I tell myself not to cry. She didn't fucking come. She didn't choose me, again. She never will.

"Mind if I join you?" His voice sounds loud in the quiet night and instead of answering, I lift my hand up, offering him the almost empty bottle of bourbon. He takes it before sitting down next to me. The sound of the bottle flipping up and draining into his mouth breaks through the cicadas in the distance.

"What are you doin' drinkin' out here by yourself? Where were you at dinner?" I grab the bottle back from him and take another sip, desperate for the beautiful burn that travels through my body with each swallow.

"Shit day."

"Well, you missed out on the big surprise. Maya's fiancé is here." My hand squeezes the bottle so tight I wouldn't be surprised if it crumbled in my grasp.

"Oh, I'm aware. Already met him."

"And?" I can feel him looking at me, dissecting me like he always tries to do. I never let him though. I tend to hold my guards up strong. The problem is, they don't feel so strong tonight.

"He's not good enough for Maya." What I really mean is, he's a piece of shit and I want to run him over with my truck.

"He seems nice enough so far. I'm not a fan of him either, but he's gettin' along with the family well enough."

"He's. Not. Good. Enough." The words sound pained when they leave my lips.

"Well, she's marryin' him in two weeks whether we like it or not. My mom has been goin' crazy tryin' to get this whole thing planned. Dad wants to walk her down the aisle… odds are he won't be around in a few months."

My mouth goes dry and my chest pangs at the thought. I should have realized the minute she said the word yes on that porch that she was doing this for her dad. She's going through with this so she doesn't destroy his one chance at walking his only daughter down the aisle. She's going to marry a man she doesn't love so her father can die knowing he gave his daughter away and she's happy. But she won't be happy. Not without me.

"She can't marry him, Andrew." The words sound defeated.

"Oh, he's not that bad, Colt. Maybe you guys should talk tomorrow. I'm sure Maya would appreciate that." I snort at the thought. That's the last thing she would ever want. The last thing either of us would want.

"Gotta say, I don't think the two of us would have much to talk about." The only thing we have in common is Maya. We have both been inside of her. We are both in love with her, or so he says he is. We both want to marry her.

"I talked to him for a bit. I don't think my father likes him, but he held up a conversation with me. And Mama likes him because he talks to her about cookin'."

"Well, isn't that just fuckin' great for you and your mama." I tip the bottle again and sigh when the burn doesn't feel as intense anymore.

"What is goin' on with you? One day you're happier than I've ever seen you and the next you're a miserable prick again. What's the fuckin' deal, man?"

"Nothin'. Just tired of city people."

"Well one of those city people is my damn little sister so you better suck it the fuck up. I'm tired of your shit, Grant."

"Noted. I'm gonna go to bed." Standing up, I don't offer the rest of the bourbon to him, instead, taking it with me. I stumble my way back into the barn and practically fall down the stairs before I reach my apartment door. The room is spinning when I open the door and suddenly, my once cozy apartment feels too big. It feels empty. I feel alone.

Throwing off my boots, I whip my hat off my head and slide against the door until I'm sitting on the ground. The silence overwhelms me and I can't stop it from happening. I can't stop the tears that come again. This time, they don't just fall for Maya.

Because, in the end, everyone leaves me. In the end, I have no family left

Chapter

FIFTEEN

Colton

It's been a week since the piece of shit showed up. A week since Maya talked to me. A week since I got wasted to try to fix my broken heart. Turns out, it only delays the inevitable. Pain doesn't go away that fast. Pain is a bitch that likes to fester and hangout for a while.

I don't go into the farmhouse anymore. I haven't had a single meal with the Turner family since Claude barged in. Andrew seems pissed at me and I still haven't figured out why Maya went from begging me to talk, to glaring at me whenever our paths crossed. Am I ashamed that I've been running on bourbon for most of the week? Maybe. Is it going to stop me? No. Not until they are off this ranch and I can move on with my pathetic life. If it wasn't for the fact that Mr. and Mrs. Turner need me, I would have left last week.

Halfway through mowing one of the fields, I feel my phone buzzing in my pocket. Seeing Andrew's name on the screen, I shut the mower off and click answer.

"Yeah?" My voice is clipped.

"I hate to ask you since you're bein' such a dick, but I need a favor."

"What?"

"Maya took Dad's old Bronco into town a half hour ago. It broke down. I'm at work and Mama is takin' care of Dad right now. Can you go help her out?" He sounds just as pleased with the request as I am.

"What about Clause? Why can't he do it?"

"His name is Claude, and he doesn't drive since he lives in the city." I try not to laugh, I really do, but I can't stop it. I laugh into the phone and to my surprise, Andrew joins in. "He's one fruity mother fucker. I think he's harmless but I don't quite get what Maya sees in him."

"Weird. I almost feel like I said that last week." I make my way toward my truck, knowing damn well I could never let Maya stay stranded on the side of the road somewhere.

"Just shut up and save my sister's ass. I'll send you her location and then let her know you're comin'."

"Don't worry about tellin' her. I'll let her know I'm on my way." I'm afraid she might run if she finds out I'm the one coming.

"Alright, thanks man." We hang up and I pull out of the driveway. Andrew's text says she's stuck on the side of Slater Street, which is a good twenty minutes from here. I press the gas and get there in almost half the time.

Pulling up to the piece of shit that should not be on the road, I put the truck in park and wait. The driver's side door pops open and my heart does an excited flutter when I see her. She's wearing those damn jean shorts and a white tank top. There's a red flannel tied around her waist which only accentuates her curves more. Swallowing hard, I almost wish she was wearing her other clothes. Since Claude showed up, he's been playing dress up in cowboy costumes and Maya went back to her old clothes. Until today apparently.

When her eyes make contact with mine, anger hits me head on. She's fuming. I watch as she saunters over to the truck, her skin glistening with sweat. Her hair is in a high pony tail, which swings behind her with each step. I feel my body harden at the site of her moving towards me and wish she didn't have this kind of effect on me.

"What are you doing here?" She doesn't move to get into the truck, instead, standing outside the passenger door and talking to me through the window. She looks at me and her face falters. I look down at what she's staring at and realize I never put a shirt back on. I'm sitting here in a pair of blue jeans, with dirt, sweat, and grass clippings sticking to my bare chest. I try not to grin at the lust evident in her eyes.

"Savin' your ass. This Bronco hasn't been driven in years. What the fuck were you thinkin'?"

"I was thinking that I had shit to do and didn't want to bother anyone. Especially you. I wouldn't have called Andrew if I knew he was going to call you."

"Darlin', if I wasn't here, you'd die of a heat stroke or get picked up by some pervert, whichever happened first." I try not to look at her, but it's damn near impossible. She's the most beautiful woman I've ever laid my eyes on.

"Both sound more appealing than getting in a car with you."

"It's a truck, and if I remember correctly, you found me pretty fuckin' appealin' last week."

"Fuck you." Her voice is laced with disgusted but I sense a small hint of my Maya somewhere deep down.

"Get your ass in the truck and maybe you can." I'm being an asshole, I know I am, but I'm still so mad at her. She disserted me after promising me the damn world.

"Never fucking happening. I'm disgusted that I ever let you touch me. Lord knows how many diseases you gave me." Her phrase confuses me, but she doesn't give me a chance to say anything. Hopping into the truck, she continues talking. "I have an appointment in Harly I need to get to. Could you bring me back to the ranch so I can figure out another ride?"

"Here's an idea, and I'm just spit ballin' here, but why don't I take you to your appointment since we are already over halfway there?" Harly, the small hipster town, is the closest thing we have to a city around here. I hate the place.

"I'm sure you're busy." She gulps and averts her eyes from me, clasping her hands on her lap. "Could you put a damn shirt on?"

"Why? We both know you like lookin' at me when I'm naked and dirty." She rolls her eyes at my words but her breathing gets a bit heavier than before. She's taking in all of the oxygen in this truck and suddenly, it feels cramped. Like the cabin is shrinking somehow and we are slowly getting closer and closer to each other.

"Colton. Can we not do this? If you are willing to take me, I would really appreciate it. But if you're going to make derogatory jokes the whole time, I'd rather go alone."

"Wasn't bein' derogatory and I definitely wasn't jokin' but yes, I'll stop. Just tell me where to go." I put my hands up in defense before grabbing a spare flannel that I keep under my seat. Throwing it on, I keep it unbuttoned and wait for her to tell me where to go.

"Um… I'm going to Blaire's Bridal." Her voice dips down to a whisper when she says the destination. My grip on the steering wheel tightens at the same time my teeth do.

"Say that again?" I better have heard her wrong.

"Jesus, Colt. I'm going to Blaire's Bridal! I need a stupid fucking wedding dress, okay?" She blows up on me and I try not to take it personally. The fact that I'm driving her to find a dress to wear while she's marrying someone who isn't me makes me want to punch something. Or someone. Named Clause.

"By yourself? Isn't it like a law or somethin' that girls are required to have someone there when they try on weddin' dresses?"

"Rub it in a little more, why don't ya? Mama is busy with Daddy so I didn't want to bother her. I don't have any friends here obviously, but you already knew that." She says something under her breath but the only word I catch is Abby. Her attitude is starting to get to me and even though we barely make it another mile down the road, I pull over again and stop the truck. Turning my body towards hers I glare into her.

"What the fuck are you doin'? You're gonna treat me like shit even though you're the one gettin' married? After everythin'?" I'm trying to stay calm. I'm trying not to get angry with her.

"Oh, yeah cause it's all my fault, right?" She's yelling at me and I feel my blood pressure rising.

"Well let's see. We were just gettin' done sharin' our hopes and dreams, sayin' we were gonna be together. God damn fuckin' like we would die without it, and then you decide to stay engaged and marry this asshole two weeks later!" I'm breathing so heavy I feel like I'm going to suffocate in this truck. "Yeah, baby girl, sounds to me like that might just be on you!"

"I'm not the one that sat there and practically confessed my love for you even though the entire time I was hiding something from you! Something big and disgusting and horrible and fuck you, Colton! Fuck you for making me admit to everything I wanted. Fuck you for making me want it. Fuck you for making me think, that just maybe, I could actually fucking have it!"

I don't think, I just act. I grab her face with both of my hands and slam my lips against hers. I throw every emotion I'm feeling into my kiss and make sure I scar her with it. She tries to pull away at first but after a few seconds, she gives in to the desire and she's kissing me back with the same ferocity. It's a sloppy, desperate connection. It's full of biting, sucking, and breathing each other in.

We move at once and she's on top of me in the middle seat of the truck. My hands grab at her sides, appreciating the way her hot skin feels under them. We are both a sweaty, sticky mess, but it only fuels us further.

"I know why you're doin' it, baby girl." My words tickle her lips as she moves on top of me. Our breath is colliding as one and I try to stare into her crystal eyes with the close proximity. "I don't agree with it. I think there's another way, but I understand why you're goin' through with the weddin'."

Her eyes flash with sadness before anger fills them again. Suddenly, she stops moving and she's trying to get off of me. No. She's not getting away with that. I grab at her again and hold her on top of me, making sure she can feel how hard I am between her legs.

"You're not goin' anywhere. You're gonna explain why you're mad at me while I fuck you until you're screamin' my name." Her quiet gasp brings a low growl to the surface. I grab at the sides of her tank top and lift it over her head while she sits on top of me with mixed emotions swimming through her ocean eyes. "Take off your shorts, Maya. Don't make me rip them. You know I will."

She swallows hard, but obeys. Her movements are slow and shaky, filled with equal parts desire and fear. Fear for how much she wants this. When she's left only in her bra and thong, I position her on my lap again. The bra comes off first, those perfect tits I've dreamt about every night spilling out for me.

"God damnit, Maya." I grab both handfuls and squeeze them, pulling a small moan from her mouth. Bringing my mouth down, I suck and nip at one of them, before moving to the other. She shudders on top of me, her hands positioned on my shoulders. "You taste so fuckin' sweet."

I pull her lips to mine again and work on my pants until they are down to my knees. Her body is hovering above mine, avoiding my hard length right below her. I shove my tongue into her mouth and explore every inch of her, desperate for more.

I distract her with the searing kiss while my hand grabs at the lace thong covering her. I rip it off in one swift movement and she gasps against my lips. Before she can pull away, I shove my tongue back into her mouth at the same time that I pull her hips down onto me, driving my dick all the way inside her in one punishing thrust.

Her scream is full of pain and pleasure and it's the most addicting sound I've ever heard. She stays still on top of me, letting her body adjust to the size of me. Letting her mind comprehend that once again, she's in my arms.

"Tell me why you're mad at me." She doesn't answer, her legs shaking on top of mine. I wait a few seconds, watching her sit there with her eyes closed and her mouth formed in a tight line. She can't hide from me forever.

Grabbing onto her hips, I pull her body weight up before slamming her back down on top of me, making her cry out. "Answer the damn question, Maya." I growl the words into her ear. "Answer the question or I'll leave my mark on you for the entire fuckin' world to see. Includin' that fiancé of yours." My mouth moves to her neck and I nip it lightly before sucking on the spot. When she doesn't talk, I suck on it harder, showing her exactly what I mean by leaving my mark.

"Fuck." It comes out of her lips in a breathy exhale. I continue to lift her up and down on my length, driving her crazy. "I talked to Abby, okay? She told me everything." Shit. That's not what I was expecting her to say. And definitely not the way I wanted her to find out. I put her down so I'm fully inside of her and grab at her face, making sure she's looking into my eyes.

"I was a stupid kid, Maya. She wouldn't leave me alone and I gave in. I'm sorry."

"She told me you guys were friends all through high school and you dated in college. She said you asked her to go to the same college as her. She said you were in love with her." The sadness in her eyes makes me both furious and happy. Happy because it proves that she does still care. That our previous conversations weren't all fake.

"Baby girl, I've never loved anyone but you." I say it before I can stop myself. Her eyes widen with the admission neither one of us has ever said out loud. "Damn. This wasn't exactly how I wanted to say it." I squeeze the bridge of my nose and finally decide to say fuck it. "I know it doesn't matter anymore. I know you're mad at me for not bein' completely honest about my past and I'm sorry about that. I know you're gettin' married to a fuckin' fairy in a week. I know we were doomed before we even started." I think back to the words I told her about her dad saving her mom from pointless hope. "Fuck… I know I'm hopin' for the impossible when I should be acceptin' the inevitable. But you need to know how hopelessly in love with you I am. You deserve to know how amazin' and irreplaceable you are. You deserve to know that there is someone out there that would give up everythin' for you just to make sure you're happy.

"I am in love with you, Maya Turner. I am in love with every little freckle on your face. I am in love with the way you bite your lip when you're thinkin'. I am in love with the way your eyebrows furrow when you're anxious or mad. I am in love with the way you yell and laugh and sing and cry. I am in love with your witty humor. I am in love with how deeply you love. Everythin' about you Maya. I wouldn't be me without you."

She doesn't answer me. Her mouth hangs open in awe and tears flood the corner of her eyes. Instead of speaking, she lifts her hips and sinks down on me. I can't stop my head from tipping back at the feel of her around me and when I let out a deep shaky breath, she grabs onto my shoulders and starts riding me hard. She doesn't stop until we are both moaning and panting against each other.

I try to hold off, to prolong this so it doesn't end, but when she screams out my name with her climax, I can't stop it. I squeeze my hands tight with my loud groan. My hips thrust forward deeper into her with my release and when I'm completely empty, I pull her to me and wrap my arms around her small frame. I hold her there, refusing to let her go. Cause that's exactly what she's going to try to do. Leave me.

Her hands push against my chest and she sits up so she can look at me. I wait, silent and desperate for her to say it back, but knowing she won't. The tears are still pooling in her eyes and when the first tear drops, she finally speaks.

"I've wanted to hear you say that my entire life." It's not a happy statement. It's full of misery and despair. "But it doesn't matter now. I made a promise to stop being selfish. Being with you is the most selfish thing I could ever do right now. I need to put my family first and if my daddy's last dying wish is to walk me down the aisle and watch me get married, then it's going to happen."

"Then marry me. Marry me in a week and we will figure it all out. Please, Maya, don't marry him." I'm begging her. I'm begging her for the impossible.

"Don't be crazy, Colton. You can't marry me in a week. We live across the country from each other. Our lives are so different." The tears keep falling from her eyes, proving how much this is hurting her.

"I'll move to New York with you. I'll do whatever it takes. I'll find a job and–"

"No. I would never make you do that. You hate the city. You'd resent me for the rest of our lives. I've made up my mind, Colton. There's nothing left to say. It's time to deal with the pain." Before I can respond, she slides off of me and throws her clothes back on. I stare straight ahead, trying to ignore the pain that just keeps coming over and over again whenever I'm with Maya. The empty cold that's taking over now that she's not touching me.

"That's not fuckin' fair, Maya."

"You're the one who told me that life wasn't fair. That we need to accept the inevitable and stop hoping for the impossible, right? So, take your own advice. Please. Don't make this any harder than it already is." I hear the desperation for me to accept it and agree. I hear her falling apart on the inside.

"I know you love me too." I'm just embarrassing myself at this point, but I can't stop.

"Sometimes love isn't enough." When she says it, I can't stop myself from laughing. Anger boils up inside of me at how easily she is giving up on what we both know would change everything. How easy it is for her to give me up. I slam my hands against the dashboard, unable to control myself, making her flinch in the seat next to me.

Trying to calm myself down, I pull my pants back on and move over to my seat. Throwing the truck into drive, I speed onto the road and say one last thing before we sit in painful silence the rest of the way to Harly.

"You and I both know our love would have been everythin'."

Chapter

SIXTEEN

Maya

His sentence replays over and over in my head. *Our love would have been everything.* God, why couldn't he just accept it and move on? Why did he have to confess his love for me? Hearing those words come out of his mouth were the most deadly, magnificent words I've ever heard. I had never felt so alive and so doomed at the same time before.

The tears haven't stopped streaming down my face since we ended the conversation. I watch as the truck pulls up to the sidewalk in front of the small boutique sporting the name *Blaire's Bridal* across the front in white letters. The last thing I want to do is shop for a wedding dress right now. Not with streaks of tears running through my makeup and a hole slowly consuming my heart with every painful beat.

"Thank you for driving me." The words come out in a whisper and I don't dare look at him as I open the door to leave. The sound of the engine cutting out makes me falter for a second, and when I look back into the cabin, Colton is already out of the truck and slamming the door behind him. He's at my door in seconds and he holds it open for me step out.

"What are you doing?" When I move to stand, I feel wetness between my legs. Jesus. The evidence of what we just did is coming through my shorts. My face heats up with embarrassment and I suddenly feel like I'm standing on this open sidewalk, completely naked.

"If you're dead set on makin' the worst decision of your life, I'm not lettin' you do this by yourself. I'll help you find a dress since your mama can't be here." His sentence makes me forget about my current situation for a second as I dart my eyes up to his face. He isn't looking at me, instead, he's moving into the truck and grabbing something from the glove box. When he returns, he hands me a napkin and then turns around, blocking me in between the open truck door and his huge frame.

The small gesture is enough to bring more tears to my weak, pathetic eyes. I quickly clean myself up, kneeling slightly so no one will see. "I'm good now, thank you." He moves, turning around and grabbing the napkin from my hand before throwing it in the garbage can next to us.

"You don't have to come in with me, Colton. I'll be fine on my own. I don't really care what dress I wear."

"Why aren't you wearin' your mama's dress? You always said that was the dress you were gonna wear when you got married." He walks forward, towards the boutique, and I know there's no convincing him not to come in with me.

WHAT HAPPENS WHEN YOU BREAK

"Doesn't feel right." We both know why it doesn't feel right but neither one of us elaborate. Colton opens the door for me and when I pass through the opening, he places his hand on the small of my back. Tingles spread where we touch and I fight back the urge to push into his hand more. When Claude touches me, I want to pull away. I want to slap his hands off and tell him to keep them to himself.

Luckily, Mama and Daddy saved me in terms of having to sleep with Claude. While they are pretty progressive in certain ways, they like to pretend to be old fashioned. They made Claude sleep in the guest room even though they know we live together. He wasn't too happy and tries to sneak into my room almost every night, but I push him away. I haven't even let him kiss my lips since being here.

"Hi, sugar!" The owner's sweet accent flows through the room. I find her behind a small desk and give her my best smile. She's wearing a yellow sundress and her brown hair falls down in waves. She's quite beautiful with her green eyes and tan skin. "You must be Maya Turner."

I put my hand out to shake hers when I reach her and nod my head. "Yes, it's so nice to meet you. Thank you for making an appointment with such short notice. It's a bit of a rushed wedding given the circumstances." I explained to her why we needed this to come together so fast on the phone and she was very understanding.

"Not a problem, I'm honored you picked my boutique." Her sad eyes leave mine and find something behind me. When I see the spark of desire in her eyes, I know exactly what she's looking at. Or rather, who she's looking at. "Is this your fiancé?"

I hate the way she's looking at him. I want to tell her yes. That he's off limits. That he's mine and she needs to stop undressing him right in front of me. But, he's not mine. "Um, no. This is just a friend of mine." The way her body stands a little straighter and her smile shines a little brighter makes my eye twitch.

"Well, just Maya's friend, I'm Blaire. It's nice to meet you." She walks out from behind her desk and extends her hand to him. He takes it, staring right at me with a slight smirk on his face. I want to slap that smirk right off.

"Pleasure's all mine, darlin'. My name's Colton." He uses the nickname he has called me since we first ran into each other at the pond and judging by the look in his eye, he did it just to mess with me. Asshole.

Her flirtatious giggle makes me roll my eyes and without her instruction, I head straight into the four aisles of white fluff. Once upon a time I wanted a big princess gown, but right now I want something simple and cheap. Something that won't draw attention, not that anyone is going to be there. Something that I can hide away in a small bag in the back of my closet and never think about again.

"What are we lookin' for today, sugar?" She follows me into the back of the boutique, still eyeing Colton who's walking next to her.

"Simple, elegant, nothing flashy or big. Price doesn't matter but I would rather it be cheap." I sound so clipped and emotionless. She doesn't seem to notice, but the way Colton is staring at me shows me that he does. That he's worried about me and hates every second of this.

"Alright, I can work with that. Why don't y'all go sit near the dressin' area and I'll pull out a few dresses for ya." I give her a tight smile and nod my head, walking over to the plush benches surrounding a huge three pane mirror. I feel Colton sit on the same bench but refuse to look over at him.

"When I get married, I'm wearin' Mama's dress cause it's the prettiest, puffiest princess dress in the world. I know I never wear dresses, but my weddin' day is gonna be the day that I surprise everyone." His voice mocks mine, repeating the words I used to say as a child. I hate how much he remembers about me.

"Shut up." I grit my teeth through the words and hold back the middle finger that wants to shove itself in his face. He just chuckles at me before standing back up and walking towards the rows of bright white.

Turning my attention back to the mirror in front of me, I take in my reflection. I look like shit. My hair looks frizzy and greasy. My face is streaked with tears and the buckets of concealer did nothing to hide the bags under my eyes. The difference between Maya a week ago and this mess of a person in front of me is actually terrifying. I look like I do when I'm dealing with a stressful case and don't sleep for days on end.

Speaking of work, I have been avoiding it at all costs. The case is slowly slipping away from me and if I don't start focusing, I'm going to lose it and Wickins is going to go free. The asshole deserves to be behind bars. He can't roam the streets to potentially do this again.

"Alright, let's get you into that fittin' room." She carries a huge handful of dresses and I barely acknowledge them or her. Standing up, I make my way into the room at the same time Colton sits down and places one knee on top of the other.

"Do you have... do you have any under garments?" I feel awkward asking the question, since most people would wear underwear when they know they are trying on dresses. Most people don't have a beast of a man named Colton ripping their underwear off without warning either.

"Of course, I'll go grab something from the back." She's gone for a few seconds before returning. I put the white thong on quickly and then she starts helping me get into a dress.

The first one is a simple silk spaghetti strap dress with rouching in the front. The back has white pearl buttons going from the butt up to my mid back. She asks if I want a veil and I quickly decline. When she opens the door for me to walk out, my breath shakes in my lungs. The thought of having Colton's eyes on me feels too intimidating right now. Especially in a wedding dress.

"Go on, sugar. Go see what you look like in the mirrors." I walk out on shaky legs and when Colton's eyes land on me I feel like I'm going to be sick. His stare is full of fire. I swear he's burning the thin fabric with each caress of his hazels. I try not to look at him as I walk towards the area he's sitting, but I can't keep away. It's like he's a magnet pulling me to him.

His Adam's apple bobs in his throat and with each step I take, I can't help but feel like I'm walking down the aisle to him. Something I have wanted forever and will never have. His eyes drag down my body, taking in the soft material covering my curves. He knows exactly what I look like under this dress, and I know for a fact he's picturing it right now.

When I reach the step up in front of the mirrors, I hesitate before looking at myself. Knowing I have to, I finally take a deep breath and look into the intimidating mirrors. I can't deny that it looks good. From my neck down I look like a bride, ready to walk down the aisle and cherish the best day of her life. But the minute I look at my face, the illusion is shattered. The sadness coating my features taints the dress and suddenly, I hate the way it looks.

"No, not this one," I say it matter of factly.

"I think you look amazing, sugar. What do you think, Colton?" I turn my attention towards him and find his eyes glued to my backside.

"Not this one." That's his only answer and I can't help but shrink into myself. I suddenly feel naked and ugly. I feel like my curves are too big and my stomach isn't flat enough. I nod my head and start to retreat, following Blaire into the dressing room. When I pass Colton, his hand grabs onto my arm, stopping me. I turn to look at him and he stares straight into me.

"You look absolutely gorgeous in this dress, Maya. You're the prettiest God damn woman I've ever seen in my life, you hear me?

But I might kill someone if anyone sees you in it. You might as well be naked in this thing."

I gulp and nod my head in understanding. Turning back around, I walk into the dressing room and try not to look flustered. Changing out of the dress, she puts me in two other spaghetti strap dresses that neither Colton nor I are impressed by and then she has me try on a form fitting chiffon dress with straps that hang delicately off my shoulders. The bodice is snug on my body but the skirt billows out just slightly, not enough to be considered a princess dress, but enough to leave some imagination to what's underneath.

We walk out of the fitting room and the minute Colton looks at me I know this is going to be the one I pick. His stare makes the breath in my lungs disappear. It makes my heart skip a beat. It's a look full of awe. A look of love. Of astonishment. It's the look I would have wanted my husband to have on my wedding day when I was a kid.

I look in the mirror and instantly know it's the one. I barely need to look at it to know. It lays perfectly against my body and looks modest and sexy at the same time. "This is the one." I turn around and look at Blaire, ready to leave this place and forget about the wedding in general.

"He said you'd pick that one." She smiles at me and then looks down at Colton. "You win."

"What?" I furrow my brows at her and wait for her to explain.

"Colton picked that one out. Bet me that you'd choose it." She walks into the fitting room and before I follow her, I eye Colton. He sports a smug smile on his face and shrugs his shoulders before winking at me. The one wink sends butterflies off on a race deep inside my gut. Flipping him off with a barely visible smirk, I walk into the dressing room after her.

She walks out once the gown is off and leaves me to get dressed. I take my time, needing to avoid Colton's gaze for a few minutes. I imagine Claude standing in his position today. If he was picking out my dress, he'd pick something out that had thousands of gaudy diamonds and barely covered my skin. He has no idea what I like. And yet somehow, after half a lifetime of not seeing me, Colton knows me better than I know myself.

Meeting them both outside, I take in Blaire leaning against the register counter, pushing her tits out for Colton. He is saying something and she laughs a little too loud before reaching out and putting her hand on his arm. It's embarrassing how hard she's working to get his attention. And it's embarrassing how much it pisses me off.

Walking up to Colton, I slip my hand in his arm and put my head on his bicep. "This is why every girl needs a gay best friend. They know you better than you know yourself." I don't know why I say it, but the look of surprise on both of their faces makes it worth it. She looks between the two of us, and when I squeeze Colton's arm he chuckles lightly and plays along.

"What can I say. I have better taste than you, baby girl." He uses the nickname to make him sound more flamboyant, but it leaves a mark on my heart every time he says it.

"I had no idea you were gay. I guess that makes sense." I can't stop the snort that escapes me when she says that.

"Alright, how much do I owe you?" I let go of Colton's arm and to my surprise, he walks out of the shop.

"Nothin', sugar. Colton already paid for it. That was part of the bet. He said if you picked this dress, he'd pay for it. You got yourself one amazing best friend. I kind of wish he wasn't gay, though."

"Trust me, we're all better off with him being gay. Thank you for your help, Blaire. I'll come by to pick up the dress early next week after the alterations. It was a pleasure meeting you."

Walking out of the shop, I find Colton standing against the truck with the biggest smirk on his face. He left so I couldn't argue with him when I found out that he paid. "You're an asshole." I give him a genuine smile and shake my head.

"A gay asshole apparently." I try, and fail to hold back my laugh.

"I'm paying you back. I can pay for my own dress, you know." I hop into the truck and wait for him to get in as well. Instead, he comes to my door and opens it back up.

"I know you can, Miss Lawyer, but you will be doing no such thing. You can repay me by buying me lunch. And a drink."

"Right now?"

"Yes, right now. Let's go." He waits for me to get out and then shuts the door behind me.

"Isn't it a little late for lunch?" I check the time on my phone and see that it's four.

"Okay then you owe me dinner and a drink. Even better." He grabs my hand and pulls me along the sidewalk. This is a bad idea. A terrible idea in fact. Not that it can get any worse. We just screwed in his truck on the side of the road. He admitted he was in love with me. I'd say that's as bad as it gets.

"Everyone's going to worry where we are." I pretend to fight it, but I'm also walking alongside him without hesitation.

"I already texted Andrew and told him that the appointment is takin' longer than we thought and we are gonna grab a bite to eat after. Everyone is aware."

"You had this planned the entire time, didn't you?" I glare at him but can't hide my smile.

"Well, I was plannin' on askin' Blaire to dinner but when you announced that I was gay, I had to find someone else to eat with. You were the second best option at the time." I whip my head in his direction when he stops talking. He's not looking at me, instead, he's smiling smugly at our surroundings.

"Sorry for raining on your parade. I was just getting a little tired of watching her eye fuck you the entire time."

"It's alright, darlin'. No need to apologize for bein' jealous. It happens to the best of us." I consider fighting him on it, saying I wasn't jealous and lying through my teeth. But there's no point. We both know I was.

"Where are we going anyway?"

"It's right around the corner. A little Mexican place I've heard is the best in Texas." I raise a brow at him, not expecting that to be his answer.

"I figured you'd be bringing me to some barbeque place or another dive bar. Why Mexican?" I can't help but salivate at the thought of tacos and margaritas.

"Mexican used to be your favorite. And judgin' by your Instagram, you're a fan of tequila." I think back to the one picture I've ever posted of a margarita. It was three years ago.

"You been stalking me, Colton Grant?" The thought brings a smile to my face. I love the idea of him keeping tabs on me through the years.

"Stalkin'? Not a chance. Admirin' is more like it." I shake my head at him while my broken heart starts to piece itself back together again for all of the wrong reasons. "You have quite the impressive life out in the city, darlin'."

"It looks a lot better on social media. Honestly? It's lonely. Anyone I go out with are coworkers of either mine or Claude's. I don't have any real friends out there." The admission sounds more depressing than I expected it to.

"If it makes you feel any better, the only people I see are your parents on a day to day basis. The closest friend I have most days is Margo."

"Margo?"

"One of the Longhorns. She's a great listener." I laugh at his joke and appreciate the light conversation. We finally reach the restaurant and Colt holds the door open for me. The air smells of fresh salsa and tortillas and my stomach rumbles loudly. The lights are dim enough to provide some privacy for each table and the huge bar in the corner is lit up by green, red, and white lights. It looks freshly renovated with the distressed wood and black iron accents.

"Table for two please, ma'am." Colton speaks with the hostess while I smile at the bustling wait staff passing by. Everyone smiles and says hi on their way past. It's such a big change from the city. Back home, no one smiles let alone greets you. Thinking of the city as home doesn't even feel right anymore. Nothing feels right anymore.

"Ready?" Colton steals me from my thoughts and I nod my head. He gestures for me to go first before placing his hand on my back like he did hours before at the bridal shop. It both comforts me and makes my nerves sky rocket.

When we get to the table, Colton pulls out my chair for me and I almost laugh. I hold it back and sit, waiting for him to join me on the other side. "I don't think anyone has ever pulled my chair out for me before."

"Bullshit. I've definitely pulled your chair out for you before." He grabs a menu and hands it to me.

"Yeah, right before I was about to sit down so I'd fall on my ass." We both laugh at the memory.

"I did do that a few times, didn't I? But back to the subject at hand, how has your fiancé never pulled out your chair?"

"Have you met him?" I raise a brow at him and he chuckles low.

"Unfortunately." The waiter stops by and takes our drink orders. I somehow convince Colt to have a margarita with me. "Last time I had tequila I blacked out in college."

"Looks like I'm in for a real treat then tonight, cowboy." I wink at him and he smiles back at me. I find myself mesmerized by this version of him. The carefree, sarcastic, boyish version. He tends to hide him away, unless it's just the two of us, and I'm desperate to see more.

Our drinks come out and Colt raises his glass. "I have a proposition." I bring my glass halfway up and wait for him to continue. "Spend the next week with me. We work together anyway, so it won't look suspicious. Just spend time with me before… before the day. I won't pressure you to leave him. I won't touch you unless you want to be touched. I just want to hear you laugh. I want to listen to your stories. I want to be able to talk to someone who will answer with more than just a moo." I can't hold back the small giggle at his corny joke. "See? I want to be able to hear that as much as possible before you leave."

I contemplate for a while even though I know exactly how I want to answer. Bringing my drink the rest of the way up to his, the glass clinks loudly, sealing our fate for the next week. "You've got yourself a deal, cowboy."

By the end of dinner, we have each had five margaritas. My body feels full from the five tacos I demolished, but light and relaxed from the buzz. Okay, maybe it's a little more than a buzz. The gleam in Colton's eye along with the pink tint of his cheeks makes him even more gorgeous than normal. It almost hurts to look at him.

"How's the tequila treatin' ya?" I smirk at him, knowing he's feeling it.

"Definitely prefer bourbon, but it does the trick. I can tell you like it which means I like it, darlin'." I smile as I take another sip of my drink.

"Judgin' by the five drinks you've downed, you like tequila more than you're lettin' on."

"You're right. I fuckin' love tequila. Apparently, tequila turns you Texas. I love hearin' your accent come through." I didn't even realize my old accent was present, but hearing that only makes my already wide smile even bigger.

"I missed my accent." The admission is something I normally wouldn't admit to without the help of tequila.

"I missed everythin' about you, Maya Turner."

"Yeah… you've said that a few hundred times already." He furrows his brows and gives me a devilish grin.

"That a problem?" I bring my glass up to my mouth with his question, looking at him over the rim of my glass. His jaw ticks when I blink at him slowly. "Don't you look at me like that, darlin'. Only bad things can come from that look."

"Bad things, huh?"

"Real bad things. Things I can't stop thinkin' about doin' to you." I blink at him again and I swear I see his irises turn a shade darker. "God, you're trouble on tequila."

"No. I'm trouble on Colton. You make all of my morals go out the damn window. When I'm with you I want to throw everything away and be selfish."

"Me too, baby girl. I would run away with you right now. Leave everythin' behind and figure it out on the way." My buzzed mind hears this and decides it's the best idea I've ever heard.

"So, let's do it. Let's get in the truck and just drive. Let's go to the ocean and watch the sunrise. Let's go to the mountains and climb the highest peak. Let's go to the desert and dance under the stars."

"I know you're jokin', but I would do it in a heartbeat."

"What if I'm not jokin'?" My mouth moves before my brain can tell me to stop. Not that my brain would protest. It's currently bathing in a bath of margarita, with a do not disturb sign hanging on the door.

"Then I'd say let's pay this bill and start drivin'." My heart races with his words. It's the best idea I've ever had. I can't think of a single thing that could go wrong. None. Nothing.

"Get your ass out of that chair and into my truck right now, baby girl." He's looking at me like he wants to devour me and a spark of electricity runs through my body. I jump out of my seat and watch him throw money down on the table before following close behind.

My body is buzzing and humming uncontrollably. I've never felt so alive. I've never wanted anything so bad in my life. I jump into the truck as my brain sloshes around in the tequila. We should get more tequila.

When Colton gets in the truck, I voice my amazing idea and suddenly his face falls. "What's wrong?"

"We can't do this, Maya. You're drunk and I've got a good buzz goin'. If I drive off with you, I'll be takin' advantage of the situation." He sounds so conflicted when he speaks.

I listen to his words and my brain decides to get out of her warm alcohol bath. It flips over that do not disturb sign and starts yelling at me to get it together. It starts reminding me of Daddy being sick. It starts reminding me of all of the hard work Mama put in to make the wedding special. It starts reminding me of my job back in the city.

"Fuck." I slouch in my seat and the high from my adrenaline starts to wear off until I feel like a shell of a person. "I really wanted to Colt. It sounds like a dream."

"I know it does, baby girl. I would love to travel the world with you. Just not when you're too intoxicated to think straight." His hand rubs my shoulder before he grabs me and pulls me closer to him. I place my head against his arm and take a deep shaky breath.

"I'm really sorry, Colton. For ruinin' our dreams." Drunk Maya doesn't understand why I am marrying Claude. Drunk Maya thinks I'm being a pussy and avoiding what I truly want. Drunk Maya knows that my daddy wouldn't want me to marry someone I don't love.

Why does drunk Maya seem more logical than sober Maya? Why do I feel like I have to do this or I will forever disappoint my family? Maybe because I've already disappointed them so much.

"My dream is that you will be happy. If he makes you happy, that's all that matters." I think about lying and saying he does. Then I think about telling the truth and saying he doesn't.

In the end, I don't say anything at all.

Chapter

SEVENTEEN

Colton

"That's not happenin', Maya. No fuckin' way. You've finally lost it." I shake my head at the girl standing in front of me. It has been two days since our night out together, which means she is getting married in five days. Five fucking days.

"Come on, Colton. I'm going to do it either way. I just figured you'd want to be there in case anything goes wrong." Her eyebrows go up and she gives me those puppy eyes I have such a hard time saying no to.

"Trigger isn't like Jax. You can't train him to like you." The thought of her getting hurt trying to train the wild animal makes my stomach turn.

"If I recall, Mr. Grant, you said the same thing about Jax almost fifteen years ago." She gives me a knowing look and I grit my teeth, trying to come up with another excuse that will convince her not to do it. I know it's hopeless. When Maya Turner gets an idea in her head, she doesn't forget it. She doesn't back down. She's ruthless.

"He's gonna kill you. And then I'm gonna bring you back to life just so I can say I told ya so." She laughs and steps closer to me. We have been working together every morning. Right now, we are cleaning out the stables. Luckily, Claude refuses to help with anything around the ranch. He loved the idea of wearing flannels and cowboy hats, but he hasn't stepped foot outside since showing up.

"He's not gonna kill me. Also, we are changing his name. Trigger is such an aggressive name."

"Which is fittin' since, you know, he's an aggressive horse!" She's now standing right in front of me and I can't help my heartbeat from increasing with her closeness. Clasping her hands together, she sticks her lip out in a pout.

"Pretty please, Colt. Give him a chance… give me a chance." I groan and let my eyes pierce into hers.

"You better stop poutin' or I'm gonna bite that lower lip of yours, darlin'." I watch as she sticks her lip out farther, teasing and tempting me. Right before I'm about to grab her and follow through with my promise, she sucks it back in and bites it herself. I find my teeth jealous of her own, wanting so desperately to be the one biting down on her pillowy flesh.

Sighing, I know I can't deny this woman. "Fine. We will try to tame the beast. But we are gonna take it slow. I don't want you gettin' hurt."

Her squeal makes me smile and when she throws herself into my arms, I inhale her vanilla scent and grab onto her. Picking her up off the ground, I spin her around, desperate to hear her laugh.

We spin for a few seconds before I stop and she pulls away to look down at me. Her laugh still sits in the air, surrounding us in the beautiful sound.

We blink at each other and I let her body slowly drag down against mine, until we are face to face. I know she wants to say something. I can see it in her eyes. I can see it in the way her mouth opens and closes, just barely. I look down at the movement and find myself transfixed, desperate to feel them on me again.

"I…" she stares down at my lips now too, just as mesmerized by this moment as I am. Our hearts beat against each other's, our breath dancing in the small space between us.

"I know, baby girl. Me too." She could have said so much with that one word.

I want you.

I need you.

I love you.

No matter what she was going to say though, I feel the same way. I know exactly how she feels. I will always know exactly how she feels.

Dropping her down to the ground, she clears her throat and takes a shaky breath. "Should we go see him?" I almost forget about who she's talking about.

"Lead the way, darlin'. Let's go get our asses kicked by a horse."

SHE DIDN'T LISTEN. SHE NEVER DOES. I TOLD HER TO STAY ON THE fence, away from Trigger, while I went in and tried to get a handle of him. Most times, I just get a saddle on the wild horses and ride them long enough to tame them. It's dangerous and exhausting and definitely not something Maya should be doing.

"Get out of here, Maya," I whisper shout to her, since we are both now standing inside the ring.

"No. I need to get close to Turant. Just let me try something."
I furrow my brows at her.

"Turant?"

"It's his new name. Turner and Grant makes Turant," she
answers so nonchalantly, but something about her response makes
my heart flutter in my chest. She must see the look on my face
because she speaks again. "What?"

I clear my throat and look away for a minute. "Nothin'." I
can't hide my growing smile. "I like it." No, I love it. I love her.

"Good. Now, let me try, please?" I go against every part of
my being by saying yes to her. I watch, with bated breaths, as she
slowly moves toward the horse.

"Hi, sweet boy. I know you're scared, and I don't blame you,
but I'm not going to hurt you. You're completely safe with me,
Turant." She continues forward. I watch the horse eyeing her, but
he doesn't move. He doesn't buck or jump. I feel like he's not even
breathing, completely mesmerized by Maya. I don't blame him.

"That's it, you're not aggressive, are you baby? You're just
misunderstood. You're scared and trying to protect yourself.
I know how that feels. People are scared of me too back home.
People think I'm mean and aggressive, but I'm just trying to
protect myself and the people who deserve justice. I'm just trying
to make my way through this world without getting trampled. So,
I'd appreciate it if you didn't trample me today, okay sweet boy?
We're in this together."

Her soft voice is hypnotic. I know she's talking to Turant,
trying to calm him with her voice, but I feel like she's speaking to
me. Like she's trying to tame my frantically beating heart.

The horse nudges and shakes his head slightly, and Maya stops
where she stands. "It's okay, Turant. I'll go slow. I just want to give
you an apple. I just want to pet you and give you love."

She doesn't move forward, his head nods to the side and his
foot rises and falls, rubbing into the dirt harshly. "Maya... please

come back here." I have my hands up and I'm slowly making my way to her. She senses my movements and puts a hand out to stop me.

"Let me try something else. Don't move or you'll scare him." I stop in my tracks and take a shaky breath, terrified of all of the shit that could go wrong. When I hear her speak again, my breath hitches in my throat. It's the most beautiful sound I've ever heard.

"She put him out. Like the burning end of a midnight cigarette. She broke his heart. He spent his whole life trying to forget." The lyrics to *Whisky Lullaby* flow through the air, soft and sweet. She used to sing when we were kids, but nothing like this. And God damn if her voice isn't the most angelic thing I've ever heard.

She continues to sing to him and I can see in Turant's eyes that he feels the same way I do. That he's so intrigued by the beautiful being in front of him. That he wants her to get closer to him, to sing to him, to take care of him.

She's barely two feet away from him at this point and he hasn't moved a muscle. His eyes stare into her, both transfixed and terrified. He wants to trust her, but he's scared to. I know the feeling. It's so easy to trust those eyes. It's so easy to believe every word coming out of her mouth.

I have to hold my breath when she reaches out to touch Turant. She's still singing, the soft melody flowing through the air, and when her hand lands on his mane, he flinches. His eyes are wide as he stares at her, confused by her. She's now petting his hair and moving towards his face, bringing a piece of apple up to his mouth. He sniffs it, never taking his eyes off her, and then finally, after what feels like minutes of me not breathing, he opens his mouth for her.

I can practically feel her smile shining through even though her back is to me. She continues singing, petting his mane while he finishes off his apple. I watch as she reaches up and pets his nose, letting her voice coax him into submission. He lowers his head for her and makes it easier for her to rub between his eyes. When she leans in to kiss him, I almost lose my shit. I start to walk forward, terrified that he's going to attack her, but stop myself.

I stop myself because not only is Turant letting Maya kiss him, he's nuzzling into her like he can't get enough. He's brushing up against her cheek and trying to get as close to her as possible. The horse that both Andrew and I could barely contain. The horse that bucked and kicked the minute we tried to get next to it. The horse we were ready to get rid of because he attacked every other horse we had.

In less than two minutes Maya Turner managed to calm the beast and make him fall in love with her. I can see it in his eyes. I can see the respect, the curiosity, the desperation to be near her. She gives him one last kiss and then slowly backs away, keeping her front facing him, always making eye contact. Her song slowly comes to an end, the soft voice fading out until the air is quiet around us. I find myself missing it more than I should.

When she finally reaches me, standing at the edge of the fence, she turns around so we face each other. Her smile is radiant, the biggest smile I've ever seen. She looks so proud, so happy, so in her element.

"Go ahead, say it." The pride radiating off of her is magnetic. I feel my own bubbling up when she looks at me.

"You, Maya Turner, are absolutely fuckin' magnificent." I scoop her up into my arms, making her squeal. Turning around, I walk out of the corral and push her up against the closed gate, her legs wrapped around me.

"That's not what I meant." She's practically glowing with her happiness. I watch as she reaches for the cowboy hat on my head and then places it securely on her own. God, I love her in my hat. "I was looking for a 'you were right' so I could say I told ya so."

"You can still say I told ya so, darlin'. And I promise you, you're always right. Everythin' about you is so damn right." I don't mean to, but when I say it, I squeeze her tighter against me. My hands are holding her up under her ass and the movement makes her gasp in my arms. I instantly feel my body harden with the sound.

"Told ya so," she whispers it so low, her eyes staring straight at my lips, parted slightly. I try to stop myself, I really do, but the adrenaline surging between the two of us and the look in her eyes makes it impossible.

Dipping my head low, I softly press my lips against hers. I barely graze them, letting the tingles sweep through me from the contact. She's so incredibly addictive. She fits so perfectly in my arms, against my lips, everywhere we touch.

She's the one that intensifies the kiss. Her tongue snakes out and licks my lip before she pulls it into her warm mouth. The smallest suck is all it takes to turn me wild. I press her hard against the gate even though I know the rusty metal is probably digging into her. She accepts the pain and when I devour her with my tongue, making sure I taste every inch of her mouth, she grabs onto my hair with tight, punishing hands.

We kiss for what feels like hours, letting our mouths be selfish and take what they want. She keeps pretending she doesn't want this. She keeps pretending she won't allow herself to be selfish. I know she won't be able to deny it. Deny this.

I'll be patient though. I'll sit here and let her make her own decisions. But in the end, she's going to come back to me. Whether it's in a week or a year, we will be together. I'll do whatever it takes for that day to come. Whatever it takes to make sure she doesn't feel any guilt or negativity towards this.

Because after the last week, I realized something. This isn't going away. When Maya told me she was marrying Clause, I thought us being together was impossible. I thought I was being a hopeless romantic. But I wasn't. We aren't the impossible, we are the inevitable. We are written in the stars. Some way or another, Maya will be my end.

Chapter

EIGHTEEN

Andrew

"Mama, do you think this weddin' is really a good idea?" We are sitting in the kitchen right now, just the two of us. Claude is up in Maya's room, Dad is sleeping, and Maya and Colton are working outside. I should be at work, but my next few appointments were canceled so I came home for lunch.

"What? Of course it is, Drew. Don't be silly. Why would you say that?" She doesn't turn to look at me from where she stands at the counter. She's making sandwiches while I cut fresh peaches and oranges.

"I don't know." I lower my voice so Claude can't hear me from upstairs. "Somethin's off about Claude. I think he's fakin' it for us. He told me he had to answer emails and phone calls for jobs earlier, but I walked past his room and heard him yellin' at a video game on his phone. I think he's moochin' off Maya."

"Don't be ridiculous. He's a great chef. Did you taste his food? He's so talented. And if he makes Maya happy, that's all that matters." Mama finally turns to me and one of her brows is raised, daring me to fight her on that.

"Is she though?" Her sigh almost makes me drop it, but I can't. "I'm just sayin', she doesn't seem happy around him. I felt like she was the happier before he showed up." I think back to when I see Maya being the happiest and realize it's always when she's out working on the ranch. She's out there almost all day at this point. She used to love working with the animals, so it makes sense.

"She's stressed, Drew. She isn't used to seein' Daddy like this and she's gettin' married in less than a week. Just pre-weddin' jitters."

"Then why are we havin' this weddin' so soon? If she isn't ready, shouldn't we stop? What does Dad think about all of this?" I don't want to upset Mama, but I know she's the one pushing this. She cares so much about Dad getting to walk his daughter down the aisle that she is willing to ignore all of the signs that it might not be best.

"Your father will never like a single boy that your baby sister is with, you know that. But he told me as long as she's happy and this is what she wants, he would love to be there for her big day." She stops and thinks for a second, her eyes glossing over. "He's dyin', Drew. He's never gonna see you get married. He's never gonna meet his grandbabies. He's never gonna celebrate another birthday or Thanksgiving or Christmas with us. Please, don't take this from him too. He is the best man in the world and he deserves to experience this."

"Okay, Mama, I understand. I didn't mean to upset you." I stand up and pull her in, hugging her tight.

"I'm not ready for him to be gone. What are we gonna do?" My own tears threaten to spill over with her question. I can't imagine this world without Billy Turner in it, but I have to be strong for my mom. I have to be strong for the family.

"We're gonna take it day by day. I'm always here, you know that. And Dad will always be with us. No matter what happens, he'll always be here." We hug for a few more minutes before I kiss her on the cheek and pull away. "I'm gonna go get Colton and Maya for lunch, okay?"

"Thank you, sweetheart. I'm sorry for gettin' all emotional on you." I give her a smile before walking out of the house and towards the stables. My mom has a point. Dad deserves to at least see one of his kids get married. Maya got engaged to the guy, so she must love him. Just because Colton and I both think he's not good enough for her doesn't mean she shouldn't marry him.

The stables are empty when I reach them so I head over to the horse's fields. My mind is still racing with thoughts of Dad dying and Mama crying when I see Colton standing over by the small corral that holds Trigger. Walking towards him, it takes me a second to see the black cowboy boots attached to the two legs wrapped around him. Legs being held up in the air and pushed against the gate. Legs that are attached to a girl who my best friend is currently grinding into and sucking face with.

I snicker to myself, deciding not to disturb him. He's pulled this move a few times in the past and I know he's had a lot on his mind lately. He needs a good lay. Leaving him alone, I go and look for Maya. Maybe I missed her in the stables. I search through them again, taking a good ten minutes to look in the other barns as well, and come up short. When I am walking back towards the house, I finally see her walking towards me from the horse fields.

"Hey, it's—"

My voice cuts out when I look at her feet. She's wearing black cowboy boots. I stop in my tracks and look back up at her face.

Her cheeks that are flushed. Her eyes that don't look directly at me. Her mouth that looks swollen. No. Fucking. Way.

She walks past me and gives me an uncomfortable smile. "Hey Andrew." Before I can respond, she's past me and halfway to the house, practically jogging away from me. I don't think, I just move. I move in the direction that my piece of shit best friend was before. I move in the direction that this mother fucker just took advantage of my baby sister.

When I spot him, my eyes see red. My ears ring and my hands clasp at my sides. He's walking towards me, with a satisfied smirk on his face. "You're home early." I don't answer him. I walk right up to him and pull my fist back before slamming it straight into his smug face. I feel his nose crack beneath my fist and the sound of it is gloriously rewarding.

"What the fuck?" He grabs at his nose as blood pours out of it. I pull my arm back again to land another punch but he pushes me hard in the chest and makes me stumble back. "That's a bad idea, Drew. What's going on?"

"You're a piece of shit!" I yell the words at him, too angry to say anything else. He looks at me confused at first and then the realization blooms in his eyes. He knows exactly what's going on.

"Andrew, I can explain." His hands go up in defense and the fact that he's admitting to it sparks another raging fire inside of me. I throw myself at him, dragging him to the ground before laying another punch against his face.

"You son of a bitch! She's my little sister! She's engaged! She's not some girl you can stick your dick in!" My own words are making me angrier when I hear them out loud.

"It's not like that! Please, Drew." Another punch to his face shuts him up.

"Our dad is dyin'! She's gettin' married in a week! You're takin' advantage of a girl who's vulnerable and scared!" I'm screaming at him still, the anger only getting worse.

"I'm not takin'–"

"Shut the fuck up. I want you gone. Get off my family's ranch. You're not ruinin' the last memories we have as a family. You're not gonna fuck everythin' up because you wanted to get your dick wet." I move to get off of him and turn around, still fuming from what I just witnessed him doing to Maya.

"Andrew." The despair in his voice actually makes me stop walking, but I don't turn around. "I love her."

"Well, she doesn't love you. She's gettin' married to another man. Get the fuck off this ranch. You're not welcome here anymore. If I see you back here, I'll shoot you myself."

Maya

ANDREW SCARED THE SHIT OUT OF ME WHEN I SAW HIM WALKING towards me. If he had showed up ten minutes earlier, he would have witnessed Colt screwing me up against the gate for all to see. Was it irresponsible and stupid? Yes. Did I have any control at that moment? No. It's like the combination of adrenaline and Colton's stare made me forget about all of the reasons we shouldn't be doing it.

God, I'm going straight to hell. Making my way up the stairs, I avoid Claude's room, needing a quick shower. I feel dirty for one too many reasons. When the hot water shoots out of the upstairs shower, I quickly undress and step under the jet. It hits my skin in punishing streams, as if it knows what I am doing. As if the water is trying to discipline me and tell me to be a better person.

I accept the painful heat scorching my skin. I accept it when I scrub over my body with a rough towel. I accept it when it feels like blisters may form on my flesh. When the first tear threatens to fall, I shut the water off and step out into the small bathroom. The white walls can barely be seen through the steam enveloping the room. I look at the mirror on the wall and barely make out my reflection. Not that I'd recognize it if I saw myself anyway.

Using my hand, I wipe away the steam coating the glass. My skin is bright red from head to toe. My features look conflicted. While I look exhausted and stressed from the bags under my eyes and my washed out complexion, my eyes shine through. My eyes shine with images of the last few hours. Of my time spent with Colton. They shine with his reflection.

Making my way to my room, I stop at Claude's door when I hear him talking. The sound of his soccer game echoes through the door.

"Si je gagne, je peux faire ce que je veux de toi à mon retour." His French is muffled through the door, but I hear it. I hear him telling someone that if he wins, he gets to do whatever he wants to them when he gets back to the city.

I hear someone whispering in answer. I can't hear what she's saying, but I can hear the feminine tone of her French accent. I wait for the anger to show up, but it doesn't. I actually find myself smiling, on the verge of laughter.

"Oh baby, oui. Continuer de parler." He tells the unknown woman to keep talking and the groan that follows has me standing a bit straighter. I'm listening to my fiancé have phone sex with someone in my parent's guest room. In the middle of the day. With someone he plays video games with. My snort escapes me and I slap a hand over my mouth, worried he heard it.

Running back to my room, I close the door behind me and finally let myself laugh. My back is pressed against the cold wood, soothing the heat on my skin. The heat I made myself endure for feeling guilty. When all along, he's been cheating on me too. I think back to a year ago when he came home wasted at two in the morning with his hair completely disheveled and his shirt buttoned wrong. I believed him when he told me he was just exhausted from work. I believed him when he said he was drinking wine when he was coming up with recipes after closing and spilled some on his shirt. I believed him when he said he must have buttoned the new shirt wrong when he got dressed to come home.

I know it's because I didn't really care. Even then, the thought of him cheating didn't upset me. It more so pissed me off since I was providing him with a house to live in. He was coming home to me and still expected sex almost every night. Not that I complained in the moment. Back then, all I ever really wanted from him was sex. Now I don't even want that. Not after experiencing it with Colton. Not after he ripped me apart and put me back together so no other man could have me.

I get dressed in a clean pair of shorts and a tank top before brushing out my tangled hair and applying some concealer to my eyes. Making my way down the stairs, I don't tell Claude that it's lunch time. I'm too busy thinking about seeing Colton when I get down there. With his content smirk, his devilish eyes, and his kind heart.

When I round the corner to the kitchen, I find Mama humming to herself alone, filling glasses with iced tea. Andrew and Colton aren't here yet. "Hi Mama." I greet her with a kiss on her cheek before grabbing napkins and plates to put on the table.

"Hi Mayflower. How was your mornin'?" She places the iced tea back in the fridge before bringing all of the food to the table.

"It was amazing. Colton and I decided to give Turant a chance."

"Turant?" I forgot that no one knows the beautiful horse's new name.

"I mean, Trigger. We named him Turant though. I didn't like Trigger. He's not aggressive, he's just scared."

"Ahh. I don't know, Maya, I saw that horse when the boys brought him in. He's one of the meanest horses I've ever seen." I sit down in my seat and watch as she takes the one to my right.

"No, he's not mean. He let me feed and pet him. He was just overwhelmed and scared. I think I'll be able to ride him soon. You'll see." Grabbing a half of a sandwich, I pick at it while thinking about Turant.

"You've always had a way with horses. Used to call you the horse whisperer. I'm happy to see that hasn't changed." She pauses for a second and I think the conversation is over. "Maya, I just want to tell you how proud of you I am. And how grateful I am that you are willin' to change all of your plans so your father can be there to give you away. It means the world to us both."

"I know Mama… I'm happy he's going to be there too." I give her an almost genuine smile, meanwhile I'm picturing my soon to be husband jerking off right above us to another woman's dirty talk. Not that I can judge.

"And I was thinkin', I know you had plans of your own to get married in a few months. So maybe you can still have both. This is barely gonna be a weddin', and then all of your friends and Claude's family can be at the bigger one in a few months. And… maybe I can finally come to the city and see where you live for the next one."

I debate my mom's words. The thought of having one wedding with this man is nauseating, let alone having two. *So why even have the first?* The thought crosses my mind and suddenly, I'm overwhelmed by the best idea I've ever had.

Why even have the first? Because I want my dad to walk me down the aisle. But that doesn't mean I have to actually get married. No one has to know it's not real. Mama and Daddy don't get hurt, I don't marry Claude, and then when Mama asks about us later, I just tell her we didn't work out. I tell her we got a divorce.

"You're a genius, Mama!" I make her jump with my excitement before a huge smile covers her face.

"I didn't expect such a reaction. I'm so happy you like the idea. I already have everythin' planned for this one. You're gonna get married out by the magnolia tree, I'm havin' Pastor John officiate, we are gonna play–"

"No. I don't want to get married by the tree. I want to get married by the... pond." It's the first place I can think of. I refuse to get married, fake or not, to Claude under the tree that means so much to me and my family. "And I already have someone I want to officiate. Tell Pastor John thank you but we don't need him. In terms of everything else, you can take full rein."

She looks a little taken aback, but she smiles at me with a nod of her head. "Whatever you want, sweet pea. It's your day." No, it's not.

Scarfing down the rest of my sandwich, I excuse myself from the table and make my way up the stairs. I need to talk to Claude. He is going to have to agree to this, whether he likes it or not.

I'm too excited about my plan to even realize Colton and Andrew never showed up for lunch.

Chapter

NINETEEN

Maya

I don't knock. I'm sure he thinks the door is locked, but I know this lock has been broken since I was five years old. I need to catch him in the act if I want to make sure he can't deny it. I wait for the right moment. I wait for him to say the words I know, since he's said them so many times to me in French.

"Je jouis!" He grunts the words letting her know he's coming and I barge right in, a huge smile on my face.

"Hey Clau–" I cut off when I see him in the position he's in. When I see him lying on the bed with his head back, his release squirting up against his bare chest. When I see him fumble to cover himself up, his movements sloppy from the intensity of the orgasm coursing through him. I look down at his phone on the bed, still on a call with someone named *Juliette from work.* Oh shit, I remember her. I always thought they were a bit too close.

"Ma belle!" His voice is still hoarse, since he's fighting between fear and pleasure. The fear from me catching him and the pleasure from his dick still spurting jizz all over himself. It's actually quite comical to watch.

I pull out my best acting skills and cover my mouth with my hand, shaking my head back and forth. "What is… How could…" I let a tear fall down my cheek and then pretend to get angry. "Explain yourself Claude Francois."

"Maya, it's not what it looks like. It is nothing. Please, ma belle." He starts to clean himself up and clicks the end call button on his phone. Does he think I didn't see it? God he's dense.

"How long has this been going on?" Do I feel guilty about this? Yes, a little. But it needs to happen. This will benefit us both.

"It's not like that. It's just, you haven't been home and even when you are, you're always focused on work. I'm a man, ma belle, I have needs." I bite my tongue so hard to keep from laughing. He has needs? Good lord.

"I'm sorry I wasn't enough. I could feel us drifting apart. I could tell we weren't really in love anymore. If I'm being honest, I haven't been happy with you in a long time." I sit down on the bed and pretend to be sad. I pretend to be heartbroken.

"I still love you, Maya. It's not that."

"Well, I can't marry you now, Claude. You know that, right?"

"Oui, I… I understand. I didn't want this to happen, ma belle." He looks down in defeat. I can sense him stressing out. I can feel the worry radiating off of him and I know exactly what he's thinking. He's worried about where he's going to live if he's not with me.

I sigh, wiping the tears away. "I know you don't have anywhere to go if you aren't living with me…" His face whips up to look at mine and hope circulates in his dark eyes. "And I don't want to put you out, I still love you too, as a person." I pause for dramatics and then continue. "So, what if we make a deal?"

"What do you mean?" He looks nervous, like he's about to make a deal with the devil.

"I will let you stay at the apartment for as long as you need until you are back on your feet. In return, you are going to pretend this never happened and go through with the wedding. For my dad's sake. He wants to walk me down the aisle and so help me if I don't give him his dying wish."

"So, you want me to marry you still?" I huff, trying not to get aggravated.

"It won't be a real wedding. It won't be officiated by someone actually certified to marry us. It will all be for show. My mom and dad don't need to know anything." He looks at me like I'm crazy. Honestly, I think I am. Maybe this idea is insane. Maybe I'm a terrible person and I've lost any glimpse of sanity I had. But I think it could work. And I think he'd be stupid to turn this offer down.

"Maya... I mean, why don't we work through this? Why don't we try to save what we have and actually get married still?" He's pleading, but it's long past over.

"No, Claude. I wasn't sure about us before I caught you doing this. This just solidifies my feelings. I'm sorry but I don't want to marry you anymore. I just want to give my dad one last important memory that he can carry on with him when he passes."

Judging by the look on his face, he's going to say no. He's going to tell me I'm nuts and go back to New York. "Alright. It's a deal." He puts his hand out for me to shake and I almost do, until I realize he just jerked himself off with that hand.

"Why don't you go clean yourself up. We don't need to shake on it." I get off the bed and right myself before walking out of the room. That went so much better than I expected. Now, I just need to let Colton in on the plan and figure out who I can pay to fake officiate our wedding.

I make my way down the stairs and find Andrew talking to Mama, eating lunch finally. Colton is still nowhere in sight.

"Have you guys seen Colton?" I stand near the counter, plopping a piece of peach in my mouth from the large tray. Andrew turns to me when I speak and his eyes hold so much anger. It doesn't seem directed at me, but I can sense it there.

"He had to leave. Not sure when he'll be back." The words are clipped. He turns back to his food and tries to end the conversation there.

"Did he say where he was going? I need to talk to him."

"Somethin' about havin' to help out another ranch or some shit. He probably won't be back until after the weddin'." That doesn't sound like Colton. There's no way he would up and leave without a single word to me. Especially after our last encounter with Turant.

"Um, that doesn–"

"That's all I know Maya. I'm eatin'. Go spend some time with your fiancé why don't ya?"

"Okay... sorry I bothered you." I turn away from him and make my way outside. Pulling out my phone, I dial Colton's number. It rings and rings, before going to his voicemail. Hanging up, I shoot him a text and decide to leave it at that for now. I have to go figure out the next part of my plan. I know exactly who is going to help me.

I don't ask when I take Andrew's car. Not with the way he just treated me. Fuck him. Putting it in drive, I search for local tattoo shops and find that there are only two in the area. Perfect. Time to go find myself an officiant.

Luck is on my side today. The first place I put in my GPS happens to be Harrison's shop, which saves me a good thirty minutes. When I find him, he greets me with a huge smile.

"Well, if it isn't Miss Maya Turner. I was worried about you, girl. You disappeared on me at the bar."

"Yeah, sorry about that. Kind of a long story." A story I don't plan on telling him.

"What can I do for you? Finally here for that tattoo?" I had no plans to get a tattoo while I'm here, but now that I'm standing in his shop, my body itches to get something done.

"Yeah actually, I'd love one." I don't even have to think before I say what I want. "Can you do a magnolia flower?"

"Of course. I gotta say, I didn't peg you for a flower tattoo kind of girl." He motions for me to follow him into the back. "Where do you want it?"

This one, I have to think about. I don't want it anywhere obvious. I want it hidden. "Um, can we do it on my rib? Right below my heart?"

"Going for one of the most painful places for your first, huh? If you say so." He winks at me before getting the table ready, telling me to take my tank top off and cover myself up with a small towel he provides. I would normally feel weird about a random man seeing this much of me, but I know Harrison is batting for the other team.

"Do you have a picture you want to use?" He sits down in front of me and brings everything over that he needs.

"No. You can be creative with it. Just, nothing too big. And I don't think I want much color... if any. You can decide that though."

"My favorite kind of client. Alright, just do me a favor and stay still. It's gonna hurt but you get used to it. The shading is the worst part." I nod my head, trying to calm my nerves and excitement.

The initial contact surprises me. It feels like someone is snapping a rubber band against my rib over and over again. It's not as bad as I expected, but it definitely doesn't feel good. "So..." I grit my teeth through the pain. "There was another reason I came here today."

"Trying to convince me to go straight again for you? I knew it." He gives me a devious smirk and I try to laugh through the searing pain at my side.

"A girl can dream, can't she?" He hits a soft spot and I wince, trying desperately not to move. "Anyway, I have a favor to ask you. Or, more so, a favor to ask your partner."

"I'm intrigued. What can Dan help you with?"

"I need him to officiate my wedding." I decide to rip the band aid off, since there's no point in wasting time.

"Sweetheart, Dan can't legally marry you and your fiancé. I mean, I guess he could take a course online easily enough, but why would you want him to do it? You don't even know him."

"Exactly. I don't know him, so my parents don't know him. I don't need him to be certified. We can tell my parents that he is and then he can marry Claude and I and it won't be legitimate." He stops working and looks up at me, confusion and worry covering his face.

"Um, Maya? I'm really not supposed to be tattooing someone who's intoxicated." I laugh at him and then realize he's completely serious.

"I'm not drunk Harrison. It's hard to explain." I close my eyes and try not to think of the pain in my side.

"Well, try me. We've got time." Shit. I'm going to have to explain it if I want them to say yes.

So that's what I do. I spend the next thirty minutes explaining the shit show that is my life. I explain that my dad wants to walk me down the aisle. I explain that I'm in love with Colton. I explain that Claude is cheating on me with someone else too. That he has been for a long time. I explain everything to him, word vomiting a story I haven't told anyone before.

"So, I need to get faked married to give my dying Daddy the chance to walk his only daughter down the aisle. I need to get fake married so Claude and I can go our separate ways and I can try to figure out the shit show that is Colton and my relationship. I need to get fake married so I don't break Mama's heart during a time she is already so heartbroken."

He doesn't talk at first. Somehow, he managed to continue tattooing me through the entire story. I'd almost assume he didn't hear anything I said if it wasn't for his eyes widening every now and then with my words.

"That's um... a lot." He uncomfortably laughs before continuing. "But it's also beautiful. I understand where you're coming from. You know, I saw Colton staring at you at the bar that night. I haven't seen him since high school so I didn't recognize him. But I saw the look in his eyes. I saw the same look Dan has for me. I knew he was a man in love with one single look."

I can't help but smile, somehow forgetting about the pain at my side when I picture Colton. "Yeah, I know the look."

"I can't guarantee Dan will say yes, but I'm going to try my hardest to convince him. As long as I get an invite to this fake wedding. And as long as Dan doesn't get in any kind of trouble for impersonating a priest."

"Woah, woah, woah. I never said impersonate a priest. That's a felony. He's not impersonating anyone. He's simply coming in and saying a few nice things and then saying you may now kiss the bride. I'm the one telling my parents that he was certified online. Easy peasy. And yes, I couldn't imagine having my fake wedding without you there."

He laughs, shaking his head, before pulling his hand away from my ribs. "Alright, partner in crime, we're finished." Applying a small layer of ointment, he has me stand up and walk over to a tall mirror in the corner of the room. I take a deep breath before looking at the art he just spent the last forty-five minutes working on.

What I assumed was just going to be one flower is actually three delicate flowers attached by a thin curving branch. Almost the entire thing is black, but fading into the dark lines of the petals are soft shades of white and baby pink. It's even more beautiful than I could have imagined. It's perfect. I can't help but picture each flower representing the generations before me. My grandparents, my parents, and then hopefully, one day me. When I get married, for real, under their magnolia tree.

"It's perfect, Harrison. Better than I could have ever imagined. Thank you so much." I feel a tear slip out and fall down my cheek, but I wipe it away before he can see it.

"Let's wrap it up and then get you out of here." He takes his time wrapping up the intricate art before telling me I can put my shirt back on. When we reach the front of the shop, I pull out my wallet to pay him.

"No, this one's on me. To make up for the other first I fucked up." I can't help but laugh. Each interaction I have with Harrison makes me like him so much more. He's changed completely from the player that took my virginity at prom.

"Thank you, Harrison." I pull a one hundred dollar bill out of my wallet without him seeing and quickly throw it in the tip jar. Grabbing a pen and business card off the counter, I write my number on the back and hand it to him. "When Dan gives you his answer, this is my number. Let me know what he says."

Taking my number, he smirks at me. "I knew you were trying to put a move on me. Gotta say, it's a weird tactic."

"But it worked, didn't it?" I raise my brows twice at him and we both crack up.

"I'm glad you're back in town. Even if it's just for a little. This town needed Maya Turner back."

I leave after we say our goodbyes, the words he says sticking with me. Why did it feel so right when he said this town needed me back? Why did I want to agree with him and say I needed this town?

And why does the thought of moving back here sound less scary and more like a dream?

Chapter

TWENTY

Maya

"Colt, I don't know what's going on, but call me. Please. I'm really worried and I need to talk to you." I leave the third voicemail on his phone, my stomach dropping lower with each one I leave. It's been two days since I saw him. Two days of me doing ranch work on my own. Two days of Andrew being weird with me. Two days of having to pretend Claude and I are very much in love.

The only thing that's keeping me sane is spending time with Daddy. We have been switching off between movie night and sitting out on the porch every other day. Tonight, we are supposed to be sitting out on the porch. He's waiting out there for me as we speak.

I make my way down the stairs and find him sitting on the porch swing, staring out at the lightning bugs dancing through the sky. "Room for one more?"

His bright blues turn towards me, the gleam in his eye as present as ever. "Of course, squirt. There's always room for my girl."

Taking a seat next to him, he offers me some of the blanket that covers him. I snuggle in close and rest my head gently on his bony shoulder. "What are you thinking about out here all by yourself?"

"Memories. Memories of takin' over the ranch after my father. Of meetin' your mama. Oh havin' you and Drew. I've been doin' a lot of that lately. Rememberin' the past." I smile into the darkness, letting my eyes get lost in the twinkling lights floating through the peaceful night.

"What's your favorite memory?"

"Now that's an impossible question. How can I have a favorite when they are all so perfect?"

"Hey, they weren't all perfect. Remember when Andrew snuck out into the field to get drunk with his friends and they accidentally let all of the horses out without knowing?" That's one of my favorite memories. He got in so much trouble after. It was karma for him not letting me come out with him.

"Oh, lord, don't remind me of that. Their rock music scared those horses damn near to death. Took me days to get them all back in the fence. I could have killed your brother that day."

"And the time I was building a volcano for science and mixed up the measurements. That explosion could have been heard three towns over." We both laugh, his deep chuckle vibrating through my chest.

"You destroyed the kitchen. We were still cleanin' up red shit over a year later." His laugh turns into a cough and I grab at his hand, lifting my head off of his shoulder to look him over. "I'm okay, squirt..." Another cough. "It's just a cough."

But it's not. It's one of many noises that I'm now terrified of. A cough used to just be a cough. A groan was just a groan. A sniffle was just a sniffle. A deep breath was just a deep breath. Now, they hold so much power. They hold so much fear and worry that that's going to be the last sound I hear from my dad. That this cough is going to be the beginning of the end. That a deep breath is going to be his last.

When the coughing subsides and his breathing evens out, I let myself relax against him again. "I'm sorry, I'm still not used to this."

"I don't think I'll ever get used to it either. But the good news is I'll be six feet under soon so you won't have to get used to it."

"Dad!" I gawk at him, disturbed by his words. "Don't say that. That's a horrible thing to say."

"If I can't joke about it, I might as well be dead already. I'm not scared of dying, Maya. It's gonna happen whether we are ready for it or not." I stare into his eyes, amazed and terrified by the strength this man possesses.

"If you aren't scared of death, what are you scared of?"

"I'm scared of your mom bein' alone. I'm scared she's gonna lose herself when I'm gone." He closes his eyes before continuing. "I'm scared my kids aren't gonna find happiness. True happiness, like your mama and I have had since makin' a life together. I'm scared I'm gonna leave my family here to fend for themselves and they aren't gonna be okay. That everythin' we did to create a life for you guys is gonna disappear the minute I'm gone."

"Daddy, that's never going to happen. We are all strong because of you. You raised us to be tough, hard headed, and a little bit crazy. This world is nothing compared to the Turner family. Besides the fact that we are going to miss you more than words can describe, we are going to be okay." I grab onto his arm and try to pull myself into him as much as possible.

"Promise me you'll be here for your mom. She needs her babies. She needs you, Maya." Two weeks ago, if my dad asked me this, I wouldn't have been able to promise him that. I would have given him an excuse and said work is too busy, I'll try but I can't guarantee I can be here when she needs me.

"I promise. I will always be here for Mama, no matter what happens."

"Thank you, squirt. I knew I could count on you. So... about this weddin'." I cringe when he brings it up. That's the last thing I want to talk about. "I know your mama is bein' a bit pushy. I've always dreamt of the day I could walk you down the aisle, but I don't want you doin' it for the wrong reasons. Do you really want to do this?"

This is my time to shut the entire thing down. He's giving me an out, he's letting me stop the wedding from happening. He's being self-less and giving up a dream of his to make sure his kids are happy... He's willing to tell his already heartbroken wife that all of the hard work she put into this day is for nothing because it's not happening.

"I really want to do this, Daddy."

"And Claude? He seems... a bit..." I can't help but laugh at his loss for words.

"He's something, that's for sure. But he has a lot of good redeeming qualities." I try not to feel guilty lying. He definitely had a few redeeming qualities, but those are long gone.

"As long as you're happy, squirt." I think back to Colton saying those same words to me. It's what people who truly love you want. They don't care about the outcome, as long as you are happy. I smile at the thought, desperately missing my other half.

"I'm happy, I promise." That's not a lie. When I think of Colton, I'm more than happy. When I think of Colton, it feels like everything in this world is going to be alright. Like there is no pain and suffering. Like there's nothing left but me and Colton.

TWO MORE DAYS. IT'S BEEN TWO MORE MISERABLE DAYS. I'M OFFICIALLY getting fake married tomorrow. Luckily, Dan agreed to do the ceremony and everything is coming together nicely. I picked up my dress yesterday and it fits perfectly.

The only problem is Colton is still MIA. I haven't gotten a single text or call and his phone is now sending me straight to voicemail. I could kill him. But, when I think about killing him, I start to worry that maybe something happened. That he is already dead. The thought is too unbearable to think. I don't want to live in a world where Colton doesn't.

Fed up with this shit, I find myself running up the stairs to Colton's apartment. When I open the door, the place looks exactly the same as always. There's dirty laundry in the corner and dishes in the sink. Why would he just leave without cleaning or grabbing some of his stuff? That makes no sense. Snooping a bit more, I come across something that makes my heart drop.

His phone is sitting on his bed, completely dead. He doesn't have his phone. Now I'm really starting to panic. He's been gone for four days without his phone or any of his belongings. Running from his apartment, I go to the only person who will know what's going on. My asshole brother who has been giving me the cold shoulder since Colton left.

I march into Andrew's room without knocking. He's sitting at his desk, doing paperwork, and when I throw the door open, he jumps in his seat.

"Jesus. What the fuck, Maya?" He doesn't meet my eyes while I storm over to him.

"No, what the fuck Andrew is more like it! What did you do? Where is Colton? I'm sick of this shit." I can practically feel the steam coming out of my ears.

I see it, the anger filling his eyes at the mention of his name. "Why do you care so much? Just leave it, Maya. You're gettin' married tomorrow." I am about to scream again, but the look in his eyes makes me stop. How did I not realize this before? He knows.

"You know." It's not a question.

"If he ever comes back here, he's a dead man. I swear to fuckin' God Maya, I'll kill him." I can't stop my eyes from rolling. Since when is he the overprotective brother?

"God damnit Andrew Turner. Get your head out of your ass. He has treated me better than any man ever has. He has been there for me more than you have and you're my own brother. He's always been the one and part of me thinks you know that." I consider admitting it out loud to him, deciding it's time for him to know. "I love him, Andrew."

The most deafening silence sits between us. He doesn't give away what he's thinking. He just stares at me, dissecting me with his blazing eyes. I wait. And wait. And wait... for him to say something but he doesn't.

"For the love of God. Stop acting like it's such a surprise. You saw how obsessed with him I was when we were kids."

"Was this happenin' back then too?" He's looking at me in disgust, clearly upset that we have been hiding this from him.

"No. Nothing ever happened between us. Not until now." His laugh surprises me.

"That's great. Nothin' ever happened until you were, you know, ENGAGED!" he yells the word, getting in my face.

"You and I both know Claude isn't the one for me."

"But you're marryin' him tomorrow, Maya."

"That's what I'm trying to tell you! I have a plan. I'm not actually marrying him. I can't marry him... but I can't disappoint Daddy either. I can't let Mama's hard work be for nothing."

"So, you're marryin' him but not marryin' him. You've lost it." Andrew shakes his head, throwing his hands in the air.

"The wedding is going to be exactly how Mama wants it, but I picked who officiates it. We don't have a marriage license and he's not certified so the wedding won't be real. It will just be for show. Mama and Daddy will never find out, I'll move back to the city and eventually tell Mama that we got divorced. Everyone wins."

"That's insane. Seems to me like Claude definitely doesn't win. Have you told him about your little plan or are you gonna hide it from him too?"

"Yes, he knows about it. He agreed to help me... he's cheating on me. Has been for a while now."

"Aw, it looks like you two are perfect for each other then."

I grit my teeth, losing my patience with him. He can be such a stubborn asshole. "Screw you, Andrew. It's happening, whether you like it or not. I love Colton, whether you like it or not. I don't give a shit if you don't agree. Hell, I don't give a shit if you decide not to be there tomorrow. All I give a shit about right now is where Colton is."

His head shakes while his hand rubs across his face. An exasperated sigh leaves his mouth. "I told him to leave. I don't know where he is, Maya. I was mad. I had just witnessed the two of you..." He doesn't finish the sentence, and I'm grateful for that. "I told him... I told him I'd shoot him if he ever stepped foot back here."

"What is wrong with you? He's your best friend."

"Was. He was my best friend."

"God, Andrew. Don't be so dramatic. Is it really worth throwing away a lifelong friendship? You always knew we loved each other. It's just a different kind of love now. Why is it such a big deal?" I know I said I don't care if he agrees, but I do. Deep down, I care about what he thinks.

"You're my baby sister. I trusted him to be with you and never look at you the way other men do. To never have those kinds of feelin's for you. It's hard to explain, but as my best friend, he should know you are off limits."

"I'd understand that if we were still kids. And back then, he did respect that. He was never inappropriate with me. But, we're adults now. Everything's different. Don't you want us to be happy?"

"Of course I do, Maya. But... I don't know. Just give me a minute to digest this shit." I don't talk for a second, letting him grasp everything I just told him. I don't talk even though my brain is screaming at me to find Colton and my heart is pounding in my chest. It feels like ten minutes go by before I finally say something.

"Drew... I need to find Colton. He doesn't know about my plan yet. He thinks I'm actually going to marry Claude. He told me he loved me and... and I didn't say it back because I was scared. I need to tell him how I feel."

"I really don't know where he is, Maya. Honestly? Your best bet is to go to the local bars. That's where I would go if my best friend kicked me out of my house... I'm sorry for how I reacted. He's still my best friend, I just don't know how to handle this."

I want to comfort him, I really do, but the only thing on my mind right now is getting to Colton. I need to find him and tell him to come home. I need to tell him I love him. I need to tell him about the plan. Turning around, I book it out of his room. It's almost dinner time, but I don't care at this point. Andrew will cover for me; he owes me now.

Time to go get my man.

Chapter

TWENTY-ONE

Maya

I've been to four bars. Four out of the five bars in our area. I should have assumed this was hopeless. What are the odds that he's at one of them at the exact same time I show up to search for him? He could easily show up after I leave and I would have no idea. Stopping at the last bar in the area, the one we all went to that night, I say a small prayer to anyone listening. A prayer that I'll find him. That he will come home with me.

That prayer isn't answered when I enter the packed bar. The music is blaring and I try to find Colt's face in the crowd. I search every inch of the place. From the seats at the bar, to the dark corners, to the same bathroom he had me pushed up against the door in. I search the entire room and Colton Grant is nowhere in sight. This was a hopeless attempt.

He could be anywhere. I know how worried he always was about my brother finding out he had feelings for me. I can't blame him for running when Andrew threatened him. I can't blame him for deciding I wasn't worth the pain of his best friend hating him. But, as much as I can't blame him, I can't believe he's willing to give everything up. After how much he begged me. After everything he confessed to me. How could he throw it all away after a bad interaction with my brother?

Deciding my hopes and prayers were doomed from the start, I take a seat at the bar. The same bartender from last week comes over to me with a grin on his face.

"I remember you, blondie." He grabs a glass from behind the counter. "Jack and coke, right?"

"Actually. I'm going for something a little stronger. Double Bulleit on the rocks." The face he makes is expected. I get that face anytime I order straight bourbon. People don't understand how a girl like me could like such a 'big boy drink.'

He whistles low. "Damn, blondie. You somehow just got hotter." I can't help but snort at his comment. The fact that a girl ordering a certain type of drink automatically ups her ranking on the beauty scale is disgusting. And not surprising.

"Just get the damn drink, please." I offer him a smirk and wait for him to pour my bourbon, trying not to let my mind wander to Colton. I watch as he pours a hefty glass, definitely more than a double, and decide he's not half bad.

"You never did tell me your name." He slides the drink across the bar and I accept it graciously, taking a big swig of the amber liquid. I let the spicy oak flavor burn my tastebuds before swallowing it down. It lights a fire everywhere it touches, waking me up from the inside out. I already feel better with the one sip.

"You never asked. My name is Maya." I put my hand out for him to shake. His huge hand encloses around mine and swallows it whole.

"I'm Brandon, but my friends call me Andy."

"Nice to meet you, Brandon." I purposely use his full name. I'm not his friend. I'm just a girl he thinks he can get into his bed tonight. I'm sure it works wonders most nights, since he's relatively attractive. But my heart and soul belong to another man. My body is his and only his.

"Ah, so we aren't friends yet, blondie?" He fakes heartbreak with a hand against his chest. I give him a soft snicker and shake my head. "And to think, I was gonna let you drink for free."

"Trust me, Brandon, you don't want to be friends with me." I take another sip and savor the taste.

"That have anythin' to do with Colton Grant starin' you down the other night?" I almost choke on my mouth full when he says it.

"What?"

"The whole damn bar could feel the tension radiatin' between the two of you. He didn't take his eyes off you all night. I thought you two were gonna start fuckin' in the middle of the bar." I give him a fake laugh, my cheeks heating up a bit.

"How do you know Colton?"

"Went to school two years ahead of him. We used to be friends but these days, Colton doesn't have friends. Besides Andrew." He gives me a smirk before adding, "And you apparently."

"Yeah, our relationship is, uh... complicated." I down the rest of my drink, letting him refill it for me. "Have you seen him in the last few days?"

"Uhh, let's see. I saw him four days ago, I think? He looked pissed. Came in here and started drinkin' in the afternoon. Didn't stop until I cut him off. We were closin' down and he kept ramblin' on and on about somethin'. He was wasted."

"What was he saying?" I feel myself lean into the bar, desperate for some sort of clue as to where Colton is.

"Mentioned leavin' town. Said he had to go find a ranch with a pond or some shit. Said he wasn't welcome here anymore. I don't know. He wasn't makin' sense. That's all I can tell ya."

I don't say anything, trying to keep myself calm. Trying to keep the anger from bubbling to the surface. He actually left. He went to find another ranch to work on. One bad experience with my brother and he throws me away like I'm nothing. The tears threaten to appear but I blink them away.

"You okay, blondie?" He must see my change in demeanor, since his voice suddenly turns soft.

I sniffle and bring my drink up to my lips. "Yeah, I'm fine." I don't say anything else. I don't look at the bartender or give him a chance to start another conversation. I just sit here, holding back so many emotions, while I finish my drink.

Once it's gone, I leave cash on the counter, tipping him over double what my bill should have been. Walking out of the bar, I know I won't be back again.

Once tomorrow is over, I'm going back to the city. I'm going back to my old life and forgetting about Colton Grant for good.

Chapter
TWENTY-TWO

Maya

The sun is shining bright and the birds are chirping too loud. It doesn't match today's mood. Today is full of sorrow and pain. Today is full of lies and deceit. I look in the mirror and find my eyes puffy and swollen. I look hungover even though I only had the two drinks last night. The redness in my eyes can't be tamed. The grease in my hair didn't dissipate with my shower. I feel bloated and sweaty.

The knock on my door startles me, making me nearly twist my ankle with my jump. "Come in," I say while moving towards my bed. The door opens and Andrew walks in, a somber expression on his face.

"You ready for this, baby sis?" He seems just about as excited for this day as I am. I don't answer him, which is answer enough. "You don't have to do this. We can figure out somethin' to tell Mama. Dad will understand. He wouldn't want you doin' this for him, fake or not."

"It's happening. What's the point of backing out now? Colton left me. He gave up and left. At this point, all I want to do is get this wedding over with so Daddy and Mama can be happy and then go home."

He pauses before talking, his eyes dropping to the floor. "You're goin' back to New York?"

"Already have a flight booked for tomorrow. I need to get back to my job. I need to start my life over again and try to move on. I can't do that here." The thought of staying in this town a second more than I have to is enough to make me vomit. All I see is Colton.

"What about Dad? What about Mama when he..." He doesn't finish the sentence. "Just stay with us. Let us be here for you."

"And tell them that Claude, my new husband, is going back to New York without me? That I'm just going to stay in Texas by myself and start a new life here? Be realistic, Drew. That can't happen and you know it."

His defeated sigh lets me know I won this argument. "We just got you back... I don't want to lose you again. Not durin' a time like this." I hear the emotion in his voice and tears spring to my own eyes.

"Drew... I just... I don't know how to be here. I'm in love with him. I see him everywhere I look. I can't be here any longer. Let me get my life figured out. Let me try to get over him on my own. Let me build my strength and then I'll come back. I'll visit all the time. I won't leave you guys like I did last time."

"You promise?" I walk over to him now, hugging him tight. His arms squeeze me like a vice, refusing to let go. I take more comfort in it than I expect to. I don't normally consider Andrew as the protective, comforting type, but right now, this hug is exactly what I need. I feel like nothing else can get to me in his arms. Like he will make sure no one hurts me again.

"I promise, Andrew. I love you." He squeezes me a little tighter when I say it. Before he can answer, we hear a sniffle at the door. Pulling apart, we look over and find Mama watching us with her hands clasped in front of her chest.

"That just made my mornin'. My two babies lovin' each other," she talks while she moves across the room. When she reaches us, she pulls us into another quick hug. "Alright, time for you to go Andrew. I need to get Maya ready and you need to go help Claude."

The barely audible groan that leaves Andrew's mouth makes me snort. Mama doesn't seem to notice since she stays quiet and walks over to my bed, opening up my makeup bag.

"Good luck with that." I smirk at him before turning around to walk towards Mama. Before I even take a step, I feel a sharp pinch on my side and squeal, spinning back around to swat at him. He's gone before I get the chance, his loud chuckle flowing through the room as he leaves.

"Come here, come here. Let's get you ready." I try not to groan. The last thing I want to do right now is get ready and put a wedding dress on. All I want to do is wear pajamas and stay in bed all day, sulking in my self-pity.

TWO HOURS. IT TOOK TWO HOURS TO GET ME READY. ONE OF THOSE hours consisted of me arguing with my mom about what kind of makeup to do. She wanted bold and beautiful. I wanted plain and simple. We finally agreed to meet halfway and do a natural face with a red lip.

My hair is curled and clipped in a delicate updo. There are ringlets dangling around my face, framing it softly. Getting into my dress was the hardest part of the day. Not because it didn't fit, but because my body almost refused to get into it. I couldn't get myself to lift my legs to step into the soft fabric. I couldn't get myself to stick my arms through the sleeves. It's like my body was rejecting the dress.

When I look in the mirror, I look like a real bride. The white material sinches my waist and billows out softly around my legs. You'd never guess I was a broken mess on the inside. Not unless you look deep into my eyes. The eyes that hold so many memories of Colton. So many dreams and wishes that were shattered by the coward himself.

"You look gorgeous, sweetie. Claude better know how lucky he is." I let the sentence sit in my brain for a while. It couldn't be farther from the truth. No one would be lucky to have me. I was engaged and cheated. I went from a woman about to be married, to a woman in love with the man of her dreams, to a woman who lost them both.

"Alright, ready? It's just about time for the ceremony." Her voice interrupts my thoughts before I have enough time to start crying. I sniffle and nod my head yes before peeling my eyes off the mirror and walking out of the room.

We take Andrew's car the short way to the pond. When we get out, I let my eyes take in the decorations. There's a mowed path in the field leading to the pond. White rose petals line the edges, the sun glistening off of them.

I look two thirds of the way down the path and find my dad standing with a cane holding him up. His back is to us, as he stares at the pond in front of him. I can barely make out a small alter in front of the dock, where four people stand. I know it's Claude, Andrew, Harrison, and Dan, since no one else is attending. The only other person who knows about today is Colton. And he won't be coming. As much as I desperately wish he was here.

We make our way down the path, my feet numb and my legs shaky. This whole ceremony feels like a joke. I guess it kind of is. I can't help but feel embarrassed by it. Like I'm a kid playing dress up, performing for the adults.

When we reach my dad, he turns toward me and gives me a genuine smile. It makes me feel slightly better about the entire situation, but not completely. His eyes water with emotion while my mom gives him a hug, his eyes never leaving mine the entire time. Once they let go of each other, my mom continues to walk down the path, leaving us alone.

"I feel like I shouldn't call you squirt right now, squirt." I laugh through the tears threatening to fall. "You look so beautiful, Maya."

"Thank you, Daddy. You don't look too bad yourself." He laughs like I said a joke, but I'm being completely serious. He looks so handsome in his black suit. My mom had it fitted for his thinner frame, so it sits snuggly on his body. He looks less thin, less weak, covered up by the expensive material.

"Should I go change? I don't wanna take away from the bride's beauty on her big day." His shoulder nudges against mine softly, his bony frame pushing into me.

"The bride got her beauty from you so no matter what you wear you'll be taking away from her." I grab onto his arm, trying to make us look graceful while still trying to hold him up. The cane on his other side is helping him as well.

"True, but she's got me beat. She looks so much like her mama too. She got all of her amazin' qualities. Her eyes, her freckles, her smile. She reminds me so much of her mama on our weddin' day." I try to smile at his words, I really do. But the fact that I'm tricking him niggles at the back of my mind. Does it make it better if a lie benefits someone and saves them from pain?

"Thank you, Daddy. Should we get going?" I point my head in the direction of the alter and he nods in agreement. We start our descent down the grass aisle, the silence surrounding us. A few steps in, music starts flowing from a speaker near the alter. A soft melody glides through the air towards us, the guitar strings making my heart drop down into the empty pit of my stomach.

Alan Jackson's voice singing *Remember When* assaults my ears. My vision goes blurry from tears and my heart rate picks up, threatening to explode inside of me. I can practically see Colton. Hear him. Feel him when the lyrics to this song reach out to me. This became our song the minute we danced to it by the magnolia tree. This became our song when we reminisced on old memories. When he told me he hoped we could have a life similar to the words Alan sings about.

I keep walking but my limbs start to shake. My legs wobble under me and my arms tremble in my dad's grasp. A tear escapes and falls down my face, leaving a wet trail in its path.

"Squirt, are you okay? You're tremblin' like a leaf." My dad's worried voice sounds distant through the panic setting in. The panic that I am desperately trying to push down. The panic of knowing that Colton, the only man I've ever loved, left me. That I will never again experience the kind of passion and beauty that I did with him over the last few weeks.

I can't hear the song through the fog which makes the panic subside slightly. I nod yes to my father, my own breath being the only thing I can hear now. Somehow, my legs manage to continue to move down the path. Somehow, I make it past Harrison, my mother, and Andrew standing on either side of the aisle. Somehow, I make it to Claude and Dan standing at the dock, right under the alter. Somehow, I avoid thinking about Colton long enough to kiss my dad on the cheek and stand across from the man I can't stand.

Somehow, I make it through the short ceremony, unable to hear a single thing that Dan says, until it's over and I'm left even more broken than I already was.

Chapter

TWENTY-THREE

Maya

Clink, clink, clink.

The sound of my dad hitting his knife against the side of his champagne flute full of water interrupts my conversation with Harrison. We are all sitting outside at two picnic tables set up in a small clearing in the woods. Mom and Andrew strung twinkling lights through all of the branches of the trees and turned it into something I could only compare to an enchanted forest.

There are roses all over the ground and tables, with light music playing in the background. My mom cooked prime rib and there's a small two tier cake sitting on a circle table. I turn my attention to my dad and wait for him to speak. He's staring at me and Claude, sitting right next to each other. Well, I wouldn't say right next to. I made sure to put a good foot between the two of us so no part of me touches him.

"I want to make a toast to the happy couple." I almost laugh but hide it with a smile. "I can't tell you how happy I am to be a part of this day. I still remember the days Maya would dress up in her mama's weddin' dress and ask me to walk her down the aisle when she was only ten years old. Those are some of the best memories I have to this day.

"So, the fact that the two of you gave me the opportunity to do it in real life, is something I will never forget and never be able to thank you for properly. I wish the two of you the most happiness in the world. I wish the two of you a life full of laughter and smiles. I wish the two of you an endless supply of love that will last for generations to come."

I don't realize I'm crying until Harrison hands a napkin to me from across the table. I accept it with a smile and continue to listen to him while I wipe my eyes. "I know we haven't done much for you in the last few years, but we wanted to make up for that in some way. It's not much, but it's something.

"Your mother and I wanted to pay for your honeymoon. It's a month long trip exploring Europe. From Italy to France to Greece. It's completely covered and you can book it for whenever you are ready to go, since you're so busy with work, squirt. I know it's not much, but you deserve to see the world and try to find somethin' that could possibly compare to your beauty. I highly doubt you will though.

"Anyway, enough of that sappy crap. To the happy couple. May everyday be the best day of your life. Let's eat and you guys better start drinkin'. You have to cover the liquor I'm not allowed to drink anymore!" Everyone laughs, clinking their glasses, while I stand up and make my way over to him.

Pulling him into my arms, I cry against his shoulder, suddenly so thankful for this day. The day I dreaded. The day I felt so much hatred towards. Seeing the look in my father's eyes. Hearing his gratitude. It makes every horrible part worth it. I'd do it a million times over to make him feel this way.

"Thank you, Daddy. I love you so much." I turn to my mom and pull her into a hug too, so grateful for the both of them. "You guys don't have to cover a honeymoon. You did more than enough already. Today was beautiful, thank you for making everything so perfect." Everything except for who I was getting fake married to.

"We aren't takin' no for an answer. We are coverin' your honeymoon and that's final. Now go have a good time with your new husband. Get drunk, you deserve it." I don't argue that, walking back to my seat and downing the last of my champagne. I need the alcohol to take the edge off.

I grab my phone off the table, taking it with me to the small bar full of alcohol. I grab the bottle of champagne, opting out of a glass, and make my way through the clearing and towards the pond. It's only a few yards away, so I'm there within minutes with only the stars and twinkling lights guiding my way.

I take a seat on the dock and let my feet dangle into the cool water. It's so dark here, I can barely make out the water below me. It just looks like a dark hole, ready to suck me into it. Ready to consume me like the hole that's already consuming my heart. I look down at the phone in my hand and find Colton's number. Maybe it's the champagne, or maybe it's the emotions coursing through me, but I press call. I know he doesn't have his phone. I know it will go straight to voicemail.

The beep rings in my ear and I take a shaky breath. "I've left a few of these already. All of them full of worry and desperation..." I pause for a second before continuing. "Well, this one is a bit different. This one is for me. For my closure.

"You confessed your love for me and then ran. You ran when my brother found out. You ran when one thing went wrong, because it was the easy choice." I close my eyes, trying desperately not to cry. "I got married today. And tomorrow, I'm going home. I'm leaving the ranch and moving on with my life. Moving on from you.

"So, this is the last message. This is me letting you go and being okay with you moving forward in your life without me. I hope you find your happy ending. I hope you find the big family you deserve so much. Thank you for showing me what I want in my life, even if you weren't able to give it to me. I will always love you, Colton Grant. Goodbye."

I press the end call button and stare down at his name on the screen. My fingers don't want to do it, but I force them to click the delete button and rid Colton's name from my phone completely. To rid him from my life for the second time.

"Mind if I join you?" Mama's voice makes me jump. I turn towards her and wipe away any stray tears from my face, forcing a smile.

"Of course." I scoot over on the dock and let her take a seat next to me. Her lacey white dress compliments her tan skin well, even in the dark night around us. Her hair is in a beautiful braided bun and her makeup, which I barely ever see on her, looks effortlessly beautiful. We sit in silence, me admiring my mom's features while she looks out at the water, calculating something.

"So, where is he?" The question catches me off guard and I stare at her with a blank look.

"Where's who?"

"You know exactly who I'm talkin' about, Mayflower." The certainty in her voice confuses me and I swallow hard, trying to figure out what is going on. "I may be old, but I'm no fool."

"Mama..."

"Maya Turner, I see the way you look at that boy. I've seen it since you were a wee thing runnin' around after him and your brother." She looks at me now with a soft smile.

"Why didn't you say anything? What about... but you let me... I don't understand, Mama."

"I knew all about your little plan, missy. I heard some of your conversation with your brother. I knew you weren't plannin' on actually gettin' married. I knew Dan wasn't certified to marry anyone."

"Then why let me go through with it? Why do all of this if you knew it was all fake?" I know the answer the minute I ask. The sad look in her eyes proves me right.

"Because I love your father with all of my heart. Because he deserves to have somethin' good to remember in the middle of all of this sufferin'. Because it's always been his dream to walk his little girl down the aisle. If havin' this fake weddin' brings that man even a semblance of joy, it's worth it.

"And you, Maya Turner, will never ever tell your father about this little white lie. He doesn't have much longer and I will not have him be heartbroken durin' his last days. This secret stays between me, you, and your brother."

"I won't Mama." I can't help but feel like we are both doing the wrong thing, pretending I'm now happily married to Claude. But, the thought of my dad knowing I'm going to be moving back to the city by myself is a lot worse.

"So, where is he?" She grabs my hand and squeezes it, pulling me in closer to her.

"He left. He got scared and moved on."

"That sounds like a load of cow manure to me. I saw how that boy was lookin' at you the last few weeks. I saw the look in his eyes. He loves you, Maya. I can't believe he would just throw that away because he was scared. Colton Grant doesn't scare easy, Mayflower."

"I thought that too, but trust me... he left. He went to find another ranch job. He gave up on us all." Her hand wipes at the tears falling down my cheek.

"Look at me." I do as I'm told and the hope in her eyes overwhelms me. "Eventually, the ones we love always come back. No matter what, time may go by, but they always come back."

"So, I'm just supposed to wait for him? I'm supposed to stop my life for him? I'm supposed to hope and pray that one day he decides I'm worth the fight?"

"Sometimes all you can do is wait, Mayflower. It hurts like hell, but sometimes waitin' for that person to realize what they gave up is all you can do." I know she's talking about me leaving them and the pang in my chest echoes through the rest of my body. "And no. You aren't supposed to stop your life. You live life to the fullest. You do everythin' you want to do and then one day, when he decides to get his head out of his ass, you can decide if you want him to be a part of all of the amazin' things you have created for yourself."

I sniffle away the tears, ugly crying to the point that my makeup is definitely ruined. "How do I do that, Mama? What am I supposed to do?"

"Whatever you damn please. You go to Europe. You focus on work. You spend time with friends. You come visit family. Hell, if you wanna find another man in the meantime, you do that too." She pauses for a second and then continues. "Just not Claude... please."

I laugh through my sobs. "I thought you liked Claude."

"I think he's a great cook but he's as lazy as they come. I have never seen a grown man sleep as much as him. And he drank all of Andrew's beer... and he never helped me clean up. You know how I feel about manners." I shake my head at her with a smile.

She's right and I can't help but compare him to Colton in that sense. The way Colton doesn't offer to help, instead just getting up and doing it, no questions asked. The way he is always up before the sun rises. The way he treats people, no matter who they are. The way he treated me when we were together... like I was more important than the air he breathes. Like I was the only thing in the world at that moment.

Mama pulls me in close and puts her arm around my shoulders. "Colton is an amazin' man, Mayflower. But he has a lot of demons from his past. I don't know why he left, but I do know that it takes a lot of strength to trust God with your heart. It takes a lot of bravery to let Him bring someone else into your life after the people you love are ripped from it so horribly. Give him time. He's a strong young man, but even the strongest can't compete with a broken heart. And the thought of breakin' an already patched up heart is even worse."

"He... he asked me to marry him. Instead of Claude." The realization that I could have so easily just said yes. I could have said to hell with everything else and took the leap. I could have been standing under the magnolia tree, happier than I've ever been, marrying the man of my dreams.

"We both know that's not the weddin' you and Colton deserve. If you two ever get married, it has to be completely your day. Not a day tainted by the memory of Claude. Not a rushed weddin' that wasn't meant for the two of you." She kisses the top of my head, rubbing her hand up and down my bare shoulder.

"But Daddy won't be there... for the real thing. Whenever it happens, if it ever happens, he won't be there." I hold by breath, trying to stop the emotions from seeping out of me and into the cool air.

"Oh, sweetie. Your father will always be with you. He will be watchin' over you, cursin' out all of us for lyin' to him, as you walk down the aisle for real next time. No matter where he is, he wouldn't miss it for the world. He will always be there when you need him. When any of us need him."

It's my turn to hold onto my mom. I grab her tight in my arms and we both cry. Because this time next year, my daddy won't be here. This time next month, the love of her life will most likely be gone. The man she has spent most of her life with. The man she has loved fiercely every single day since they met... The man I took for granted and lost half a life with.

"I'm gonna miss him so much, Mama."

"I know, sweetie. Me too... me too."

Chapter

TWENTY-FOUR

Colton

Beep.

Beep.

Beep.

My eyelids feel so heavy. Like there are weights holding them shut. I can see blinding light behind them, but I can't convince them to open up. As if the signal is getting lost somewhere between my brain and my eyes.

I can feel an uncomfortable bed underneath me, and the smell of antiseptic burns my nose. *Come on, Colton. Open your damn eyes.* I desperately try to pry them open, finally seeing a semblance of the bright light when they open a sliver. That light blinds me, making my sore eyes pierce with intense pain.

I take a deep breath, which makes my lungs sting and burn, finally getting my eyes open enough to see where I am. I squint around the room and see white everywhere. The walls are white, the bed I'm lying on is white, the curtain covering a window is white.

The beeping continues next to me, and I just barely get my head to turn in that direction. The heart monitor next to me beeps away, showing someone's heart rate which is slowly increasing. Is that mine? Is the machine attached to me? I look down at my body, finding it covered in a thin hospital gown with an IV sticking out of my arm. What the hell is going on?

I try to sit up, but the movement makes my head pound. My vision suddenly goes blurry and everything around me starts to spin. It doesn't stop me though. I need to figure out what's going on. I need to find Maya.

"Woah, big guy. Where do you think you're goin'?" A feminine voice invades my head and I try to turn in the direction of the sound, but the movement makes the spinning even worse, threatening to make me throw up all over the place.

"Where... where am I?" My voice sounds foreign to my own ears. It sounds hoarse and raspy, like it hasn't been used in days.

"You're at the hospital, Colton." The masculine answer takes me by surprise until I realize there are two people in the room with me. And that I know who that masculine voice belongs to.

"Officer O'Neil?" I turn towards him as I say his name. He is sitting in a seat next to my bed, somehow completely unseen by me before. I haven't seen him since my parents passed... since he told me that his best friend, my father, was dead.

"Kathy, do you mind goin' to get the doctor? I'd like to talk to him for a minute." The heavy set nurse nods her head with a smile, walking out of the room and leaving me with a ghost from my past. I have been purposely avoiding him. Seeing him only makes me think of that dreadful day. The day I got the call about my parents.

"Why am I in the hospital?" I look over at the man with white hair sprouting from under his cowboy hat and covering his jaw. His mustache has only grown since I last saw him and the wrinkles coating his skin are deeper and more pronounced.

"Boy, what the fuck were you doin'? I could kill you for bein' so stupid. You almost took care of that for me though, dumbass."

"What are you talkin' about?" I feel my jaw tick, my temper rising with the way he's talking to me. My whole body hurts and I can barely think straight through the intense pounding in my head.

"You're lucky I found you. If it was someone else, you'd be fucked." He shakes his head, his thin lips frowning at me.

"George! Tell me what the fuck happened!" I don't mean to yell, if you can even call it that. It comes out in a jumble of cracks and hoarse wheezes.

"You were in an accident six days ago. I found you on the side of the road, with a damn telephone pole through the hood of your truck. You were wasted. What the fuck were you thinkin'? I thought you were dead when I found you!" I can hear the emotion coursing through his voice. I always admired the deep timber as a kid, wishing one day I would have a voice as gravelly and intense as his.

I don't speak at first, trying to piece together the information he just threw at me. I was in an accident six days ago? I don't remember any of that. The last thing I remember is... shit. The last thing I remember is Andrew punching me. The last thing I remember is me leaving to give him space. I got out of there so fast that I didn't even grab my phone.

I remember being drunk at the bar, talking to the bartender. I remember telling him about my plans to find a ranch with a pond and a swing. A ranch for my Maya. After that, I don't remember anything. Wait...

"You said six days ago?" I sound frantic when I speak, desperate to hear his answer.

"Yes, dumbass. Six days ago." I ignore the endearing name, too consumed with the fear and disappointment coursing through me.

Six days...

Six days after Andrew punched me.

One day after Maya was supposed to get married.

No. She couldn't have done it. Not after we were so happy together. Not after our dinner in the city. Not after our afternoon with Turant. Except, that was six days ago.

Six days...

Six days of Maya thinking I left her without a word.

Six days of Claude being there when I wasn't.

My heart rate picks up, the machine beeping faster for the world to hear. I start to move again, throwing the covers off of my body so I can get off the bed. I look down and find a huge cast on my right leg, covering most of it. How did I not feel that before?

I decide it doesn't matter. I'll destroy my leg if it means getting to Maya. I try to stand and fall back down on the bed. I don't let it stop me. I attempt to stand up again, but right when I'm about to, George pushes me back down on the bed.

"Move. I need to get to her. I need to make sure she's still here."

"I don't know what you're ramblin' about. But you're not goin' anywhere. You have a severe concussion, bruised ribs, and a broken leg. You've been out for days. You don't remember anythin'. You need to let the doctors take care of you until they agree to discharge you. I'm not lettin' you leave."

"Fuck off, George. You can't stop me." I glare at him, wanting more than anything to push the old man out of the way and run past him. Run to my girl. But I'm too weak. I can't run and I can barely see three feet in front of me.

"Fuck I can't, boy! I could get fired for this shit! I didn't report that damn accident because you were drivin' wasted off your ass! I pulled a favor with a doctor I know to make sure he didn't ask any questions as to what happened. You could have killed someone! You could have killed yourself!" His whispered shouts hit me hard and I sit back on the bed, defeated.

"Shit." I run my hand through my hair, letting the reality of what I could have done take over. I could have ruined someone's life. I could have killed someone's parents, someone's daughter, someone's son. I was reckless and stupid because I was so upset about how Andrew reacted. I don't do reckless. At least, not since Maya showed up again.

"I'm sorry... I'm so sorry." I feel the first tear fall, followed by others. Each tear represents someone specific.

The first falls for my mom.

The second falls for my dad.

The third falls for Maya.

TWO TORTUROUS DAYS GO BY BEFORE THEY LET ME LEAVE. OFFICER O'Neil refused to contact the Turner family, saying he doesn't want to be associated with this. He doesn't want anyone else knowing he was involved. I asked the nurse for a phone, but once I had it in my hand, I realized the only number I knew by heart was my own. I tried calling it and it went straight to voicemail.

So now I'm sitting in the back of George's old station wagon, my very broken leg resting on the seat with my crutches on the floor in front of me. My head still feels foggy, but I'm getting better with each day that passes. I'm not as weak as I was a few days ago.

"I'll drive you most of the way down the driveway but that's it. I don't want the Turners knowin' I was involved in any of this shit. Your truck is sittin' at Mike's shop in town. Yet another favor

I pulled for you. You're lucky I love you like a son. Even though I haven't heard from you in years."

"Thank you, George. I'm sorry I haven't reached out... I just couldn't. Not when—"

I cut myself off, not wanting to talk about them. George looks at me through the rearview mirror, a knowing look in his brown eyes. He nods at me once, telling me he understands, and then we spend the last five minutes of the drive in silence. When we reach the house, I thank him again and get out of the car.

The short walk down the driveway feels a lot longer on crutches. I haven't quite gotten the hang of them and the dirt road doesn't make it any easier. Seeing the white farm house makes a spark of life shoot through my chest. Even if Maya is married, which deep down I know she is, at least I get to see her. At least I get to give her a hug and explain everything.

Deciding I need a shower before seeing her, I forego the farmhouse and walk to the barn. Making my way up the stairs is a lot harder than I expected it to be, and it takes me almost ten minutes to make it up them and into my apartment. My apartment which smells like rotting food and dirty laundry. It smells worse up here than it does down in the stables.

I walk the short distance to my bed and find my phone sitting there, exactly where I left it a week ago. Plugging it in, I wait for it to charge and take a quick shower. Okay, a not so quick shower. Trying to keep a full leg cast dry is not an easy task. Especially when you're as tall as me in a shower as small as mine.

When I finally smell more like myself and less like a hospital, I get dressed in a pair of loose basketball shorts and a hoodie. Not my normal attire, but it's about the only thing I can get on over my cast right now.

I grab my phone as I plop down on my bed. When I open it up, my heart sinks. There are dozens of missed calls from Maya along with messages and voicemails. I listen to the earliest ones first, hearing her soft voice asking me where I am and begging me to come back home. My heart contradicts itself by feeling full and breaking at the same time. I love that she wanted me home but hate that I put her through this. I click on the last voicemail, dated yesterday, and wait for her soft voice to fill my ears.

"I've left a few of these already. All of them full of worry and desperation... Well, this one is a bit different. This one is for me. For my closure."

My breath halts when I listen to her words. She talks about me leaving her. She talks about me taking the easy way out. No. I didn't leave her. I'd never leave her.

"I got married today. And tomorrow, I'm going home..."

No. That's not possible. She couldn't have left. She wouldn't have left. I continue listening, my eyes watering with the horrible words attacking my ears.

"So, this is my last message. This is me letting you go—"

The rest of her message drowns out. I can't hear her voice over my racing heart. I can't hear her voice over my brain screaming at me to find her. To get her back. To do something. The only word I hear come through the receiver is her last.

"Goodbye."

Fuck that. It's not goodbye. It's never going to be goodbye. Not for us. I'll find her. I'll fight until I die to make sure she knows her worth. To make sure she knows I would never give up on us.

Standing, I move as fast as I can, grabbing some clothes and throwing them into a bag. I need to talk to Andrew. I need to explain myself and ask for his help. I need to convince him that I would do anything for his sister. That she belongs with me. I make my way to the farmhouse and when I finally make it into the house, I find Andrew and Mrs. Turner sitting in the kitchen, talking to each other.

They both turn to look at me at the same time and shock, relief, and fear flash across their faces. Mrs. Turner stands first, rushing over to me so she can help me sit down. But I don't want to sit down. I want to leave. I want to run after Maya.

"What on Earth happened, Colton? Are you okay?" Her worried voice makes my heart squeeze.

"I got in an accident... I've been in the hospital for the past week. I'm okay, I just—"

Andrew throwing his arms around me in a hug interrupts my next sentence. "I'm so sorry, man. I don't know what I would do if somethin' happened to you. I don't know what I'd do without you in my life. You're not just my best friend, you're my damn brother. I'm so sorry for makin' you leave."

I feel the words get clogged in my throat, emotion shoving them down. I hug him back, forcing my tears to stay hidden. "It's okay, Drew. I understand why you did. I know how it must have looked. But you need to know that I really do love her. She means the—"

I cut myself off when I remember that we have an audience. Andrew pulls away from me with a small smirk on his face, sitting back down in his seat to watch this play out. I chance a look at his mom, terrified of the woman that practically raised me as her own. She's standing there, staring me down with one brow raised and her arms crossed in front of her body. I wait for the confusion, the anger, the disappointment that's bound to come my way.

"Do you think I was born this mornin'?" She shakes her head at me before turning to grab a glass from the cabinet, leaving me a bit disoriented in my seat. I watch as she pours iced tea into the glass and then places it in front of me before taking a seat.

"I don't know why you felt like you couldn't come to me, Colton. I like to think, or I like to hope, that you see me as a mother figure after all of this time."

"Of course, I do. You always have been... but I don't understand, Mrs. Turner."

"Oh, good heavens. If you're gonna end up marryin' my daughter you should probably start callin' me mama finally." I turn towards Andrew, the confusion plastered across my face. He just smiles at me with a knowing look on his face like I'm the only one missing something here. Like what she's saying makes the most sense in the world.

"How'd you know about us?" I aim this at Mrs. Turner before looking back at Andrew. "And how are you okay with her sayin' that?" I think back to the last time I saw him, when he threatened my life.

"I always knew Maya was in love with you, I just didn't know you felt the same until she came home after all this time. You two weren't very good at hidin' it. And Andrew decided to stop bein' a cave man and realize that you are the best thing that could ever happen to Maya."

"And Billy? Does he know?" I can't believe what I'm hearing. I almost feel like I'm still in the hospital and dreaming this entire conversation up.

"Lord no. Not because he wouldn't approve, but because I don't think he can handle the news. Not after walkin' his daughter down the aisle to an entirely different man three days ago."

My heart drops. "So, she really is married? She really left?" I look down at my hands, not wanting them to see the pure despair shining through my eyes. "I won't give up. I'm gonna get her back. No matter what it takes. I want to spend the rest of my life with her."

"We know you do, sweetheart. And I truly believe you will. I truly believe you will be the reason our Maya comes back to us. The reason our Maya finally comes home." I smile at her words, remembering how excited I was a week ago to start searching for a home for us. I wanted to surprise her with a ranch of our own. A home that had everything she ever dreamed about.

"I didn't leave her... I just want you to know that. I left for the night to give Drew some space, but I had a plan. I was goin' to look for a house. She told me how much she wanted a ranch of her own someday and I wanted to give that to her. I wanted to bring her back to us for good and give her the life she deserved... and then I got in the accident and she married Clause."

"What do you mean look for a ranch of her own? You should have came to me." She scolds me and for the second time in the last few minutes, I'm confused.

"What do you mean?"

"That girl has been obsessed with this ranch since she was just a baby. She has loved this place more than the two of you combined, even though she left it behind. Don't go searchin' for somethin' when the perfect place is right here."

"We aren't takin' this ranch from you. This is your home."

"Sweetheart, I'm not givin' you my house." She swats her hand at me with a laugh. "You're gonna buy the field with the magnolia tree on it, right through the tree line. You're gonna build my baby her dream house and bring her home to me one day. Got it?"

How did I not think of that? How did I let that idea slip my mind? It's the perfect place. It has everything she could ever want and more. I feel overwhelmed by the emotions coursing through me, finally feeling like maybe, just maybe, I am going to get my happy ending. We are going to get our happy ending.

"Why did she marry Clause? Why did you guys let her go through with it? You know she doesn't love him." I'm not accusing them of anything, I just don't understand.

"For the hundredth time, his name is Claude, man. And she's not married to him." Andrew says the words but they don't quite register.

"Um, she told me she was. She left me a voicemail."

"Sweetheart, we had a ceremony for her dad's benefit. We wanted to give that to him. But it was a fake weddin'. They aren't actually married. She was upset. She thought you left her. She thought you gave up. She's tryin' to pick herself back up right now. That's why she went back to the city. To forget about you and try to mend her heart until you were ready."

"I have to find her." I start to stand up, almost falling down because my broken leg is long forgotten in my mind.

"Woah there, Colt. She isn't goin' anywhere. You need to rest. You look like shit." This comes from Andrew and I glare his way, not wanting to wait a second longer.

"He's right, sweetheart. You need to rest and she needs to focus on work." Mrs. Turner touches my arm reassuringly.

"With all due respect, I can't do that. I can't sit here while she's out in the city thinkin' I deserted her. I am goin' to the city. I won't stress her out. I won't force her to come back with me. I just need to tell her I'm still here. That I'm hers. And then I promise I'll come back and take care of the ranch."

"I'm not worried about the ranch, Colt. I already told Mama that I hired another physical therapist to cover the practice. I can focus on the ranch for now. If you go to Maya, don't worry about rushin' back. Be there for her. Figure out your lives. And then come back home when you're ready. Bring her home when she's ready."

"I promise, I will."

Chapter

TWENTY-FIVE

Maya

I've been in the city for barely a week now and I'm ready to rip my hair out. The job I once adored is driving me to drink. Literally. I have been drinking more than I ever have the last few nights. I have also been avoiding my apartment, since Claude is there. I spend all day at the firm getting everything ready for trial and at night I stay tucked away in my office drinking bourbon and eating take out. I haven't been getting back to the apartment until after midnight every single night.

I'm sitting in my office right now, getting ready for a meeting with my team. We have a character witness coming in to discuss John Wickins. I have read every report over and over again the past three days. All evidence leads to John, except for the loose end called his step son. The schizophrenic mentally unstable step son who was seen in the area on the day of the crime. The step son that hated John and his new family more than anything.

We need strong witnesses to help prove our case and put John behind bars. That son of a bitch will not go free after what he did to his wife and son. I'm hoping this new witness is enough to take him down.

Shifting in my seat, I pull at the tight clothes on my body. I used to love wearing my work clothes. I used to love how it felt walking down the street in a pencil skirt and blazer, my heels clicking against the sidewalk with each step. Now they just feel tight and uncomfortable. They feel over the top and showy. I'd much rather be wearing a flannel and a pair of shorts.

I picture Colton's blazing eyes when he first saw me in the jean shorts I bought. The way he undressed me with those hazel orbs, making me squirm under his gaze. Every time that man looked at me, I felt like I was going to light on fire and melt into a puddle. Just thinking about it now makes my insides clench and my mouth go dry.

Checking my phone, I jump out of my seat when I realize I'm five minutes late to my meeting. I'm never late. That's not what I do. I'm the one that shows up fifteen minutes early, yelling at everyone else for showing up on time. At least, that's who I was.

Running to the conference room, I trip on my heel and drop my file on the ground. "Shit," I mumble under my breath as the papers scatter across the hall. Nothing is going my way today. I'm a disheveled mess. I'm on the brink of tears. I'm losing it.

Bending down, I crawl across the cold tile, grabbing at all of the thrown papers. I feel my hair fall out of the clip on my head and curtain around my face, making it hard to see in front of me. I continue to swear under my breath, annoyed at the fact that my neatly organized papers are now completely disorganized.

I crawl towards the last few papers, blowing the hair out of my face and praying no one sees me. I spot the last piece, and right when I'm about to grab it, a black dress shoe steps right on top of it. My first thought is that it's my boss and I immediately feel my cheeks blaze with embarrassment. I'm on my hands and knees in front of my boss, looking like a complete mess.

I realize it's not him when I see a cast covering the other foot, awkwardly sticking out from gray dress pants. I try to remember who has a broken leg in our office but can't come up with a single person.

"I love seein' you on your knees for me, baby girl." His voice turns the blood inside of my veins into ice. It can't be him. He can't be in New York. I let my eyes trail up his body, taking in the tight pants around his huge thighs, his perfectly tucked white button up, and the gray suit jacket that does a terrible job hiding what's underneath.

When I reach his face, I feel my heart drop into my stomach. The same features I remember from just two weeks ago burn my insides. His hazel eyes, his thick beard matching the short brown hair on top of his head, his plump lips positioned in a deadly smirk. The only difference is the once perfectly tanned face is now covered in bruises and scrapes.

My first instinct is to grab him and ask him what happened. To hold him tight and tell him I'll take care of him. But then the memories hit. The memories of him leaving me. The memories of having to fake marry Claude on my own. The memories of crying to Mama about how much I love him.

I rip the last piece of paper out from under his shoe and then stand up, fixing my skirt and wiping off my blazer. Glaring straight into the eyes I've dreamt of almost every night, I attempt to pass him. My path is blocked when he brings one of his crutches up until it's positioned parallel to the ground, between him and the wall.

"Move. I have a meeting." I don't look at him as I talk, knowing if I look into those eyes of his too long, my tough façade will crack.

"Maya, let me explain." He reaches out to me and I step back, avoiding his touch.

"Move. Now. I'm not going to leave my team waiting. I'm not going to leave them wondering where I am." He flinches at my words, knowing I'm directing them at him, and I feel a small bubble of pride rise in my chest.

"I deserved that. But I'm not goin' anywhere. I'll be right outside the door when you finish your meetin'."

"Don't bother. I have nothing to say to you Colton. It's too late. I'm married, remember?" I don't know why I say it. It's a complete lie, but I want to hurt him the way he hurt me. I want to make him suffer and feel like shit for leaving me the way he did. I look back down at his leg and wonder what happened to him. I want to ask so bad, but I refuse to stand here any longer.

"Sure you are, darlin'. I'll see you when you're done." I'm already walking away, trying to ignore his hypnotizing voice. I need to focus on this meeting. But I can't. Not now. Not after seeing him. Not when I know I'm going to have to talk to him once this meeting is done. Part of me wants to prolong it as long as I can. To keep this meeting going for hours until he gets tired of waiting and leaves.

I open the glass door and walk in, all eyes on me. I give everyone an apologetic smile and take a seat at the table across from John's neighbor. I'm about to start talking when I see movement through the glass wall outside the office. Colton sits down on one of the few benches in the hallway, back to us, waiting.

I'm never going to be able to focus.

"MISS TURNER?" MY NAME PULLS ME FROM MY THOUGHTS AND I look around the room, until I find my boss, Mr. Kerington standing near the door. His glasses sit high on his sharp nose and his peppered hair lies in perfect waves. His usual black suit hugs his slim body. "The meeting was adjourned ten minutes ago. May I speak with you?"

"Oh, shit. I mean, no, not shit. I mean." I huff in annoyance, hating how flustered I sound in front of my boss. "Yes, of course. Sorry, I was just thinking about the case."

"That's what I wanted to speak to you about. It's come to my attention that you have a lot going on in your personal life." He doesn't sound angry, if anything, he sounds concerned. His blue eyes are creased with worry, making his already present crow's feet more defined.

"I'm sorry about that. I don't know why he's here and I'm going to get rid of him." I stand up so we are at the same level, rather than him standing and looking down at me in my seat.

"That's not what I'm referring to, Miss Turner. Your father's sickness. You're wedding being cancelled." His mention of my wedding surprises me. "The office talks, Maya. I know you spend most nights here by yourself. I know you've been distracted from work."

"I'm sorry, sir. I'll do better. I can assure you I am focused on this case. I won't let you down." Nerves bubble up with what my boss is about to say. He's going to fire me for being distracted.

"You never have let me down, and I have always been able to rely on you when I need something. Which is why I want to make sure you can rely on me when you need something."

"Sir?" I have no idea what he means. That's not what I would expect a boss to say right before he fires someone.

"Before you freak out, I'm doing this for you. For your own well-being." Great. He's firing me and somehow making it look positive. "I'm taking you off the Wickins case."

"Wait... you're not firing me?" I barely register his words, besides the fact that they didn't consist of *you're fired.*

"What? Miss Turner, in the short time you have been here you have become one of our best prosecutors. Of course, I'm not firing you. But I am putting you on leave. You need to take care of yourself. Figure out your personal life and spend time with your father."

"With all due respect, Mr. Kerington, I know this case like the back of my hand. I brought in our witnesses. I can take him down."

"I've been preparing Keith for this the past few weeks. I'm sorry I had to do it behind your back, but I knew you wouldn't focus on your personal needs if you knew about it."

I almost laugh but manage to hold it back. Keith Stanley is practically senile. "Sir, Keith already has so much on his plate. I don't think it's fair to add more to it."

"Alright, Turner. Tell me one full sentence that was said during this meeting with your character witness and I will keep you on the case." I start to talk, ready to throw something at him and prove myself, when the words cut short. I search every corner of my brain and can't remember a single word that was said during the meeting.

"I... I can't. I'm sorry." My words come out in a defeated sigh.

"No, Maya, I'm sorry. I'm sorry for everything you are going through. Take the time off. Let yourself heal and then come back to the office when you are ready. There will be a spot here for you when you do."

"Alright, thank you, sir." While I don't want to give up so easily, I also feel a wave of relief fill my body. Work has been killing me with so much on my mind and I haven't been able to put my all in this case. I was worried deep down that I wouldn't win with the way I've been acting lately.

I leave the conference room and walk into the hallway. I almost forget Colton being here, until I look down at the bench and find it empty. Did he leave? Half of me hopes he did and the other half is embarrassingly disappointed that he did. I make my way to my office and when I look through my glass walls, the disappointment disappears, replaced by nerves.

I see him sitting in the chair across from my desk, his back to me. I take a minute to look at him. To look at his soft brown hair cut short on his head. To look at his broad shoulders stuffed into the suit jacket that I both love and hate. He wears that suit better than any man I've ever met, but I much prefer him in a flannel and cowboy hat. I much prefer him dirty and sweating from a long day on the ranch.

Sighing, I open my door and then proceed to close it behind me, trying to provide us with an ounce of privacy. I walk over to my desk and sit down in my seat, feeling his eyes on me the entire time. He dissects me while I avoid his eyes completely.

"What are you doing here, Colton?" I still don't look at him. I tidy up the files on my desk and move them around randomly, acting like there's an order to what I'm doing.

"I came to get you back. To explain everythin'."

"To explain why you left me when one thing went wrong?" I still don't look up. I pick at my fingers on my lap.

"Baby girl, did you happen to look at me? Were you even curious what happened?" I finally look up at him and catch the slight smirk splayed on his lips. The smirk that could bring any woman to their knees.

"I just figured you hurt yourself on that new ranch you were working on." I shrug my shoulders and stare at his nose, his cheeks, his forehead. Anything but those golden eyes of his.

"What? What new ranch?" He sounds genuinely confused, which only confuses me more.

"I know what you told the bartender that night at the bar. I know you told him you were leaving to find another ranch to work on. I know you gave up on my entire family because Andrew threatened you. I was pissed at him when I found out how he acted, but we both knew how he would react. I was willing to work through it. I was willing to deal with the repercussions if it meant being with you."

The silence sits between us and I regret opening my mouth. I had no intention of saying this much to him. I was planning on making this short and sweet and then going home. Well, not necessarily sweet.

"Maya..." The way he says my name makes me finally look into his eyes. The desperation floating through the one word is enough to make me forget my anger. At least, for a second. "I wasn't goin' to find another ranch to work on... I was plannin' on givin' Andrew time to relax before comin' back and talkin' to him. I was plannin' on tellin' him that no matter what he said, I would never give you up. I would never leave you."

"Cut the crap. You did leave me! You told Brandon you were leaving to find work somewhere else!" My voice rises without me meaning to, but hearing the lies he's spewing hurts more than I thought it would.

"Who the hell is Brandon?"

"It doesn't matter, Colton. I'm married and you're too late. You made up your mind two weeks ago. Just leave." I'm trying to push him away. I'm trying to keep my heart from breaking even more.

"Oh, baby girl, I know you're not married to that fruit fly. And I know that it's never too late with us. We are written in the damn stars. There's no world where we don't end up together." I feel tears spring free and try desperately to hold them back. "When I left that day with Andrew, I went to the bar to give him time to breathe. I got a little too drunk and... and I stupidly decided to drive."

My heart stops at the same time he pauses his sentence. I know what he's about to say and I feel fear creep up my spine. Fear for what could have happened. Fear for the thought of Colton not being on this planet.

"I crashed the truck on my way to..." He cuts off mid-sentence and looks over at the window facing the city. Emotion swirls in his eyes and practically seeps out of his skin.

"On your way where?" I whisper the words, worried if I talk too loudly, I'll scare him off and he won't finish his sentence.

"It was supposed to be a secret... I didn't want to tell you, but I had plans to find you a ranch. To find you a place with a pond and a swing and enough land for Jax and Turant and any other animal your heart desired. A place where you could still be a tough ass prosecutor in a nearby city, and have the dream home you have always wanted.

"My drunk ass thought that night was the perfect time to start lookin' and then boom. I crash and end up in the hospital with no way to contact anyone. I'm so sorry you thought I left you, baby girl. I would never leave you. You're everythin' I've ever wanted and more. You're my life, which means my existence is pointless unless I'm with you."

"Are... are you okay? Are you in trouble?" I'm so overwhelmed by everything he just told me that I don't know what to say. The one overpowering emotion is my worry for him, so that's what I go with. His deep laugh tickles my ears and I inhale sharply with the butterflies flying around in my stomach.

"I forgot I was talkin' to a lawyer. Don't worry, I'm not in any trouble. A friend helped me out." I know exactly who that friend is without him saying his name. Officer George O'Neil. The only man who would risk his career to save another. The man that always made sure Andrew and Colton never got in trouble as kids.

"That's good." I'm trying to hide how giddy I feel right now. I'm trying to control the burst of adrenaline running through me, begging me to stand up and kiss this man. "Are you okay physically?" I eye the cast on his leg.

"I have a concussion, but I'm used to those from football. A few bruised ribs and a broken leg can't keep me down either, darlin'. Not when somethin' as amazin' as you is on the line."

I try to think of what to say next. I try to think of a reason to turn him away. A reason to be mad at him. A reason that this won't work. "Daddy thinks I'm happily married... he thinks I'm about to leave for Italy with Claude... I can't just show up and tell him it was all fake and I'm with a completely different man. I promised Mama I'd never tell him the truth about that day."

"So don't tell him. He doesn't have to know. When you visit your family, tell him the truth. That you are so happy and in love. Just leave out the fact that it's with me. I'm not goin' anywhere. I'll be wherever you are. If you're here, I'm here. If you're in Texas, I'm in Texas. If you're on the fuckin' moon, you bet your ass I'm figurin' out a way to get there too."

I feel tears fall down my cheeks through my laughter. I just stare at him, too in aw by his words. I expected him to give me a lame excuse about running off. I expected him to tell me he wants me back because he realized he was wrong. I never expected him to tell me there was never a doubt in his mind. I never expected him to admit to wanting to find a home for us when he was gone.

"Please say something before I make even more of a fool out of myself." I don't say anything. Instead, I stand from my seat and slowly walk towards him.

One step.

His eyes trail up my body, making the once uncomfortable clothes I was wearing feel nonexistent.

Two steps.

His eyes reach mine and I watch as the golden flecks sparkle and dance with my reflection.

Three steps.

His eyes don't blink a single time as I finally reach him. I don't have to tell him to stand up, he simply does it by himself, somehow knowing exactly what I am going to do next. I keep my eyes glued to his, swallowing hard at the lump of emotion stuck in my throat. The emotion that only Colton Grant can bring out of me.

"Kiss me." I barely get the whisper out before his lips are on mine, branding me with their burning touch. It's like we were never separated. Like the last few weeks never happened and we are right back on my parent's ranch, talking about our hopes and dreams. Only, now, I truly believe those hopes and dreams are going to become a reality. I truly believe this is our time.

We kiss, forgetting about the world around us, until I hear a catcall coming from outside of my office. I remember my boss saying the office talks and pull apart from him, not wanting this to escalate and travel through the entire firm. I look up at him and smile, forgetting all of the worry in my life and focusing solely on him.

"So, baby girl, now what?" I think for a second, trying to decide what we are supposed to do now.

"My boss is mandating I take a leave of absence."

"Shit, is that cause of me? I'm sorry I showed up here. I thought it would be this big romantic gesture like in the movies and then I realized I was probably distractin' you from your work."

I shake my head at him with a soft chuckle. "No, cowboy, it's not because of you being here. He knows about my dad and the wedding being called off. He wants me to take time to focus on myself and be there with my dad."

"Hm, I like your boss already. Unless he's hot and into you. Then I'll have to kill him." I laugh again, loving the feeling since I haven't in a few days.

"He's about thirty years my senior. Trust me, you don't have to worry about him." I pull him in for a hug, basking in the way he feels holding me. He feels like home. "I want to go visit Daddy at some point, but I'm not ready to after the whole wedding fiasco.

By the way, you missed a very weird night. My mom knew the entire time."

"Yeah, Mrs. Turner filled me in on that before I came here... it scares me how much that woman knows."

"Do you have a passport?" I smirk at him, staring straight at the bright golden flecks in his eyes,

"Course I do. What are you thinkin'?"

"Wanna crash my honeymoon?"

His deep chuckle vibrates through me and I feel it down to my toes. "Damn, baby girl, I thought you'd never ask."

Chapter

TWENTY-SIX

Colton

I wake up to the morning sun warming my eyelids. There's a warm breeze brushing against my face, making me open my eyes to see where it's coming from. I take in the room around us. The four post canopy bed that feels like a cloud. The coastal décor filling the expensive hotel room. The sheer white curtains flying into the room from the open terrace doors.

The only thing missing from this scene is my Maya. I look to my right at the spot on the bed where she was sleeping and find it empty. Sitting up, I throw on my boxers and make my way to the terrace. When I look out on the white balcony, the view takes my breath away.

It's not the crystal clear water that surrounds Greece that takes my breath away. It's not the rainbow of colors in the sky with the rising sun. It's not the scattered white architecture with royal blue rooves below us. It's the girl who is standing with her arms against the railing, looking over the water. It's her blonde hair flowing with the wind, looking like glistening strands of silk. It's the curve of her body, kissed by the sun over the past few weeks, barely hidden under the sheer slip she's wearing.

Walking up to her, I cage her in from behind, placing my hands on the railing on either side of her. "I hate not wakin' up to you, baby girl." She places her head against my bare chest and sighs deeply, relaxing into me. I can feel her smile even though I can't see it.

"Sorry, my stomach was bothering me so I thought I'd come out here for some fresh air."

I look down at her with concerned eyes. "Are you okay? Are you hungover?" While we have been traveling across Europe for the past three weeks, we have definitely been indulging ourselves in all of the necessities: good food, alcohol, and sex. I think back on last night, remembering that we called it in early and barely drank anything. She shouldn't be hungover.

"No, I'm okay. Just a bit nauseous. Nothing a little fresh air and water can't fix." Her tone sounds off, proving to me that she's lying about being okay. I grab her arms and turn her around, forcing her to look me in the eyes. The normal light blue color of her irises appears darker this morning, making my stomach flip.

"Baby, what's wrong? I know somethin's botherin' you. Let me in, please." I coax her with soft words while my hands brush through her hair. She doesn't answer at first, closing her eyes and letting her head relax into my hand.

"I... I'm late, Colt."

"Late for what?" I furrow my brows at her, confused by what she means. I didn't think we had anything planned for today.

"No... I mean... my periods late." She still hasn't opened her eyes, and I just stare at her, desperate for her to look at me again. "I didn't realize it until this morning, when I woke up feeling so sick, but I'm over a week late. I'm never late, Colton."

My heart speeds up in my chest when her words sink in. The world around me stops and suddenly I'm thrown into my own head. I see flashes of our life together. Of a baby crying in Maya's arms, as she looks up at me from her hospital bed. Of a blonde haired, blue eyed little girl taking her first steps. Of Maya cheering us on as I teach her how to ride a bike and then a horse and then drive a car. Of her going off to college and then getting a job and having kids of her own. So many scenes flash through my mind, preventing me from speaking.

"I'm... I'm sorry. I'm probably not pregnant. It's probably just the stress." I pull myself out of my head and find Maya looking down at her feet. Shit. She thinks I'm upset. She has no idea how much I want this.

"Baby girl," my voice is coated with emotion. I feel tears brim the edge of my eyes. "Do you think... do you really think you are?" My smile can't be contained. She must hear it in my voice because she looks up at me, suddenly. When her eyes dart to my lips and find the cheesy grin, her lips wobble.

"You're... you're not upset?" I place both of my hands on her cheeks, making sure she can't look anywhere but at me.

"Maya Turner, I've never been so happy in my entire life. I've never wanted something more than I want this. More than I want you. More than I want that baby girl." She laughs through the tears soaking both her cheeks and my hands.

"We don't even know if I'm pregnant. Why do you think it's a girl?"

"Just a feelin'." I bend down and put my hand on her stomach. The small magnolia flower that Maya got on her ribs is just barely visible through the sheer fabric of her dress. I didn't think she could get more perfect, but the tattoo proved me wrong.

When I touch her stomach, it's completely flat. Somehow, I feel a connection to it, like the tiny clump of cells inside of Maya can feel me and I can feel her. "She's in there, baby girl. And I already love her almost as much as I love her mama. That little Magnolia in there is gonna be the luckiest girl in the world because you're her mama."

She pulls me into her arms without warning, sobbing against my bare chest. I bring my hands around her and place one of them on the back of her head. "I love you, Colton Grant."

"I love you more, Maya." I pull away and look down, ready to kiss her, when she gives me a sad smile. "What's wrong, baby girl? This is amazing news, isn't it?"

"Yes, of course... if I am pregnant, I'll be really happy. But... I feel horrible. My dad has no idea about us. He has no idea how happy I am and how in love with you I am. He won't be able to know about this baby." She puts her hand on her stomach, rubbing it in small circles.

"Can I be honest with you?" She nods her head in answer, staring up at me with wondering eyes. "I think we should tell him. I think he'll be happy. And I think findin' out he could have a granddaughter on the way will give him somethin' to look forward to. Somethin' to fight for."

"Weren't you the person who told me not to hope for the impossible? He stopped treatment. He has a few months at most, not nine."

"But bein' a part of our journey is gonna make whatever time he has that much better. Seein' you happy with the man you love is gonna make him forget about the pain that much more." I watch as she debates my words. I can see the war at battle inside of her brain.

"You might be right. I don't know. Maybe we should go visit them when we get back. After we figure out if I'm actually pregnant."

"I'll do whatever you want, baby girl. How about I order some room service and you relax out here while I grab you a test?" I kiss her forehead, still giddy and jumping up and down on the inside. I have always wanted kids and the thought of a baby that's half me and half Maya is almost too good to be true.

"Thank you. It might be too early, but it's worth a shot." She stands on her toes and places a kiss against my lips, before I pull away and walk back into the room.

After I order her everything on the breakfast menu, besides coffee, I get dressed and head outside. Looking up at the bright blue sky above this amazing city, I smile wide.

"Please, God. Please let it be true. Please give me the family I've always wanted."

Chapter

TWENTY-SEVEN

Maya

My hands shake as we exit the airport and the humid air hits our faces. Colton's hand on my back supplies me with enough confidence to keep moving, but the fear bubbling up inside of me for what's to come can't be suppressed. What if this kills him? What if he tells me I'm a disappointment? What if he never talks to me again and I lose out on his last days?

"Baby girl, deep breaths. Try not to stress out. It's not good for Maggie." I snort at his name for our little miracle. He has been calling her Magnolia since we found out, and just yesterday shortened it to Maggie. You'd never guess this burly cowboy with more muscles than a Greek God would be so sappy.

When I took the test a week and a half ago, he sat right next to me on the floor of the bathroom, his knee bouncing up and down. Those two lines slowly faded into existence and before I could even take a breath, Colton had me in his arms. His tears mixed with mine as he whispered sweet nothings into my ear, promising a beautiful life ahead with our little flower.

Since then, he hasn't left my side. He made me take three more tests just to be sure, and I can barely escape him to use the bathroom by myself. I haven't been able to carry anything, he's been making sure I eat enough, and on the plane, he kept his hand on my stomach the entire trip, as if to protect her. It's the cutest thing in the world and his excitement over this new chapter in our lives makes me love him even more.

"What if he hates me?" I look up at his hazel eyes and beg them to take all of my stress away.

"Now, that's by far the craziest thing I've ever heard you say, Maya Turner. That man could never hate you. You're his little girl. He loves you and he is gonna love our little girl with just as much fierceness. Whether he's here with us or watchin' down on her."

I nod my head in agreement, meanwhile my fingernails are being gnawed off by my teeth. He grabs my hand and brings it down to my side, engulfing it with his own and refusing to let it go. I take a deep breath and place my other hand on the bottom of my stomach, trying to take comfort in her. The minute I make contact with the spot, my nerves instantly calm and I feel lighter. Like she's trying to tell Mommy that everything is going to be okay.

I feel tears spring to my eyes and look down at my stomach. I know she is just a bundle of cells right now and she isn't aware of anything, but I already feel so connected to her. Like my entire life has been leading up to the moment she was made. The moment she will come into our lives.

I spot Andrew's car parked in the huge line of cars and we make our way to him. When he gets out to greet us, he has a smug smirk on his face. "It's gonna take a long time for me to get used to seein' the two of you together. How was the honeymoon you little love birds?"

He pulls me in for a hug and the entire time, Colton keeps a hand on my shoulder. It's comical how protective he's being over his girls. When we pull apart, I mold myself back to Colton's side while they shake hands.

"It was absolutely beautiful," I answer him as he puts the bags in the back of the car. Colt opens the front door and gestures me to sit. "No, you can get the front. I'll sit in the back, baby."

"I don't want you gettin' car sick. Sit before I pick you up and put you in the car myself." He places a kiss against my temple and I bend over to get in. When they both get in the car, I place my hand on my stomach for comfort and look back at Colton, my eyes darting between his. He puts a hand on my shoulder and rubs it, reassuring me that everything is going to be okay. Andrew clears his throat, and I realize instead of driving, he's looking between the two of us.

"You two okay? You're actin' weird." I look back at Colton and I nod my head at him, deciding we should have one more ally on our side when we tell Mama and Daddy.

"We have some news. We found out a about a week ago," Colt pauses and waits for me to finish. Andrew stares at me with his mouth open, as if he already knows what I'm about to say.

"You're going to be an uncle." The silence that takes over the cabin of the car is like nothing I've ever experienced. Andrew stares at me, a blank, unreadable expression on his face. I feel my heart race while my stomach plummets to my feet.

"You're... Y'all are... You're pregnant?" The astonishment in his voice isn't making me feel any better. I nod my head slowly, my body refusing to speak again. "I'm gonna be an uncle?" The blank look morphs into a wavering smile as his eyes begin to glisten. "I'm gonna be an uncle!"

I don't have time to react before my body is being pulled into the middle console of the car. Andrew hugs me hard, his arms wrapped tight enough to prevent my lungs from filling with air.

"Careful man, she's fragile right now." Andrew pulls away from me and I roll my eyes.

"I'm not fragile, cowboy," I say with a smirk.

"Not you, baby girl. My other baby girl is the size of a pea. Gotta keep her safe." I know he's joking around by the glint in his eye and the lopsided grin plastered on his face.

"It's a girl? I'm gonna have a niece?" Andrew bends awkwardly and grabs Colton's hand before pulling him in for a hug. The smile on his face is like nothing I've ever seen on him.

"Colton's convinced it's a girl but we won't know the gender for a while. I'm only a few weeks along."

"I'll take that bet. Twenty bucks says it's a boy." I watch as Andrew puts his hand out for Colton to shake, trying to seal the bet.

"Forty and you're on." He clasps hands with my brother and I shake my head with a laugh.

"You two can turn anything into a competition. You just find out I'm pregnant and the first thing you do is gamble on it. Asses." Colton jumps forward and places a kiss on my cheek while Andrew laughs.

"Only bettin' cause I know our little Maggie wouldn't let her daddy lose. It's gonna be a girl, just you wait." I have to admit, I agree with Colt. Something deep down is telling me that it's going to be a girl.

"What are you gonna tell Dad? That the baby is Claude's?" The mention of his name makes the air in the car shift. Anger rolls off Colton's body in suffocating waves. He hates that my dad thinks I'm married to him.

"We are going to tell him the truth." I grab Colt's hand and smile at him. He squeezes my hand back and gives me a quick wink while taking a deep breath.

"Mama Turner isn't gonna be too happy about that." Andrew raises a brow at us and I swallow down my nerves. "We promised her we wouldn't tell him."

"Well, circumstances are different now. He deserves to know he has a granddaughter on the way. He deserves to know Colton is the one that I'm in love with."

"First time I've ever heard you say that out loud... damn." Colt laughs at Andrew's words, clapping a hand on his shoulder.

"Get used to hearin' it, man." I can't hold back my smile. Colt's right, we truly haven't stopped saying it since we officially got together five weeks ago.

"So... how are we goin' about this? What are we gonna tell him?"

"You, Andrew, are not going to be telling him anything. We just need your support after we tell him. Or, after I do. I want to talk to him myself first. I think he'll take it the best if it's just the two of us." I swallow hard, the fear of my father's reaction resurfacing again.

"We will do whatever you need from us, baby girl. If you wanna talk to him alone first, we will support you and give you your space."

"Thank you, Colt. I think that's best." The cabin is silent for a second, all of our minds racing and thinking about the worst case scenarios. At least, that's what I'm thinking.

"Alright, you love birds. Let's get this over with."

Chapter

TWENTY-EIGHT

Maya

"I know you're the size of a thumbtack right now, Maggie, but can you give Mama a little courage? I really want your grandpa to know about you but I feel like I'm going to throw up before I get in there and I can't tell if it's because of you or because of the stress. Probably a little of both, huh?"

When we got to the ranch, we snuck into Colton's apartment to avoid having to talk to Mama yet. I know if I tell her I'm planning on telling Daddy that we all lied to him, she would try to convince me not to. Andrew said he would figure out a way to get her out of the house so I could do this myself. I'm not sure what he did, but it worked because she's nowhere in sight when I walk into the farm house.

I make my way to Daddy's room and knock on the door. A soft 'come in' greets me and the sound alone is enough to make my knees buckle. He sounds even weaker than he did when I saw him last month. Finding any ounce of courage, I have left, I turn the knob on the door and walk into the room.

This is my first time being in my parent's room since he got sick. I look around at the darkened room that's full of shadows cast from the shades blocking the sun. Everything looks the same with the soft white walls covered in memories, the two floral arm chairs facing the brick wood fireplace, the four-post king size bed I used to sneak into when I had bad dreams.

The only difference is the frail man tucked under the plush covers. The only difference is the medical supplies sitting on the dresser and night stand. The only difference is the unmistakable smell of antiseptic and sickness. They all somehow make the room seem darker.

"Maya?" His quiet voice manages to sound surprised when he sees me. "What are you doin' here?"

I walk over to him with a sad smile on my face. "Surprise... I wanted to come see you. I have to talk to you about something." Standing near the edge of the bed, I pick at my fingers. My hands are itching to touch my belly.

"Come here, squirt. I missed you. How was the honeymoon?" He pulls the covers to the side to make a spot for me. I crawl onto the bed and let the cloud like material suck me in. He covers us both with the comforter and puts his thin arm around my shoulders, bringing me in so we are cuddling like we used to when I was a kid.

"It was amazing."

"Is Claude here?" I can hear the change in tone when he says his name. I have a feeling he doesn't particularly like Claude which makes me breathe out a laugh.

"That's what I need to talk to you about... I don't even know where to start." I shake my head and close my eyes, my hands shaking from nerves. "Claude and I aren't together."

The silence makes my ears ring. I feel him dissecting me with his eyes, trying to figure out what I'm feeling. "I wasn't expecting you to say that. What happened, squirt? What did he do?"

"He didn't do anything... it wasn't him. I mean, I guess he is to blame for some of this, but it's my fault. I... I'm not in love with him. I haven't been in a long time." My stomach is churning and Maggie isn't to blame for the nausea this time.

"Then why did you marry him, Maya? You shouldn't have married someone you aren't in love with. Can you get it annulled?" His eyebrows are furrowed as he looks me over. I can see his brain moving a mile a minute, trying to figure out how to fix this for me. How to take care of me. I squeeze his hand and decide I need to bite the bullet.

"The wedding was fake. I lied to you and pretended to marry Claude." I close my eyes and wait for him to scold me. I wait for him to tell me to leave. I wait for him to tell me I'm a disappointment. When his deep chuckle floats through the room, I peak one eye open to make sure I'm hearing him right. "W- why are you laughing?"

"Maya Turner, that is the most absurd thing I have ever heard in my whole damn life. Why the hell would you ever fake a weddin' and pretend to get married?"

"So you could walk me down the aisle. I didn't want you to miss out on such an important moment. I wanted you to remember me happy. I wanted you to be sure that I was being taken care of."

"You? Taken care of? Squirt, I never expected a man to take care of you. Especially that city boy. He can barely take care of himself, let alone my Maya," I laugh at the very true statement. "I have never once worried about you bein' taken care of because you're such a strong woman that you don't need someone to take care of you. You need someone to love you. To make each day brighter. To give you a reason to laugh and smile. That's what I've always wanted for you."

"Well... that's the other thing I wanted to talk to you about..." His laugh startles me again and I pause my sentence.

"Can I guess what you're about to say? I bet I know." I almost laugh now, but I hold it in. There's no way he knows what I'm about to tell him.

"I can assure you, Daddy. You aren't going to guess this one."

"You are in love with Colton." The smug smirk on his face reminds me of the way he was before cancer took over his life. I feel my brows rise into my hairline, the shock of what he just said evident on my face. "You two are about as subtle as a sledgehammer. Anyone with eyes would be able to see it."

"Why does everyone in this family know things before I tell them? And why the hell didn't anyone tell me they knew before I planned that whole fake wedding?"

"Squirt, it's your life. I want you to do what makes you happy. I want you to make your own mistakes and learn from them. Did I think marryin' Claude was a mistake? Yes. But you're a smart girl, and I figured there was a reason you were marryin' him. I figured there was a reason you and Colton weren't together. I figured you knew what you were doin'," he pauses and wipes a stray tear that I didn't feel slip out. "Boy, was I wrong about that."

My laugh cuts through the quiet sob that escapes me. "I thought I was doing the right thing. I thought if you found out about everything, something would happen to you. I thought I'd make you worse or break your heart from disappointment. I'm sorry for lying to you."

"Oh, Maya. Nothin' you do could ever disappoint me. I may look like hell, but I'm not as weak as I look. And I'm so damn proud of you. All I want is your happiness. No matter what that means."

"I'm really happy, Daddy. Happier than I've ever been in my entire life." The sentence is the most honest thing I've said to him in the last few months. "I'm in love with him."

"I know, squirt. I can see that. And that boy better not break your heart. I love him like a son, but I'll have Andrew kick his ass. And when I die, I'll come back and haunt him if I need to."

"I know, Daddy, you don't have to worry about him doing that... but... there's something else." He nods his head slightly, waiting for me to continue. He doesn't offer any guesses this time, instead, sitting quietly and letting the silence consume me. I look down at my stomach and picture my little flower. Our little Maggie.

Placing my dad's hand on my stomach, I look up at him with tears in my eyes. "You're going to be a grandpa."

I watch as my words hit him. The blue color of his eyes lightens as they glisten with unshed tears. His mouth opens and closes, no sound coming out of the gaping hole. The first tear falls and all I can do is sit here in fear of what that tear means.

"You're... you're pregnant?" He looks down at his hand that is still being held by mine, against the t-shirt covering my stomach. I nod my head, too nervous to talk and wait for something else. "I'm gonna be a grandpa?"

He doesn't give me time to answer before he pulls me into his arms and holds me tight. His soft sobs shake me and I can't hold back my own anymore. We sit on the bed, embracing each other. I picture my little Maggie between us, being cradled by her mommy and the grandpa that I pray she gets to meet.

"Please, Lord, tell me Claude's not the father." I laugh and grimace at the same time, picturing how different my life would be if it was Claude's baby.

"No! She's Colton's. She's definitely Colton's."

"She?" He pulls away and looks down at me with tears still streaming down his cheeks. A look of pure awe is plastered across his gray skin. "You mean to tell me, there's gonna be another little Maya runnin' around?"

"We don't know for sure. I haven't even been to a doctor yet. It's just a feeling that we both have."

"I'm so happy for you, squirt. You are gonna be the most amazin' Mama. I'm gonna fight like hell to make sure I meet her." He hugs me again and I cry in his arms, eyes shut tight. Sitting here, engulfed in his smell and his tight embrace, brings me back to when I was twelve years old.

Back when he would hold me until the pain or sadness I was feeling went away.

Back when he was big and strong.

Back when he wasn't sick.

Chapter

TWENTY-NINE

Maya

I threw up three times this morning. That's two more than usual. I know the reason. It's the same reason my hands are clammy and shaking on this uncomfortable chair. It's the same reason Colton hasn't stopped bouncing his leg as he sits beside me. Today's the day we get to see Maggie. The day we find out if Maggie is really a girl. The anatomy scan.

The first trimester was exhausting and amazing at the same time. I spent most mornings and nights sitting near a toilet, but the connection to our little flower has only grown stronger every day. So has my stomach. You can finally tell I'm pregnant. Before, I simply looked like a I was eating a bit too much fast food. Now, the small round pooch in my lower belly can't be missed.

I was worried I'd feel gross. I was worried my confidence would plummet. Instead, I feel more beautiful than I ever have. When I look at myself in the mirror, everything about me glows. My hair, my eyes, my skin.

It might have something to do with the way Colt looks at me now. The way his eyes sparkle with love when he stares into my eyes. I swear his hazel irises have lightened permanently since we found out about Maggie almost fifteen weeks ago. The normal brown color now reminds me of sweet honey speckled with gold flakes. The color contrasts against his tan skin and sends tingles down through my body.

Oh, that's the other thing. Since starting the second trimester, I have been hornier than I've ever been. Another reason Colt has been so happy lately. We fuck like bunnies. Every day, at least once a day. Every time I look at him, hear his voice, smell his intoxicating scent, I lose my mind. I can't keep my hands off of him and to say he feels the same is an understatement. We were never vanilla in the bedroom department, but our sex life has become ten times wilder than before.

Since Mama and Daddy found out about our little miracle, they begged us to stay on the ranch. Colt and I have been living together in his apartment above the stables and it's been exactly what I needed. Waking up every morning and looking out over the green pastures as I drink my tea has become a necessary ritual.

I worked it out with my job where I could work remote, acting more as a paralegal than an attorney, until I have the baby and figure out my next move. They have been so understanding and supportive during all of this. Being able to spend this time with my father is something I never expected and will never forget. I swear every day he seems a little stronger. He talks about Maggie more than anyone else and just the other day he told me something deep inside of him thinks it's going to be a boy.

A knock on the door makes me jump and Colton squeezes my hand softly. "Come in," I say and cringe at the shakiness of my voice. The door opens and an older woman walks in with soft eyes and peppered grays in her auburn hair.

"Good mornin', y'all. This is baby Turner, right?" The ultrasound tech walks over to the machine and types something before turning back to us.

"Yes, ma'am," Colton replies for me with a smile.

"Ah, you must be Daddy. My name's Tabitha, but you two can call me Tabs," she looks between the two of us and her smile widens as her head shakes slightly. "Well, I'll be. You two are one good lookin' couple. This baby is gonna be absolutely beautiful."

"Yes, she is. She's gonna look just like her mama." Colton looks at me when he talks and my stomach flutters. I can't tell if it's the butterflies he always gives me or if Maggie is just trying to break out of my uterus and jump into her daddy's arms. I wouldn't blame her if she was.

"She, huh?" Tabs moves back to the computer and types a few more things before grabbing everything she needs for the procedure.

"Just a feeling we have," I say as I watch her grab a tube of jelly and some large napkins. She works while she talks, lifting my shirt up to uncover my stomach and then lining the hem of my shirt and the waist of my shorts with the napkins.

"So, I'm assumin' you want to find out the gender today?"

"Yes!" This comes from both me and Colt at the same time and earns us a chuckle from Tabs. She squirts some of the clear jelly onto my stomach and I wince at the initial chill it gives me.

"Alright, y'all. Let's take a look at your bundle of joy, shall we?" She positions the wand over my stomach and moves it around in the jelly. I watch with baited breaths as our little flower's profile pops up on the screen. Her perfect little head, her soft nose, her hands reaching up and her feet kicking around. Colton's grip on my hand tightens and he practically pulls himself onto the chair with me to get a better look at the screen.

Tabs continues to move the wand around, naming off different parts of our Maggie, but I can barely hear her. Tears are flowing down my cheeks and I can feel my heart racing in my chest. This moment right here, is the most precious moment of my life. I could feel her there this whole time, but seeing her is the most beautiful thing I've ever experienced.

"Hi, baby girl," I whisper the words quietly, not wanting to interrupt the technician. My eyes are glued to the screen, taking in how perfect she is. "I don't think you can hear me yet, but I need you to know how much I love you. I will tell you every day for the rest of our lives. I love you more than anything, sweet girl."

"Well, that feelin' of yours was pretty accurate." The technician interrupts my whispers to our miracle. I look straight at her and wait for the words I've been so excited and nervous to hear.

"Congrats, Mom and Dad, y'all have a bouncin' baby girl."

Colton

I CAN'T BREATHE. I FEEL LIKE MY HEART IS ABOUT TO POUND OUT OF my chest. Today has been one of the best days of my life and it's either about to get a lot better, or plummet. We found out this afternoon, mere hours ago, that our Magnolia is, in fact, a girl. She's the picture of health and everything about her is perfect. Not that I ever doubted it. I knew from the moment Maya told me about her that she would be perfect.

Now, I'm standing out in the field, under the family tree. Under our tree. The tree where we discussed our hopes and dreams. The tree that watched over so many beautiful moments, and is about to be supplied with a lifetime of more. Because today, under this tree, is the beginning of our lifetime.

I'm distracted by the wind blowing the long grass and the sun setting, casting orange and pink light across the landscape, that I almost miss Maya approaching through the tree line. Almost. Her presence rips my attention away from everything else and I glue my eyes to her.

Her hair flies gracefully in the wind, the blond whisps caressing her flawless face. Even from across the field, I can see her intense blue eyes staring into mine. I can feel the love and want and desperation in them. They mirror my own feelings, our gazes bouncing off of each other's and colliding in perfect unison.

She's wearing a white cotton dress with thick straps on her shoulders. The material hugs her chest with small ruffles and then billows out until it hits mid-calf, hiding the sweet little bump of our baby girl. I can't take my eyes off of her. Nothing in the world could make me look away from her in this moment.

"What are you doing out here?" She finally reaches me and the smile that graces her lips takes my breath away.

"I have somethin' to show you," I pull her in for a hug and place a soft kiss against the top of her head. "How's Maggie doin'?"

"She's giving her mama a run for her money. I threw up after dinner and I feel as swollen as a tick right now."

"I'm sorry, baby girl. You look absolutely stunnin' if that makes you feel better. How about later tonight I draw you a bath and massage your feet?" I rub her shoulders before pulling away.

"God, you've gotten really good at dirty talk lately." Our laughter mixes together before she speaks again. "What is it you wanted to show me? It's getting dark."

I don't speak, I just grab her hand and walk forward with her until we are a good twenty feet from the tree, standing in between the wooden stakes I mapped out. We step over the tight pink string that connects them all and then stop.

"What is this?" She looks at each different section, separated by the bright string.

"Well, this is our kitchen." I walk forward until we cross over another piece of string. "And this is our living room, which will always have a perfect view of the sun settin'." Her silence scares me, making my heart race faster.

"And this is our room," I say as we step over yet another string. "Which will have a clear view of our magnolia tree every mornin' and every night." I hear a shaky inhale coming from her lips and squeeze her hand. We cross over the next string and I let go of her hand, letting her take in what I set up.

"And lastly, our sweet Magnolia's room." She walks forward, her back to me, and looks down at the grass. A soft sob echoes through the air when she sees what's there.

The pink blanket has a magnolia tree embroidered across the front. Starting from the top, there are names sewn in white cursive letters, listing off everyone in our families from our great grandparents on. At the bottom of the thick flowers, the name Maggie sits right in the middle, with enough space for at least two more names next to hers. Her ultrasound pictures lie under her name, showcasing the perfection we created together.

Surrounding the blanket, there are dozens of pictures sprawled out across the grass. Pictures of our life together. Pictures of us as children. Riding horses. Laughing as we race down the stairs. Cheesing up at the camera with birthday cakes in front of us.

Then, there are the pictures of us now. Of us in Italy, Greece, and France. Pictures of us smiling, laughing, and staring into each other's eyes. Pictures of Maya holding her growing stomach, staring down at our girl. Pictures Maya has never seen.

Her back is still to me as I get into position. My hands shake, reaching into my back pocket and pulling the small box out. By the time she turns around, I'm already down on one knee. The gasp that escapes her is only enhanced by her falling tears.

"I have lived the majority of my life thinkin' I was handed the short end of the stick. I felt like I had lost more than any man ever should. And then, a ghost from my past walked back into my life. She flipped my world upside down and drove me crazy. She made me angry, irrational, and completely bat shit with one simple look. But she also made me feel things I never thought I'd feel again. She made me feel like I wasn't alone. She made me feel like wakin' up every mornin' and bein' a better person. She made me feel love again.

"How does a man express his gratitude to someone for helpin' him find himself? For savin' him and makin' him realize that he was wrong all this time," I pause and swallow hard, trying to blink back the tears about to fall. "I was wrong about bein' handed the short end of the stick. God was just makin' me wait. God was makin' me wait to see just how much he had given me. Just how lucky I actually was. I've been handed a life no man deserves. A life even the best of men shouldn't be able to reach. And yet, here you are. Here Maggie is. And here I am, expressin' my love and gratitude to the most amazin' person I've ever met.

"I will spend the rest of my life tryin' to give you what you gave me. Tryin' to make every day better than the last. Makin' sure you always dance. Makin' sure you always smile. Makin' sure that little girl never wants for nothin' and will always know what love is.

"This spot, right here, is where I want to spend the rest of my life. Our life. In the house that will one day stand right where we are. The house that will be filled with memories. The house that will have a pond and a swing and a stream outside of it and whatever the hell else you want. Because you deserve everythin' you want. And I'm gonna be the one to give it to you.

"So, Maya Turner, will you please give me one last thing, even though you've already given me the world?" I grab her hand, both of our tears falling into the lush grass below us.

"Will you marry me?"

The End

Epilogue

Maya

One month after Daddy passed
REST IN PEACE BILLY TURNER...

"Almost there, Maya. Give us one more big push!" I grit my teeth and try to suppress the scream that wants to escape. Colton's hand cracks under the tight pressure of my grasp, but he doesn't flinch, letting me take the pain out on him. I take a deep breath, sweat coating my skin, and push as hard as I can.

"That's it! She's comin'! You're almost there!" The doctor's voice sounds distant with my own guttural sounds ringing through my ears. My eyes are closed, blocking out the stark white of the hospital room and all of the scrubbed up strangers staring at my exposed bottom half. Colton stands at my side, holding one of my legs up and whispering encouraging words into my ear. I don't want to hear encouraging words. I want this baby out of me.

"One more push, Maya. That's all we need. Give us your best one yet." If I could muster up the strength to roll my eyes, I would. Instead, I hunker down and push with all of my might, knowing it's the last bit of strength I have left.

My breath comes out in shaky heaves when I'm done pushing. It feels like hours of silence before suddenly, the most beautiful sound I've ever heard hits my ears. My baby girl's cry.

"Well, I guess we were wrong." The doctor's voice makes me open my eyes in fear. I watch as he comes over to me with the smallest little bundle of perfect pink skin I've ever seen. "Say hello to your baby boy, Mom and Dad."

His words don't register until he places our baby on my chest. I reach down with tears in my eyes and hold onto our perfect little miracle. The minute our skin touches, the crying stops and the sweetest face I have ever seen looks up until dark blue eyes open and take me in.

I know those eyes. Those eyes are the same eyes that have comforted me since I was a baby. The same eyes that always shown brightly with pride and love. The same eyes that stole a piece of my heart when they closed for the last time just a month prior.

"So, what's his name?" The nurse's question breaks me from the trance I was in, staring into my son's eyes. The son that smiles up at me like this isn't the first time we are meeting, but rather, a reunion we have both longed for.

"Billy. His name is Billy."

Extra Scenes

CHRISTMAS EVE

Three years later...

"What if Santa doesn't come tonight, Mama?" Billy's soft voice whispers through the dark room. The only light is coming from his nightlight, which casts small stars all over his ceiling. I look down and find his bright blue eyes staring up into mine. His small face looks worried, with his brown brows furrowed and plump lips frowning.

I run a hand through his soft brown locks, the locks that match his daddy's hair color perfectly. "Well, sweetheart, do you think you have been a good boy this year?" I smile down at him as I bring my hand down to his face and stroke his chubby cheeks.

"Yes. I eats all of my broccoli and I share with Daddy and I cleaned up all of my toys." I laugh at his innocence and then tuck the blankets around his body even more, cocooning him in the soft material. The huge embroidered magnolia tree sits perfectly across his body, with all of the members of our family written across it.

"Well, then Santa will be here, baby. He told me that he has a lot of presents for a certain Billy Grant. He's almost as proud of you as Mommy and Daddy are." He smiles up at me, his small white teeth shining in the soft glow of the stars.

"I'm proud of you too, Mama. I think you're gettin' lots of presents too." I cherish these moments with him. His heart is bigger than most and I can't believe how grown up he is. The last three years have flown by and now I have this little adult staring back at me. He's an old soul. Well, he's one old soul in specific. His grandfather's. The resemblance, both appearance and personality wise, is uncanny. Hence the fact that he has his grandfather's name.

"Thank you, Billy. Now, it's time for bed. Santa wants to come soon but he can't until you're fast asleep and dreamin'. I love you with all of my heart." I kiss the tip of his nose before nuzzling it with my own.

"I love you more, Mama."

Closing his bedroom door, I make my way down the hallway towards the kitchen. The sound of singing hits me halfway down the long hallway and I can't help but smile. *It's Beginning to Look a Lot Like Christmas* echoes off the walls of the kitchen, sounding more country than I've ever heard it with my husband's accent. The man that hates Christmas music. The man that is too big and tough for such sappy crap. His words exactly.

I turn the corner and stop myself, leaning against the wall. Standing by the white marble island, Colt is not only singing, but dancing to the music coming from the small Bluetooth speaker. His voice is at least three times louder than Michael Bublé's.

I watch him with a smile on my face as he makes two cups of spiked hot chocolate. He's wearing a Santa hat and the flannel pajamas I bought for all three of us. They are red and green, and match each other's perfectly. Yet another thing he fought at first, but very willingly got dressed into when the time came.

He moves around the open kitchen, grabbing whipped cream from the huge stainless-steel fridge, sprinkles from the dark blue cabinets, and a straw for me from the cup on top of the huge window over the kitchen sink. The window that overlooks our magnolia tree. The tree that holds onto so many memories of our family.

Memories of us climbing it as kids. Memories of us dancing under the tree for the first time. Memories of him proposing to me while baby Billy bounced in my belly. Memories of our wedding, one of the best days of my life. That tree has always been the heart of our relationship, which is why I made sure it was visible from the heart of this house. We spend the most time in the kitchen as a family. Always have and always will.

"Whatcha doin'?" I finally speak up and my voice makes him jump. He quickly stops singing and clears his throat with a cough. This only makes me smile even wider.

"Nothin', baby girl. Just makin' us some hot chocolate." I walk over to him and grab onto him from behind, wrapping my hands around his hard waist. He's a wall of muscle. Even in these pajama's, I want to jump his bones. He could make anything look good with his dark brown beard, plush lips, and light golden brown eyes.

"Really? It sounded like you were singin' along with Mr. Bublé if you ask me." I pinch his side and feel his stomach flex in reaction. Without warning, he spins around and somehow maneuvers us in the blink of an eye until I am sitting on the counter with him standing between my legs. His huge hands clasp onto the back of my thighs, right below my ass, and I suck in a breath at the feeling.

"Are you makin' fun of me, Mrs. Grant?" His face lowers to mine, bringing his mouth mere inches from my ear. His hot breath tickles my lobe and I shiver at the feeling.

"Wh..." I swallow hard, my breathing now a bit labored. "What if I was?"

His hands move up slowly, gripping me tighter and tighter. "Well, baby girl, if you were makin' fun of me... I might just have to punish you." His hands now grip my hips and he brings me to the edge of the counter, harder than he normally would. The minute his body makes contact with mine, I can tell how turned on he is.

"But it wouldn't be much of a punishment, would it? You like when I'm rough with you, don't you?" He grinds into me and I gasp at the friction. "You like when I rip your clothes off and take what's mine."

I nod my head as it falls back and hits the cabinet behind me. No matter how many times I have him, I can't get enough. He somehow got even sexier after becoming a dad. After seeing how sensitive and vulnerable he can be as a father. After seeing how much he loves both me and our son.

"What do you want, baby girl? Tell me." He brings his hands up to my breasts and puts one in each hand, squeezing them over my cotton pajamas. I moan at the feeling but his mouth cuts it short as it captures my lips in a harsh kiss. He kisses me until I see stars. Until my mind is a jumbled mess and I can't think of anything but the way they move over mine.

"Please," I whimper when his lips pull apart from mine. I'm holding onto him for dear life, begging him to keep going.

"Please what?" His voice is stern and I hate how much my body reacts to it.

"Please... please keep going." I'm panting as I look up at him. My body is humming and tingles spread everywhere he touches me. He brings his hands up to my face and stares into my eyes, putting me in a trance as I take in every last fleck of gold in his irises.

He brings his face closer again, blinking slowly at me. He's about to give me what I want, I can tell by the look in his eyes. The desperate need to be inside of me. To make me scream his name. I close my eyes and wait for his lips to touch mine again. For his tongue to invade my mouth as his hands find their way lower.

"You know, I would. But we have to wrap presents." Cold air hits me as his body pulls away from mine and I snap my eyes open in confusion. He's already holding the two cups of cocoa, walking away from me and towards the living room. What the fuck?

"That's for this morning!" He calls back behind him and I groan loudly in my spot on the counter. He's teasing me. Torturing me. All because I turned him down in bed this morning. I had a million things to do so I swatted him away before jumping out of bed and starting breakfast. He hates being denied what's his.

His low chuckle greets my ears now and I can't help but smile even though my body is screaming at me to get him back here. He's one of the most infuriating, beautiful people I have ever met. I've fallen in love with every single part of him. Not like I had to fall much farther. I've been in love with him since I was barely six years old.

Jumping off the counter, I move across the dark wood floor and head into the living room. The ceilings of the room are high, with windows taking up most of the walls. Our tree this year is over twelve-feet tall, glistening with white lights and red and gold ornaments. It sits in the corner of the room next to the white brick fireplace that is crackling away as we speak. Our huge sectional sits in the middle of the room, the light gray color matching the hint of gray in our wood floors.

Colt is now sitting on the floor in front of the tree, surrounded by a pile of unwrapped gifts for our Billy. To say he's spoiled is an understatement. And the biggest culprit there is Colt. He wanted to buy Billy a horse this year. I finally convinced him to wait on that one. He's only three, he doesn't need a horse right now. We already have four as it is. Adding one more will just make both of our lives that much more hectic.

"You're a cruel man, Colton Grant." I take a seat next to him on the floor, happy to get off my shaky legs. My body is still desperate for him, but he's right. We need to get all of these presents wrapped before tomorrow morning.

"Well then, I'm as cruel as you are gorgeous, Maya Grant." His eyes twinkle when they look at me and I don't think it's because of the glowing string lights in their reflection. I roll my eyes at him but feel the butterflies that have found a permanent home in my belly flutter away.

"Thank you for the hot chocolate." I grab the steaming mug and hold it close to my face. The warm liquid heats my hands and I can't help but shiver, wishing the rest of me was being caressed by the same warmth. Only, instead of a cup warming me up, it could be a cowboy.

Colt must see me shiver because within seconds, there is a plush white blanket wrapped around my body. I cuddle into the soft material, already feeling warmer. "You know, if you didn't stop what we just started in the kitchen, I wouldn't be cold at all." I raise one brow at him with a smirk.

"I'll make a deal with you, baby girl. For every present you wrap, an article of my clothin' comes off."

"What about when you wrap a present? Do I start takin' my clothes off? That definitely won't help me warm up." My smirk has grown into a painfully wide smile. I can't look at him without smiling. He makes me happier than anyone ever has.

"Fuck no. I'm getting' you naked myself. After we finish wrappin', I get to unwrap you." He licks his lips and looks down my body slowly. I know he's picturing me naked. Picturing me sprawled out for him.

"Alright, deal." I grab the bag of clothes I got for Billy, including a cowboy hat that matches his daddy's, and start wrapping them all into one big present. It's not the neatest, but there are other things on my mind. I write, *Love, Mommy and Daddy*, on the paper and then stick it under the tree.

Turning back towards Colt, I stare at him like I'm the child and he's my present. He shakes his head at me but starts to unbutton his shirt. His eyes don't leave mine, but I rip mine away from his the minute his shirt is unbuttoned.

My eyes trail down his tan chest moving down to the rigid muscles I can't get enough of. He slowly removes the red plaid and now he's sitting in front of me completely shirtless with every hard muscle out on display. I am having a hard time stopping myself from touching him. From running my hands across his hot skin before kissing my way across each one of his abs and down to his—

"Keep wrappin', baby girl. The faster we are done with this, the faster you get to feel my cock deep inside of you." My mouth salivates at his dirty words and a shot of electricity travels to my core. I'm seconds away from saying screw this and just touching myself. I need him. I don't think I've ever been this turned on.

I reach for more presents and while he wraps his neatly, I am a shaking, sloppy mess with mine. The good news is, he is taking care of the Santa presents and I'm taking care of our presents so there will be a very clear distinction between the two.

At this point, he is sitting there in just his black boxers and Santa hat and I am about to combust. There are too many presents left. Screw this. Throwing the wrapping paper to the side, I barely notice as it unrolls across the floor. I take off my blanket and stare right at Colt as I start to remove my pants. My mouth is hanging open and my eyes are heavy from the lust coursing through me.

"Mrs. Grant, we aren't done wrappin'. I still have two more articles of clothin' to remove." He's smirking at me the entire time he talks. He's having too much fun torturing me. Which means it's my turn to torture him.

"Fuck your game. I'll finish wrappin' after I make myself come." I throw my pants and underwear to the side at the same time I hear a deep growl in his throat. Without bothering to remove my shirt, I reach down and bring my cold hand to my sensitive core. The gasp at how sensitive I am can't be contained.

I sit back on the floor and spread my legs, staring at my husband. Just looking at him would be enough to get me off. The smirk he once wore is now completely gone and his eyes are staring at my hand. Or, rather, where my hand is currently rubbing. I moan at the sight of him taking me in. At the intensity of his stare.

He moves fast, so fast that I squeal from fear. He's on me in seconds, throwing me down onto the floor and ripping off my shirt. The wrapping paper crinkles under the weight of us. "You've always been so impatient, Maya Grant." He growls out the words against my lips, taking my hand away from my body and replacing it with his.

Where my hand was cold, his burns hot, searing itself into my skin. "You're fuckin' soaked for me. I almost feel bad for makin' you wait so long. Almost." He nips at my lip and I cry out. Before my cry even begins to fade, he shoves two of his fingers inside of me. It's almost too much to take and my mouth stays open wide with no noise escaping.

"That's it, baby girl. I love makin' you speechless." He pulls them out before shoving them back in, repeating the movement until I am thrashing against the wrapping paper. Each small movement makes the paper crackle and tear below us and the sound somehow makes me even hotter.

"You ready to come for me? You ready to come all over my fingers?" That's all it takes to send me over the cliff. I free fall, closing my eyes tight as my entire body shakes for him. I can't control the way my body moves, the sounds coming out of my mouth, or the tight grip I have on Colt's arms. The intensity of my climax takes my breath away and I start to feel dizzy when I come to.

"Goddamn, baby girl. That was so fuckin' hot." He's moving above me, removing his boxers before positioning himself over me. "Do you think you can come for me like that again? I want to feel you squeeze my cock the way you were squeezin' my fingers."

Somehow, after such an intense orgasm, I still feel a shock wave travel down my body at his words. I can't talk, so instead, I nod my head slowly, staring up at him. He's still wearing the Santa hat, and oddly enough, it makes him look even sexier

Without hesitation, he fills me up in one single move. The fullness is triple what his fingers felt like and the pain of him stretching me only makes it feel that much better. He doesn't stay still or let me adjust to his size. He moves hard and fast, forcing unnatural sounds out of my mouth.

"You're so perfect." The words come out muffled through his clenched teeth. I look down at where we are connected and watch his abs flex as his cock fills me up and then pulls back out over and over again. I'm overwhelmed with the pleasure coursing through my body. I'm overwhelmed by the pressure of my impending climax, only getting more and more intense.

"I love you so much, baby girl. Everythin' about you. You're all mine." I can hear in his voice that he's close. I can see the look in his eyes, powerful and full of desire. I nod my head, agreeing with him.

"Yes, baby. I'm yours. All of me. Forever." He groans at my words and then picks up the pace. He thrusts into me so hard the paper below us rips around my body and the roll goes flying across the floor, leaving even more of a trail of paper. Three more thrusts and my vision starts to go blurry.

The same feeling, only more intense takes over and I barely make out the sounds of him grunting as he spills himself inside of me. His movements slow until he comes to a stop. I can still feel his cock pulsing inside of me with the last bit of his release.

Our labored breaths mix together as we lay here, unmoving. "I love you more, just so you know." I try to answer his earlier sentence right before we both came, but my voice sounds more like a whisper.

"That's not possible, baby girl." He kisses my temple and then gets off of me, retreating to the kitchen. I don't even have to ask, I know he's going to get a warm wash cloth to clean me up. If Colton Grant is anything, it's a gentleman.

When he returns, he takes his time cleaning me up before helping me to my feet. "Well, we managed to destroy half of the wrapping paper we need for Billy's presents... Now what?" I look down at the mess we made and can't help but laugh. We destroyed almost an entire roll of the paper we were using for the presents from us.

"I have some happy birthday paper left over from his last birthday." Colton shakes his head with a smile and then closes the distance between us and pulls me into a hug.

"How did I get so lucky marryin' such a smart and beautiful woman?" I softly slap him on the chest and look up into his glimmering eyes. He stares down at me with so much love that it's a bit overwhelming. How can someone love me this much? How has my life changed so much in the last four years? Four years ago, I was engaged to a man who put me second to everything else. Now, I'm with the man of my dreams that kisses the ground I walk on.

"Well, you treated me like shit after not seein' me for years and then somehow managed to get me in your bed. I guess I have a thing for douche bags." I tease him with a lopsided grin on my face. He glares down at me and then grabs my face with both hands, squeezing my cheeks tight.

"And I guess I have a thing for bad ass prosecutors who think they are funny when they aren't." He bends down and licks my face, making me scream out a loud cackle. "Careful there, darlin', you're gonna wake Billy up and then I'm really gonna have to punish you."

"Ish that a promish or a threat?" My voice comes out sounding funny from the way he squeezes my cheeks together. He laughs low at the sound, eyes beaming with love, before placing a kiss on my nose and then letting go of my face.

"You're my whole world, baby girl. I hope you know that." My heart hums in my chest, threatening to burst out of its confinement and into this man's hands forever.

"As long as you know you're mine too."

"Always and forever." He bends down and gives me my pajamas, making me notice that we are both still very much naked. I throw them on and run to grab the birthday wrapping paper from the closet.

We spend the next few hours wrapping and laughing, reminiscing on the last few Christmases we have had and all of the rest to come. Tonight has always been one of my favorite nights of the year. A night when we can just be together, no other worries in our minds besides making tomorrow as special as possible for our Billy.

After we are finished, Colton scarfs down the three Christmas cookies Billy and I made this evening and drinks both of our hot chocolates that ended up cold after our little intermission. I make my way into our room, inhaling the fresh pine scent that comes from the wax melter I have on my nightstand.

The room is decorated with reds and whites just like the rest of the house this time of year. My normal gray comforter is replaced with a white one with red pillows and a plush throw thrown over it. Along with the many black and white pictures of our family, there are Christmas signs and a wreath hanging from the white walls.

LED candles are lit across every table top from the TV stand to the dressers. It's my little oasis, especially since this room also has a huge window with a window seat looking out at our tree.

I walk over to the window and sit on the plush bench covered in more holiday pillows. Looking out at the tree, I admire the Christmas lights Colton hung across the branches. He surprised me with it the first Christmas we spent together and he has been doing it ever since. The twinkling lights illuminate the outline of the tree in the dark night and I find myself tearing up at how much love and happiness it has brought into our lives.

"Ready for bed, baby girl?" Colton's voice pulls me from my thoughts and I turn towards him. His Santa hat is now missing and his brown hair is sticking up in a sexy, messy way. While his shirt remains off, he has his plaid plants back on. If I wasn't so tired, I would tell him it's time for round two, but the exhaustion is setting in quick.

I nod my head with a smile before running into our master bath and doing my nighttime routine. Once my face is washed, teeth are brushed, and hair is combed through, I return and find him lying in bed with my side of the bed drawn and ready for me. He usually brushes his teeth in the other bathroom so I have space in our bathroom to get ready for bed myself. If James wasn't his middle name, I swear selfless would be.

I crawl into bed and bring myself flush against his body, letting him warm me up as his body spoons mine. I feel his hand run through my blonde hair and sigh, feeling more than relaxed. This is my safe place. Being wrapped up in his warmth, his intoxicating scent. Feeling his heart beat against mine as his breath comes out in even puffs behind me.

"Merry Christmas, Maya," he whispers against my temple with a soft kiss.

"Merry Christmas, Colt."

Extra Scenes

CHRISTMAS DAY

The doorbell rings at exactly nine in the morning. She's never late. Hasn't been for all twenty-nine years of my life. I clean the flour from my hands on my apron and make my way to the front door. Opening it up, my mother's crystal blue eyes blink at me, slightly squinted at the sides from her wide grin.

"Merry Christmas, Mayflower!" She has a casserole dish in her hand that I take from her as she walks into the house. Her long graying blonde hair is lying down her back in waves. She used to wear it up all the time, but about two years ago she started wearing it down. It suits her tan skin and slim figure.

"Merry Christmas, Mama." I give her a kiss on the cheek and walk back into the kitchen, passing Colton in the living room as he organizes all of the presents and starts a fire.

"Where's my little man?" Mama comes running after me once she hugs Colt and meets me in the kitchen with a huge smile on her face. Billy and Mama are inseparable. From the moment he was born, I saw the look in her eye. The look that proved she saw exactly what I saw. The man that she was married to for almost her entire life. The man she loved with all of her heart.

"He's still in bed. I figured I would wait for you to get here to wake him up. Do you want to do the honors?" Her eyes light up with my words.

"Yes! I'll go get him now!" She's already running down the hallway before she even finishes talking. I shake my head at her with a laugh and continue making the waffle batter for this morning. We are still waiting on Andrew to get here, like always, and then we can start opening presents.

"Did Santa come, Mimi?" Billy's voice can be heard all the way out here and my heart swells at his excitement. Christmas is by far his favorite day of the year and the pure joy in his voice brings tears to my eyes.

I don't hear what Mama responds with, but within a few minutes, Billy's footsteps running down the hall graces my ears. Just in time for him to reach me, I turn towards him and put my arms out. He jumps into them and I spin him around, cherishing the uncontrollable giggle that erupts from his mouth.

"Santa came! Santa came!" He cheers as his little arms wrap around my neck. When I stop spinning, he stays clasped around me, his hand softly patting my back the way it always does when he hugs me. Like I said, he's an old soul.

"Of course, he did, baby. Merry Christmas." I kiss his cheek and then he brings his hands to my face, grabs both of my cheeks, and plants a kiss right on my lips. The mwah sound echoes through the kitchen and I hear Colton chuckle as he walks up to us.

"Daddy! Santa came!" Billy pulls away from me and towards Colt, practically throwing himself out of my arms. Colton is right there to catch him and when he has him in his arms, he throws him up in the air. His happy screeches flow through the house and I look over at Mama standing by the island, watching us.

There are tears in her eyes. But not sad tears. These tears hold onto so much love, so many good memories. These tears represent the hope and blessings we have been granted. These tears are accompanied by a wavering smile that can't be contained.

Because even though Daddy isn't here physically, we know he is watching over us. And we know, when his last breath left his body, he made sure a piece of him stayed on this planet. He made sure a piece of him remained in the little boy that blessed us only a month after Daddy's passing. He made sure we would never forget his humor, his wit, his charm, because Billy will always remind us of what we so tragically lost.

I walk over to her and pull her into a hug, not caring that the flour on my apron is currently being transferred onto her red flannel pajamas. She matches the three of us, something we make sure to do every year.

"Sorry, Mayflower. You know how I get when I see the three of you. You are the most beautiful family." She squeezes me back before letting go.

"*We* are the most beautiful family, Mama." I point a finger into chest softly, making sure she knows what I mean. Without her, we wouldn't be a family.

"Oh, don't you start tryin' to make me cry harder." She swats a hand at me and I laugh, pulling away before moving towards the fridge.

"Anyone care for a mimosa?" I call out and, as expected, get a yes from both Mama and Colt. "Do you want some hot chocolate, baby?"

"Yes, please! Thank you, Mama!" His voice grows distant as he runs towards the tree.

"Billy Drew Grant, don't you dare touch those presents before your aunt and uncle get here!" I yell with my back to him.

"Okay, Mama! I just wants to look at 'em." His squeaky voice is interrupted by Colton turning on Christmas music on the Bluetooth speaker. Nat King Cole's voice boasts from the small box and I find myself singing along with him.

"Here you go," I say as I drop two flutes full of champaign and a splash of orange juice on the island. They both thank me before picking them up. Mama takes a small sip and Colton manages to practically down the entire glass in one gulp.

"Are you gonna have one, baby girl?" Colton eyes me with a raised brow at the lack of mimosa in my hands.

"My stomach is a bit off this mornin'. I think I should eat somethin' first. I'll have one after we open presents." I step up on my tippy toes and place a quick kiss against his lips before going back to mixing the waffle batter.

"Nuh uh, not happenin'." He reaches for the whisk in my hand and quickly pulls it from my grasp. "Go sit down, Maya. I'll make you some tea and then finish up preppin' breakfast. I promise I won't screw it up too bad."

I'm about to interject when Mama beats me to it. "I won't let him mess anythin' up. You go sit with Billy and we will take care of this until Andrew gets here." Begrudgingly, I agree and make the journey to the couch.

By the time Colton brings over a cup of steaming ginger lemon tea, the doorbell is ringing again. "I've got it, stay put." Colton places a kiss on my forehead before spreading a blanket over my lap. I smile at him in thanks and take a small sip of the tea. I'm not sure why my stomach is so uneasy.

Today is one of my favorite days, but I have that queasy, nauseous clamminess coursing through me. I would normally blame it on work, but none of my cases have been very hard or time consuming. I watch with my mug close to my face, as Colton opens the front door. Andrew's huge grin is the first thing I see. His light hair is even more peppered with grays but his blue eyes shine just as bright as ever. He has a scruffy beard and the red pajamas he sports make him look even goofier than normal.

"Merry Christmas, family!" His boisterous voice glides through the house, alerting Billy of his arrival.

"Uncle Drew! Aunt Lia!" Billy runs to the front door and rather than jumping at Andrew, who is holding a tower of perfectly wrapped presents, he bypasses him and goes straight into Lia's arms.

Lia and Andrew got married a few months ago. I introduced the two of them when I started working for Wexel and Prat's Firm in Harley two years ago. She is one of my coworkers and the minute we met, we hit it off. Not only is she the kindest, funniest person I have ever met, she is one of the most beautiful.

I watch her as she walks into the room carrying my baby boy. She somehow makes the pajamas she's wearing look like they belong in a New York City fashion show. Her deep tan skin is flawless and contrasts against her light green eyes. Eyes that draw you in and keep you coming back for more over and over again. I think that's why she's such a good lawyer. No one can say no to those eyes.

"Hey, Lia. Merry Christmas." I smile up to her, not getting up from my seat. I just need a few more minutes and then I'll be good to go. The tea is already helping ease my stomach. I watch as she comes over to where I'm sitting and bends down over the back of the couch. Her long black hair falls around both of our faces as she places a kiss on my cheek.

"Merry Christmas, M. You okay?" She blinks down at me with concern in her eyes and I nod my head with a tight smile.

"Mama's belly hurts." Billy answers for me as he twirls Lia's hair in both of his hands.

"Oh no! Well, B, I think you should give your mommy a hug and rub her belly. Then maybe she will feel better. Do you think you can do that?" Billy's perfect little head nods up and down fast as he throws himself out of Lia's arms and onto the couch next to me. He crawls over and gives me a hug before placing his head on my stomach and using one of his hands to rub it.

"Do you feel better, Mama?" He looks up at me with a toothy grin, his ear pressed against my stomach.

"You know what? I do! Thank you so much, baby! You're a miracle worker!" I grab him and squeeze him tight, ignoring the nausea still bubbling in the pit of my stomach. His excited giggle is worth suffering through it this morning.

Standing up, I place him on the ground and walk over to Lia, pulling her in for a hug. "How are y'all doin'?" I ask as Andrew comes up behind us and hugs me from behind, trapping me between the two of them.

"We're great! Ready to start drinkin'." Andrew practically yells in my ear and I can't hold back my laugh. He's always been the loudest guy in the room.

"Let me make you two a mimosa." I sneak my way out of their arms and walk back into the kitchen. Mama is placing bacon in the oven when I get in there and I rub her arm in thanks on my way past her. Mixing up two mimosas, I bring them into the living room and pass them out before moving to sit on the floor next to Billy.

"Alright everyone, present time!"

HALF AN HOUR LATER, ALL OF THE PRESENTS ARE OPEN AND THE ROOM is destroyed. There is wrapping paper everywhere. The mimosas are gone, Andrew having finished both his and Lia's, and everyone is laughing as Billy runs around with his cowboy hat on. When he calms down enough to sit, he moves towards the tree and starts looking underneath it.

"What are you lookin' for, baby? Everyone already opened all of their presents." When he turns toward me, he has a confused expression.

"But Santa didn't bring any presents for the baby." No one speaks at first, looking at him like he has two heads.

"Did... did you tell him, Drew?" Lia's voice breaks the silence and we all turn towards her. Did she just say...

"You're pregnant?" I question in disbelief, my heart hammering in my chest. They look at each other for a second and when both of them turn towards me, they have unshed tears.

"We were going to announce it on New Year's." I can't keep the sob from escaping me as I run up to my brother and throw my arms around his head. I'm ugly crying, letting my tears soak into his shirt. I can barely hear my mom's or Colton's voices through my own excitement. I'm going to be an aunt. Billy is going to have a cousin.

We all hug for what feels like an hour, giving them both our congratulations and talking about how beautiful this baby is going to be. When we settle back down, Lia looks down at Billy with a smile.

"How did you know about our baby, B?" Lia's hand is now placed on her stomach and I can't help but feel something else underneath all of my excitement for them. I feel slightly jealous. We have been trying for a baby for almost a year now and it hasn't happened. Billy, while a blessing, was not expected, so we never had to experience the hardships of trying to get pregnant. We never experienced the hope and devastation each month.

Billy giggles and shakes his head like Lia just said the craziest thing in the world. "Auntie Lia, not your baby!" For the second time, Billy renders everyone in the room speechless.

"Billy, the baby in Aunt Lia's stomach is her baby. That's your cousin." I smile at him, not sure how to explain something like this to such a young mind. He looks at me now and then comes running over.

"But, Mama, I wasn't talkin' about that baby." His hand comes out and he places it on my stomach. My breath hitches in my throat and I stop breathing. "I was talkin' about the baby in your belly. Baby squirt."

"Wh... what did you just say?" My voice is a whisper. No one else speaks, or at least, I can't hear any of them if they are. The only thing I can hear is my hammering heart and the sound of my son's voice.

"Baby squirt, mommy. You're bein' so silly. But Santa didn't get her any presents. Was she a bad girl?" I half laugh, half cry as I throw my hand up to my mouth. Tears trickle down my cheeks and fall to the floor. "Don't cry, Mama. I'm sure Santa didn't mean to forget about squirt."

He continues using the nickname that my dad used to call me. The name I haven't heard in three years. The name that makes my throat close up and my heart squeeze from the pain of losing my biggest fan. My biggest supporter. The man that would do anything for the people he loved.

"Maya? Do you... is it true?" Colton is now holding onto my arm, his own mouth wavering as his eyes glisten. I blink at him, still too in shock to comprehend what is happening. "Do you have somethin' to tell me?"

"I... I don't know." I try to swallow the lump in my throat and wipe the tears from my face. The queasiness in my stomach hits me again full force and I jump up and run to the bathroom as fast as I can. I barely make it to the toilet before I'm heaving up bile.

My hair is pulled out of my face within seconds and a warm hand rubs up and down on my back. "It's okay, baby girl. Let it out." His words coax more heaves but nothing else comes out. I spit into the toilet bowl and grab the wash cloth offered to me by Colt, before wiping my mouth.

Leaning back, I let my head fall against Colton's shoulder. He grabs me and turns me effortlessly, putting me on his lap so he can hold me. "Are you okay?" He asks, his voice barely a whisper.

"He said squirt, baby." I can't stop the tears from falling again. They fall one at a time, as memories of my father hit me. Memories of us sitting on the swing. Of him walking me down the fake aisle. Of him rubbing my stomach and talking to Billy before he was born.

"Squirt, I want you to know... I will always be watchin' over you. And through every stage of your life. The good, the bad, the ugly... I will be proud of you. So, so proud. You're gonna be an amazin' mother. That little boy is gonna be the luckiest kid in the world."

"Daddy, how many times do I have to tell you. It's a girl." I laugh through my tears, staring down at my strong father now lying weak and thin in a hospital bed.

"I guess we will see, squirt. But I need you to know. Even if I'm not there to meet baby Grant in person, I'll still be there. And I bet you, the day that baby boy is born, it's gonna rain."

I furrow my brows at him. "Why do you say that?"

He grabs my hand, placing a shaky kiss against the back of it. "Because I will be watchin' over you. And the minute that baby cries his first cry, I'll be bawlin' right along side him. It will be quite the storm, squirt. Just you wait."

He wasn't wrong. It did rain. One of the worst storms Texas had seen all year. Colton's hands wiping away my tears brings me back from the memory.

"How does he know about that nickname? How could Billy come up with that on his own?" I cry harder thinking about my father somehow communicating with Billy. I don't know how it's possible, but I also believe in miracles. God brought me this amazing man. God brought me Billy. I know anything is possible because of that.

"I think it's time to take a test, baby girl." Colt moves over to the sink and opens the cabinet under it. Grabbing one of the dozens of tests I have stored in every bathroom, he brings it back over to me with a soft smile on his face.

I nod my head, taking the test from him and moving, shakily, until I'm sitting on the toilet. Colt takes a seat on the bathtub edge to the right of me and places a hand on my shoulder.

"Either way, Maya. It's gonna be okay. If it's negative, we try again next month. No matter what, we are gonna have an amazin' day, baby girl." I don't answer him, trying to concentrate on peeing on the stick. After a few seconds, I'm pulling my pants back up and the stick is sitting flat on the white counter.

"Come here." Colt puts his hands out for me, still sitting on the bathtub, and I carefully place myself back in his arms. In my safe place. And then we wait. It's only two minutes but it feels like two hours. Colt holds me tight, whispering soft words of reassurance in my ear. I don't need the reassurance. I feel something deep in my bones. Something screaming at me that Billy is right. That after all of this time, our tears and disappointment have paid off.

"You ready to look?" Colt kisses my hair, helping me stand up to walk over to the sink. We make the short journey hand in hand. "No matter what, I'm right here, baby girl. Always and forever." I nod in agreement, taking one last breath before looking down at the stick.

And then I start to sob.

Note from the Author

So... cliff hanger much? That was never the plan. I wanted Colton and Maya's story to be a stand-alone with a feel good happily ever after. But, as most of you are, I am so connected with these characters! I'm not promising that there will be a sequel to their story... but I'm leaving it open so one day down the road, I may be able to return to them both.

I hope you enjoyed this extra scene from What Happens When You Break. I am so grateful for every last one of my readers that support me and enjoy my stories. I promise to continue to write as long as you promise to continue to read!

Love,
G.L. Strong

About the Author

GILLIAN STRONG IS THE AUTHOR OF WHEN A ROSE FALLS, AFTER the Fall, and The Shadows. She is a part time author, part time Real Estate Agent, and full time mom of a beautiful two year old girl. Living in North Eastern Pennsylvania with her husband and daughter, she spends late nights writing, taking advantage of the peace and quiet! In her free time, she loves to read romance and horror books, cook anything and everything, and spend quality time with her family.

For more books by G.L. Strong check out her website:
www.glstrongbooks.com